A FALLING

KNIFE

OTHER TITLES IN
THE HOLLOW CITY SERIES

The Big Fear

A FALLING KNIFE

THE HOLLOW CITY SERIES

ANDREW CASE

THOMAS & MERCER

Text copyright © 2017 by Andrew Case
All rights reserved.

Published by Thomas & Mercer, Seattle

www.apub.com

Amazon, the Amazon logo, and Thomas & Mercer are trademarks of Amazon.com, Inc., or its affiliates.

ISBN-13: 9781503938922 (paperback)
ISBN-10: 1503938921 (paperback)

Cover design by Brian Zimmerman

Printed in the United States of America

For Claudia

CHAPTER ONE

Twenty-four stories up, Wade Valiant could only barely hear the sirens. Every few months, a new job would start, each one a little bit deeper into Brooklyn. Now, past Empire Boulevard, in the low sprawl that used to be called only Flatbush, Wade was working on his fourth build this year. Prospect-Lefferts Gardens, they had named it, with a debate about where precisely to put the hyphen. Developers can get into an argument about anything.

Another squad car zipped through the light below, dashing to whatever small injustice had appalled a new arrival. Wade had seen the same story from above over the past decade: Carroll Gardens, Prospect Heights, and now here. The new buildings go up and the new buyers bring Manhattan with them, complaining about their neighbors' drums or the local roti shop's late-night parties. The offenses get pettier and pettier, and soon hardened officers are mediating disputes about where to put the recycling.

The crowd below hustled along over the powder of broken leaves. Wade knew the neighborhoods he looked down on by their foliage. Cobble Hill had its ginkgoes, with the dry berries that stank putrid when you stepped on them. Elms in Park Slope, and out here, oak. No one in the crowd saw Wade or knew what species of leaves they were walking through; they never looked up. Time is money, after all, and no matter what the politicians said, money was still king in New York.

The view down had never troubled him. From his first day on the job, stepping out onto an I-beam five short stories up on what passed for a skyscraper in Trenton, Wade had been comfortable in the air. Something in the genes, he figured. From Plattsburg, Wade had a little Mohawk in him, just like the men who built the towers of Manhattan in its first heyday. Skywalkers. He was as comfortable on an elevated crane at twenty-four stories as the drones below him were at their desks, so many honeybees nestled in place, brewing money.

Under his helmet, behind the jet-black mask, Wade's face was covered in sweat. Even in November, welding was hot and mean and uncomfortable. Not like the later work, hauling the wiring and plumbing and innards into place, skipping across the I-beams, empty space below him and brooding sky above. But that would have to wait until spring. There were only a few weeks left before the job would be called for the winter. The arc flared; the joint sealed. Wade leaned back into his narrow platform and pressed the joystick to move himself another four feet.

The platform slid to the next set of joints and set itself in place with a mechanical thud. Wade knew the sounds of all the iron skeletons through which he clawed and clamored. He could hear, when he banged with a C-wrench, what was solid enough to hold and what needed another few ounces from the torch. But he still didn't know or trust the sounds of the crane. He couldn't tell which creaks were natural and which should give him pause.

It had been his busiest two years on the job. Since the edict to add affordable units had come down, there hadn't been a glass tower that the Department of Buildings wasn't happy to green-light. There wasn't a developer in town who hadn't eaten from the trough of the Department of Finance. Wade's own split-level in Baldwin had been paid for by money he had made splicing together one anonymous skyscraper after another. Wade was at a loss as to why the hordes scuttling to the subway below would rather own eight hundred and fifty square feet on the fourteenth floor in Flatbush than a two-story house with a backyard in the suburbs. But it was their party.

Steady at the next joint, Wade leaned out and clamped down his mask. The silly security railing on the platform nudged his upper arms as he bent in. The heat was getting to him. He opened up the flame and pressed harder into a thick iron joint, watching as the metal gave way, started to boil, and smoothed itself into a familiar scar. He pressed further, lurching forward. Then a sudden jolt. His platform swung from below him and into the I-beam.

Wade held the cheap railing as he rebounded from the I-beam. Something was wrong. He should grab onto the beam. But as he lunged to grip it, he dropped his torch. It tugged his belt and jerked back to him, springing toward the clamp on his safety harness. He swung his leg to protect his shin; even though the flame shut off, the barrel was hot and heavy enough to break a bone. If it had fallen, that would have been the end of it. But his harness was always in place. Safety first. Not just a slogan when you're crisscrossing the tops of construction sites all day long.

Wade gathered the torch and turned it off. He settled himself as he thought on what happened. The crane had banged into the I-beam. The platform had been thrown off its level and now his right foot was a few inches higher than his left. That needed to get fixed. You don't want anything out of whack at this height. Wade reached for his radio to call the guy in the booth below.

"Manny? You want to tell me what went on down there?"

Static. Then quiet. The equipment isn't perfect but usually you can at least hear something. Either the radio was shot or Manny just wasn't answering. Wade stepped to the edge of the platform and looked down. The cab of the crane stood squat and quiet. No sign of Manny. Not in the cab, not on the avenue, all the way up to Empire Boulevard and then the park. Across the street was a dull yellow brick conversion. Once a bank or a bakery or a warehouse, now cobbled together into a discount store, a gym, and a liquor store. They would get hold of that one soon enough. Across Empire Boulevard, Wade saw the Ebbets Field Apartments. Hulking, powerful, and dull. If the developers could ever empty that out, the zoning would let them put up almost an entire city.

Wade slung the radio back up. "Manny, if you can hear me, go ahead and take me down. Something went wrong with the platform. We should check it out."

Silence. Static. Wade wasn't worried. There are always safety redundancies on the job. The platform had a bright red switch to signal descent. Wade held it down, and it started to buzz. If Manny was in the cab, he would hear it too. Wade would be down in a few minutes. The platform still wasn't plumb.

Nothing. Wade took off his helmet. The artificial heat was gone and the sweet November cold was sliding inside him now. But he was still sweating. No longer the fierce sweat of work or heat or electricity, now it was a dull sweat. For the first time since he had been on the job, Wade felt the stirring of something like fear. For the first time, he looked over the edge of the platform and saw how far he really was above the ground.

There was a final fail-safe, of course. A manual switch to bring the platform down. It wasn't ideal; you can't see below you. You could get tangled with someone on the street if you weren't paying attention. But now it was the only way. Wade popped open the plastic case and pulled the switch to descend. The platform lurched, then started down slowly, steadily. The crisp beeping below gave pedestrians their fair warning.

And then it stopped. He was on the eighteenth floor, maybe, beside a set of welds he put in just last week. He pressed the switch to start down again. Manny, or whoever was in the cab, had overridden the command. The crooked platform started rising again. The clueless commuters kept on their way, munching their precious cranberry scones.

4

The platform lurched. Wade reached over it toward the beam. The building seemed safer than the crane now. He wrapped his arms tightly around the I-beam and started to pull himself off the platform. He'd sit on the building until help arrived. He didn't care how long. He was comfortable up here, after all. As he hoisted himself onto the beam, he breathed out. The sweat stopped. He took in the long view, the trim townhouses on Guilder Street, the rotting Victorians to the south waiting to be torn down and replaced by glass and steel.

He heard it before he saw it: a sick metallic crunch, metal on metal, loud and low pitched. The sound of bones breaking, only the bones were made of chromium-infused steel. The crane swung toward the building once more, twice more, and the girders loosed the platform from the crane itself. It was twisting sideways now, about to tumble from its perch and onto the unsuspecting crowd.

Wade watched from the girder, planted above the crumbling crane. Only as the platform finally twisted and began its fall did he realize his mistake. Safety first. Just as he had hitched his tools to his belt with a security line, he had hitched himself to the crane platform. In case he slipped over the edge.

Too late he saw the wire run taut as the platform slipped. Too late he reached for the carabiner on his belt. As his belt yanked him off the beam, he reached hopelessly to tug himself back on. His fingers cracked and slipped past the sharp edge, and he was alone, in flight, looking up at his perfect creation as six hundred pounds of metal carried him down toward the crowded street.

CHAPTER TWO

Leonard Mitchell was always at ease in a cheap suit. He didn't mind
the pinch in the shoulders or the sag at the waist. He had learned the
power of anonymity. A year ago, it had just about saved his life. He had
been investigating a police shooting when the wrong sort of bad cops
had come after him. He had stayed just hidden enough that he didn't
end up dead. But it hadn't saved his job, and it hadn't kept him from
doing six months in jail. Some thanks for uncovering a conspiracy of
dirty cops. But life goes on.

Leonard smiled as the subway skidded to a halt and commuters
filed onto the outdoor platform. The station was below ground level, but
open to the sky. From here, the line reverted to a local, creeping through
Ditmas Park, Midwood, and Sheepshead Bay before petering out at
Coney Island. That made it the last stop that catered to Manhattan
exiles. Express over the bridge and you could be at Union Square in
twenty minutes on a good day.

Leonard waited as the crowd slipped out. There were suits much
nicer than his; there were expensive bags carried by kids in one creative
industry or another; there were a few lawyers who worked in the kind of
firm where you could wear jeans. Leonard, happily invisible in crowds
like this, let them hurry out into the night air, whipping phones out of

their pockets to check if anyone had texted since they crossed the bridge fifteen minutes ago.

Leonard smiled to himself. He had been getting off at this stop for over a decade, ever since he'd moved into the Ebbets Field Apartments. With rents rising, and stuck with a city salary at DIMAC—the Department to Investigate Misconduct and Corruption—he'd had no other options. The building had the massive, grim feel of a housing project, but it had been decades since it was famous as its own little crime capital.

Now, the pickings were even slimmer. Crown Heights had long ago filled up with tech executives and preposterous rents. Even Flatbush was on its way, complete with newly nicknamed mini-neighborhoods designed to put buyers at ease. Every week, another West Indian restaurant or discount tailor closed its doors and was supplanted by an expensive soap-and-candle shop. After the past two years, Leonard was lucky enough to be staying, even at Ebbets.

Stepping out after the commuters, he thought about last summer. It seemed like years ago and it seemed like it hadn't been five minutes. His old boss at DIMAC had been murdered days after she had left for the comfort of the private sector. Leonard had been investigating whether Ralph Mulino was justified in shooting another detective on a container ship, and ended up discovering that Mulino was the only clean cop in the whole soup. A dozen officers had been sabotaging the city. And for what? To scare people into thinking they needed the police more. Fear as a political strategy; terrify people into electing a strongman as their mayor.

And when Leonard and Mulino had sorted the whole thing out, what Leonard got was six months in Moriah Shock. He had walked away from a dead cop, but that's the sort of thing you do when there are cops trying to kill you. The district attorney, keen to keep up appearances, hadn't seen it that way.

Technically a prison, but a work camp in practice, Moriah Shock is where you go to keep your nose clean and promise never to get in trouble again. It wasn't as though he'd wanted a parade, but going to lockup for thwarting a terror attack hadn't felt exactly fair.

After that, Leonard hadn't even tried to go back to DIMAC. The mayor had cleaned house, and now the place was run by Barry Schaeffer, a former personal injury lawyer who wore his uncombed white hair just past the collar and wasn't ashamed of his cognac nose. He had made millions suing swimming pool manufacturers over drowned children, or amusement parks where the roller coasters flew off the rails. Investigating cops seemed a natural progression. When Schaeffer found a big case, he could kick it back to his law firm. There was big money in corruption nowadays.

A few kind words and a handshake landed Leonard as the press secretary at the Parks Department. The biggest story of the year was announcing when there was enough snow to go sledding. After a decade in the corruption business and six months in prison, Leonard welcomed the change. Every couple of days he would tout a newly opened dog run, a freshly graded softball field, or a repaved playground. He pushed soft and pleasant stories that were barely newsworthy, and didn't even call in to complain if the papers didn't run them.

But every now and then, there was a real bit of crime. A body dumped in Great Kills. A drowning at Orchard Beach. A rape in Flushing Meadows. Nothing like twenty years ago, of course. Nothing like the Central Park jogger, wildings, or the screaming headlines of the early nineties. Still, he always picked up his step on the nights he hit a crime scene. Nights like tonight.

It hadn't happened in the park proper, but he had been getting calls about it. A construction accident on Ocean and Flatbush, at the latest condo building going in on top of the subway station. Park views, Wolf ranges, Sub-Zero refrigerators: the works. A crane had split in half, dragging a skywalker to his death, and leaving two injured on the ground. The police had the block cordoned off all day.

Leonard had referred the papers to the NYPD spokesman, but knew his commissioner would want to make a statement tomorrow. And it was an easy layover: three blocks from his house. There was nothing like getting on the scene and taking the word directly from the investigators.

The rumor was that there was going to be trouble for the Department of Buildings. The crane had passed its latest inspection two weeks ago. That meant the inspector had missed something, or someone had tampered with the crane, or the inspection had never really been done at all. Given the reputation for corruption at the Department of Buildings, the last option was most likely.

Leonard knew from his time at DIMAC how often inspectors filled in paperwork affirming the safety of scaffolds and cranes and windowsills they had never looked at. It was a lot of work, running around from construction site to construction site. Much easier to kick back and take a long lunch at a local bar. And when a developer is willing to give the inspector a couple of hundred bucks to have that lunch instead of coming around to the site, it's easier still. Aside from the Corrections Department, where guards gleefully smuggled straight razors and heroin into the jails for the price of a cup of coffee, Buildings was the most corrupt agency in the city.

As he trundled up the stairs toward Flatbush, trailing the long crowd, Leonard figured it would be an easy case. He would find out that the inspector had never looked at the crane. That the bolt had been weak for months. Buildings would run out tomorrow and inspect about fifty cranes. People could safely walk past construction sites and into the parks. And by the way, the Parks Department inspects its own equipment regularly. Maybe Barry Schaeffer would get his chance to file charges against the inspector. Or maybe he would just make an angry speech about it and head back to the upper seventies to nurse a single malt and congratulate himself.

The yellow tape blocked off the whole sidewalk from the train station up to Empire. Even the bus station was shut down. A rookie officer stood by the tape, bored, directing pedestrians around the long way.

"You gotta go around, sir."

"Leonard Mitchell. Parks Department." Leonard took out his city ID. He didn't get to carry a badge anymore, not like he did at DIMAC. The official card was usually good enough for an ordinary crime scene that was basically inside his agency's jurisdiction. Usually. But the young cop just stared at it.

"Parks Department?"

"I need information so my commissioner can make a statement."

"The park is across the street."

You can always count on a police officer to say something basically true and utterly irrelevant. Leonard slowly simmered, ready to tell the cadet just how much he outranked him, when he saw a heavy man with a wide, red face and a mismatched suit watching him. The man stepped away from the crowd of officers conferring by the twisted metal, still in place.

"Leonard Mitchell. Well, isn't this a surprise?"

Leonard looked up and smiled. "Hello, Detective."

The man with the red face gestured to the gatekeeper. "Let this one in, laddo. He's all right."

The cop lifted the tape and Leonard stooped under. He walked up to the familiar figure and shook his hand.

"So what happened?"

Detective Ralph Mulino shook his head. "Let me show you, Leonard. You wouldn't believe me otherwise."

CHAPTER THREE

Detective Mulino was not going to learn anything about this one from looking at the body. Eighteen stories, straight down. Dragged by his own safety harness when the platform dislodged from the crane, from the look of it. At least Mulino wouldn't have to listen to some so-called expert on spatter patterns or bite marks prattle on about what had killed the guy. Blunt force trauma: the simplest cause of death there is. Just thinking about it made him feel old and heavy all over again. His bad knee had started throbbing the moment he hit the scene.

From the look of it, the techs had said, he had tried to scramble off the platform but his safety harness pulled him down. If it isn't one thing, it's another. The techs had taken their notes, snapped their photos, and zippered him up; the body was off the scene by mid-morning. There would be a coroner's report tomorrow that would tell Detective Ralph Mulino precisely nothing about why. For that, he was going to have to do his own legwork. And if Mulino was familiar with anything, it was legwork.

After what had happened last year, Mulino had been as surprised as anyone that he had been given his own squad, a new rank, and a higher pay grade. At the end of last summer, he had been worried about losing his shield, forfeiting his pension, even going to jail. Alone on a container ship floating in Buttermilk Channel, he had opened fire at a man running toward him with a gun, only to learn afterward that the man had been a detective too.

He had been subject to a civilian investigation, but in the end, the investigator had been a better friend to him than most cops. Leonard Mitchell had believed him, and together they had rooted out a crime ring. The Department doesn't like it much when civilians uncover too much of its dirty work, so Mitchell himself had been scuttled to the background. He lost his job and did a short stint upstate. All the credit had gone to Mulino. The tarnish of twenty-five years of dirty looks from his superiors had been polished away in a few weeks. He figured he owed the guy in the cheap suit at least a favor or two.

After all, Mulino got everything he could have hoped for. Supervisory Detective Sergeant. SDS. The rank he'd always wanted. There is no straightforward promotional path if you are a detective in the NYPD. If you want to run the department, don't become a detective. Get promoted through patrol. Sergeants man the desk at precincts; lieutenants supervise a tour; captains run the precinct itself. Deputy inspectors, inspectors, and deputy commissioners either have real power or are just too much of a pain in the ass to fire. Very rarely you can have the detective's badge and get the promotion to SDS. And what happened to Mulino last summer counted as very rare.

So here he was, leading his own little unit. Still stuck in the strangest bureau in the NYPD—OCCB, the Organized Crime Control Bureau. Still no sign of anything that looked to Mulino like organized crime. But when you needed an investigation done, and it wasn't precisely clear from the outset that you were looking at a homicide—there was no bullet in anyone's forehead, after all—then the precincts and the homicide bureau didn't want to touch it. And then OCCB could step in.

Being in charge meant he had a couple of freshly minted gold badges that no one else wanted to work with reporting to him. Timothy Bruder had become a cop because his daddy had been a cop and his brother had been a cop and maybe an uncle somewhere had been a cop. He had made detective on his third try because the people who make up the promotional lists still liked getting free drinks at the retirement bar his father had opened in St. George. The kid looked like he needed a good kick in the ass, but giving it would be a good way for Mulino to lose everything he had worked for. There were dozens of people in the department who may not have liked Timmy Bruder, but they liked his family well enough to look out for him. Bruder would barely speak to the other detective, Aurelia Peralta, but that's because Bruder could probably barely speak at all.

Peralta herself was more muscle than mind, but at least she was in the job for the right reasons. Only twenty-six, she had graduated the academy with the highest fitness scores since they started letting women on the force. Peralta was a legwork cop, and she had opted for working the streets, nabbing guns, and making detective. Mulino saw a lot of his young self in her. He worried mainly that she'd get hurt or that she'd maybe shoot someone. There is a lot of danger in being the first person through the door.

Bruder and Peralta had spent the day talking to witnesses. Everyone saw the crane come down. Nobody was looking up beforehand. They had brought in an engineer to look over the heap of metal on the ground. They had scaled the scaffold. Mulino had been told that the building was set for occupancy come spring. He couldn't believe it. It was November already, and the site was nowhere near to sealed off. You can't do electrical work when you're open to the snow.

Mulino had been conferring with Peralta and Bruder when he saw Leonard Mitchell arguing with the patrol officer manning the tape. His first feeling was guilt. Here the guy had spent six months away and Mulino hadn't even checked up on him to see if he was okay. His second thought was surprise. He had heard Mitchell was comfortably squatting at the Parks Department. But that didn't explain why he'd be at the scene of this particular tragedy. Then he figured he might as well let the old investigator in. Having Mitchell around could come in useful.

After greeting Leonard, Mulino walked him over to his detectives. "Len, this is Detective Aurelia Peralta and Detective Timmy Bruder."

Glum stares from the two kids in the gold badges. And why not? If they didn't know anything about Leonard Mitchell, then he was a stranger to them, and at first pass the NYPD is not open for business to strangers. If they did know anything about him, they probably knew that he had worked at the Department to Investigate Misconduct and Corruption, investigating their colleagues. That was just as bad as the rat squad, without the benefit of being a cop.

Mitchell held out a thin hand. It was cold enough that Leonard should have some sort of overcoat on, but he was still in the same municipal suit. His knuckles had just started to glow red when he took out his hand.

"Leonard Mitchell. Parks Department." Presented with the hand, Peralta and Bruder couldn't find a way out. Each politely shook, and gave an introduction by rank and name.

Mulino turned away from his subordinates. "So what are you even doing here, Len? If you're with the Parks Department."

"Commissioner wants to give a statement. It happened next to the park. We take down a lot of trees with these same kind of cranes."

Peralta spoke up. "The park's across the street. And Empire Boulevard is a pretty big street."

Leonard shrugged. Mulino smiled at him. What was he going to say? His commissioner liked getting his name in the paper. It was as good an excuse as any, a terrible accident near enough to a park. It beats standing up at the podium and giving a speech about the kind of grass they are seeding the Great Meadow with this year.

"Len, I'm going to trust you not to spill the whole thing to your commissioner."

"Detective." It was Bruder this time, hoping to preserve a little confidentiality. Mulino wasn't interested and nodded to his subordinates.

"Detectives, can you start out on those follow-up interviews? We'll reconvene tomorrow and start canvassing. Don't worry. I'm going to give just an overview to our friend here."

The two underlings turned back to the street. Somewhere parked along Ocean would be an unmarked car. Their eyes made clear they didn't like being told to go, but the department is a paramilitary organization after all. That's what happens when you make supervisor. You actually get to tell people what to do.

"Len, you may have already heard there was something wrong with the crane."

"I've heard. Department of Buildings failed to inspect."

"Yeah. Well, it's easy to make people believe that. It's true often enough. It gets people to stop paying attention."

"And why don't you want people paying attention?"

Mulino looked up at the unfinished building. "This building is being put up by Hill and Associates. Are you familiar with Hill and Associates?"

A blank look from Leonard.

"Are you familiar with Eleanor Hill?"

Another stare. "Not unless she's related to McArthur Hill."

"Bingo. She's the daughter."

Leonard nodded, and Mulino could see him putting it together. McArthur Hill ran the Songhai Methodist Church in Flatbush, one of the largest in Brooklyn. He had risen to prominence twenty years earlier by denouncing police violence against black youth, long before it was popular to do so. He had led marches and twisted the arms of mayors and police commissioners. He had reminded them all that his three thousand parishioners not only voted, but that they drove vans and manned polling stations and told their less pious friends about elections. He ended up with a comfortable fiefdom with grants for after-school programs, senior centers, and other predictable gravy.

Mulino spoke. "Hill's daughter started into real estate. She fixed up a few burnt-out buildings, bought a few more, and now she's feeding on the condo boom. So if it looks like we are accusing her of anything, we not only get the Borough President calling and asking what we're up to, we get three thousand parishioners chasing us over the bridge back into Manhattan. So better let everyone think we're going to pin it on a building inspector."

"The DOB didn't miss the crane inspection?"

"Maybe they inspected it, maybe not. But there was nothing wrong with it."

Leonard looked at the twisted heap of metal, the six-inch-deep gash in the sidewalk. Something was wrong with it now. "So if nothing was wrong with it, what brought it down?"

Mulino knelt by the body of the crane. He ran his hand along the bright white iron, just where it had snapped. There were scuff marks on the paint. Six or seven, steep slashes along the body.

"You see this, Len?" Leonard leaned down to see the marks on the crane.

Mulino went on. "And on the building, when we went up, we saw paint on the girders. Paint that had come off of this crane."

"The crane fell into the building first?"

"It didn't fall. The crane was banged against the beams until it hit right on the joint and the joint gave way. Most likely the guy running the cab."

"And who was in the cab?"

"The personnel records show a man named Manuel Reeves. Been with Hill and Associates for five years. Worked on buildings himself, hurt his leg, got put in the cab. Partial disability."

"And where is Mr. Reeves now?"

"We have twenty perfectly competent officers canvassing the area asking that very question. And I just sent my detectives off to get to the source of it."

"So what do we think happened?"

Mulino smiled. Leonard Mitchell was going to come in very useful for him after all. "We know what happened. Someone in the cab banged this crane into the building until it snapped. We don't know why it happened. Tell your commissioner to give a very bland statement about how important it is to inspect cranes regularly, and maybe even throw the Department of Buildings under the bus a little. And on top of that, I have a proposition for you that I think you'll find very appealing."

"Detective Mulino, I'm all ears."

CHAPTER FOUR

Well, that was a waste. Eleanor Hill sat alone in her car in the middle school parking lot, facing the mean traffic on Empire Boulevard. Piled on her passenger seat were twenty-nine neat packets, one for each member of the Community Board. But she hadn't had the chance to hand them out. She had come to the school that night ready to pitch her latest project to the Board, hoping for swift approval so she could move on to the City Council, then the Department of Planning, and then break ground. It was going to require a zoning change, turning two blocks of boarded-up businesses to residential. And if they had only given her a chance, she was sure she could have convinced them.

Eleanor had come prepared. She had a portfolio filled with data: with five thousand units and the housing coming in at 20 percent affordable, she was offering a thousand discount apartments in a neighborhood desperate for them. She could turn a profit on the deal even if they jacked up the affordable demand to 30 percent, but you never start a negotiation at your closing number.

Plus, she had calculated the revenues for the city: jobs created, property taxes paid, sales taxes from the in-neighborhood spends on services and amenities. What dry cleaner doesn't want four thousand professionals moving in around the corner? She was going to upgrade the sewers; she was going to put in an electrical substation; there was going to be some space given back for a soccer field for the very school where they were having the meeting. Anyone reasonable would have given her the thumbs up.

But she should have known that in some neighborhoods, reason doesn't rule the day. The board meeting that night had been disrupted by twenty protesters waving signs, chanting slogans, blocking the exits. They said that the unpaid board members were in the pockets of malicious developers. The majority-black board was a tool of the sinister Jews. Tearing down an empty sugar warehouse to build housing was going to displace local families.

Eleanor Hill knew many of the protesters. They lived mainly one block up from the proposed development, on Guilder Street, a neat row of hundred-year-old townhouses. Their angry chants were a cover: what they were really worried about was that the new development would front their private backyards.

She had waited it out in the auditorium or cafeteria—whatever that ungodly room was—until after all the protesters had left. One of them kept screaming until the board chair had to call the police. As a cop dragged her out of the room, she yelled that she was being assaulted, that her life mattered, that she couldn't breathe. Never mind that most of the board, Eleanor Hill, and the cop manhandling her were all black, too. Say what you will about the demonstrators. They knew how to put on a show.

Eleanor Hill had underestimated the protesters. They were never going to let the board vote if they could help it. They were never going to look at her charts and decide the development was a good idea. But sitting in the middle school parking lot, she realized that their obstinacy was not a problem. If they didn't want to negotiate, she would simply run them down.

But the board was trickier. The board vote didn't matter in any real sense. Hill and Associates had bundled donations for the local council member, for the borough president, for the mayor, public advocate, comptroller. Eleanor knew the Uniform Land Use Review Procedure so well that she didn't even sound silly saying "ULURP." If the variance came before the committee at the City Council with a thumbs-down from the community board, all it would mean would be a few more office visits. Electeds will always come around.

But a couple of months spent lobbying city council members would be a couple of months lost breaking ground, laying the foundations, and in the end a couple of months less rent from four thousand market-rate units. Not to mention the optics. If the board approves you even though some protestors complain, eventually everyone in the neighborhood will fall in line. If the board turns you down and you build anyway, there are going to be people picketing the site, storming the open houses, filing frivolous lawsuits. It would be easier to avoid the whole headache.

Eleanor guided her Lexus toward the edge of the parking lot. She slipped her phone onto the passenger seat. Her father had called her six times during the meeting. She had noticed the first ring, just before the meeting started, and managed to silence it. That was the last thing she needed, to be the person whose phone was going off during the community board meeting.

The speeches had been canceled because of the protests. She had no chance to hand out her neat packets of convincing data. She had emailed it to the board members a week before, but she knew they hadn't read it. You have to spoon-feed people everything. The board had gone into executive session after the protest. So they had voted, but they hadn't heard from her. And she wouldn't find out for a week what they had decided. Lots of the board members, deep down, sided with the protesters. It wasn't that they wanted one kind of building instead of another. They just didn't want any new buildings at all. Eleanor thought maybe they should all move to Topeka.

There was a new guy on the board she hadn't been able to get a bead on. White, a little heavy; he had mottled hair and faraway eyes, and looked as though he had just woken up from a twenty-year nap. Trying to look professional with a tie and a sport coat, but instead only looking uncomfortable. She figured he would vote whichever way the majority was going. Or against the other white people, to prove he wasn't a newcomer-gentrifying-racist. He probably was against her. It was too bad that community board members get appointed and work for free. They don't have election campaigns you can contribute to.

Swinging out on Empire, she looked back down at the phone. Her father. He knew she was at the meeting. He knew it was important. But he had called anyway. Over and over. And sent three texts too, asking her to call him. She'd do it when she got home. She couldn't let him believe that he still had that kind of power over her. His congregation meant votes, and votes meant that he could walk into any elected official's office and get to the point without ever having to donate to a campaign. But at the end of the day, votes didn't make you rich.

Friends in City Hall won't make you rich either, not unless you skim a little off the top. And say what you would about McArthur Hill, he was thoroughly, deeply, totally incorruptible. He might play to the cameras, threaten a riot, or accuse a mayor of racism with the best of them, but graft was unthinkable. Every penny that flowed into his congregation from the city went straight where it had been earmarked. McArthur Hill could get the city to turn on the faucet, but he would never drink from it himself. Powerful but humble, if Eleanor's father wasn't exactly poor, he was a long way from rich.

Not like Eleanor. She considered herself just as incorruptible as her father, but there were plenty of non-corrupt ways to make money in this city. Born in Brooklyn in 1971, she had seen at least four rapid-fire waves of development, buildings selling for nothing one day and for millions a few years later. She had raised a little capital, made a few deals, and pretty soon she was swimming with the best of them. She made money on affordable housing and luxury condos. She made money when they put in a basketball arena and when they put in a community center. It irked her when the protesters called her names, when a community board would vote against her. She was serving the community, making mostly good things happen. Sure she took a cut, but that was the way of the world.

Her father was a worrier. He called too often and demanded too much. He wanted to know who lived in the buildings she was buying. He asked where they would move when she tore them down and put in the new ones. Sometimes he seemed like one of the protesters, leaving thinly veiled accusations that she was betraying her people. That even though a thousand affordable units would mean housing for people of every race, she was somehow in league with the moneyed interest, and could therefore never do right.

As she pulled onto Midwood and toward her own home, she thought finally on the accident. She had been called in the morning. One dead, a few injured. It happens. Construction workers had died putting up the Chrysler Building, the Empire State, both World Trades. They discovered the bends when workers digging the foundations of the Brooklyn Bridge surfaced and died. She had been briefed already. Wade Valiant wasn't married. Didn't have a family. That would make it easier. No children in the newspaper. She had heard something about a problem at the Department of Buildings. She would be happy to pass the blame back to the city.

She pulled up her driveway alongside her massive Edwardian brick home. It was ringed with terraces and broad bright windows; the original parquet floors were polished so bright you could almost see the shine from outside. The American Dream, smack in the middle of Flatbush. She stopped the car and dialed her father.

"Eleanor."

"Dad. You knew I was at the board meeting. I couldn't answer."

"Listen. I have to tell you something."

She sighed into the phone. It was going to be another of his petty grievances. "All right, Dad. Let me know."

"No, Eleanor. It's not that. Something terrible has happened. Something truly terrible."

CHAPTER FIVE

Ralph Mulino leaned back in his blonde wooden chair, his bad right knee propped up on a little stool he brought to his office for that very purpose. When they promote you, you get a perk or two. He kept his desk neat, without a computer. Wooden inbox and outbox, and the inbox was usually emptied as soon as something was put in it. The desk itself was metal, banged up, probably recovered from the basement of a school that got torn down to make way for condos, but it would do. It wasn't as though he'd been promoted to inspector, after all.

Mulino turned to his guest and spoke. "Nowadays, people don't just disappear."

Leonard Mitchell sat in front of him. Guests still got uncomfortable chairs. It seemed to Mulino that Leonard was, if anything, even leaner than he had been a year ago. At least in the face. Six months in Moriah Shock will do that to you, though. You start the day with push-ups at dawn, and you plow the dirt roads, and if the weather is right, you farm. Mulino had visited Moriah Shock once. It looked like something out of the nineteenth century. But there were no bludgeonings, no gang wars, no scalpels snuck inside to settle the scores of the criminal world. When they got out, most of the inmates never again wanted to do whatever they had done to get sent there. The rest of the prisons in the state could learn from a place like that. If only prison systems were the kinds of places that learned anything.

Mulino kept up his little lecture. "Back in my time, someone wants to run off, what can you do to track him down? You ask his friends. You have a driver's license if you're lucky. His address. The places he liked to hang out. And sometimes people would do that, try to run from us, and the Warrants squad would find them at happy hour at Moonies. But if someone really wanted to hide, back then, there was nothing we could do."

Mulino looked past Leonard for a moment. Peralta was talking to Bruder out at their open-air desks. They had both just gotten in. Give detectives a daytime tour and they will almost immediately take advantage. Eight thirty arrival becomes nine, then nine fifteen. But they had been out doing interviews last night, after all. He didn't want to be the kind of boss that cracks heads right away. Tough to strike that balance.

Mulino went on speaking. "Now, you have the Internet. This guy, Manny Reeves. He had his Facebook. He had his email. He had a cell phone. A cell phone is a tracking device; it pings your carrier constantly. We don't need a warrant to get that from the carrier. We don't need a warrant to get into his email, his social media. We call up these people and say he's missing, we get it all within minutes. So we are going to find Manny Reeves."

"But you haven't found him yet."

"No, Leonard, if we had found him yet, I wouldn't be talking to you. I'd have him in an interview room and I'd be asking him why he slammed his partner into the wall of a building hard enough to break a steel crane. I appreciated the statement your commissioner put out, by the way."

Leonard shuffled in his seat. His hands moved to his knees. Mulino could tell Leonard was uncomfortable. And why not? He had just conned his Commissioner into playing it like an accident, when they both knew it wasn't. Mulino had made sure that the new head of the Department to Investigate Misconduct and Corruption had taken up the city angle. Not just an investigation of who was supposed to have approved this crane. A full audit of the DOB's inspections of the past year. By the time they came around to issuing a report, no one would even remember.

"We have people looking into Mr. Reeves. We'll get him." Mulino had told Bruder to contact the Technical Assistance Response Unit. At TARU they hack phones, subpoena service providers, and basically operate as if they were their own little NSA. But Mulino knew TARU would back-bench his request. If you tell them you are hunting a terrorist, you have their full attention. But if you are investigating a death that may not even be a murder, they will get to it when they get to it.

"My detectives were out last night gathering data. And now the department has Mr. Reeves's data, and he is going to be found. I'm just telling you so that you don't think that's why I brought you in here."

Leonard nodded. "Why did you bring me in here?"

Mulino lifted his right leg and moved it about six inches across his stool. It ached if he walked and it ached if he left it still for too long. "The lucky part of being OCCB is we aren't limited to investigating the homicide. If our initial determination that it was a homicide turns out even to be correct."

"I got you."

"This building is being put up by Hill and Associates. Their fourth one in the neighborhood. They have three others in downtown Brooklyn. The land gets bought, the buildings go up fast; it's a rapid-fire operation."

Leonard nodded. "Welcome to New York. Ever upward."

"Yeah. Well, not every developer wakes up in the morning to a dead body on the doorstep and tries to get the building back online the next day. Not every developer is run by a woman whose father controls a quarter of the votes in Flatbush."

"I figured. You ever meet McArthur Hill?"

Mulino let out a slow breath before answering. "I had some dealings with him." You couldn't have been in the NYPD and not had some dealings with McArthur Hill. He had swept through Brooklyn like a firestorm twenty years ago, bottling local rage and selling it to the city at a premium. When he was still a beat cop, Mulino had been assigned to stand patrol at a march Hill's people had organized down the length of Flatbush Avenue, allegedly a memorial march for a man who crashed his car into Grand Army Plaza while fleeing from the police at eighty miles an hour. The crowd had walked, quiet and peaceful, for the most part. But there was a police officer every seventy feet, so every seventy feet someone sneered, or called the cop a killer, or spat on his shoes. The patrol rookies sent out for the rally had been told that their job was to stand there and take it. This kind of thing burns out if you let them have a day to be angry, the thinking went back then. But if one officer takes the bait and leaps into that crowd, then all hell breaks loose. The department assigned rookies to these marches because they didn't have union protection yet and could be quickly fired if they lost their cool.

Mulino went on. "Eleanor Hill runs the development company. It's not affiliated with the church. The father owns a stake in it, but it seems totally passive. Helped his daughter out when she was getting started. But you never know what kind of role he may play. After all, lots of people love McArthur Hill. Or at least lots of people want to please him."

"And some people don't."

Mulino nodded. That was true too. "So one guy kills another on a Hill and Associates worksite. Maybe the two of them had some personal grudge. Or maybe someone who doesn't like the company wanted to make it look bad. Somehow got to this Manny character. Or maybe, just maybe, this guy Wade knew something about what was going on with the operation. Maybe everything at that company isn't as above-board as it looks. And maybe they had a way of taking care of him."

"There are better ways of rubbing someone out than this. Quieter, certainly."

"Maybe this is someone's idea of making it look like an accident."

"Which is why you want everyone to think that you're looking only at the Department of Buildings."

"You know better than anyone, Leonard. When someone is on guard, they are not going to tell you anything. You need to catch someone after they think they have gotten away with it."

Leonard had leaned in now. Mulino could sense he was ready to be asked. Leonard's fingers were twitching on his knees. His neck a little stiffer above the collar. He wasn't going to be stuck writing press releases for the rest of his life after all.

"You want me to go after Eleanor Hill."

Mulino heaved himself off the chair and made his way to the door. He nodded to his detectives, now sitting at their desks shuffling through their Daily Activity Reports, and closed the door. He took out a piece of paper and slapped it on the desk in front of Leonard. "Hill and Associates has put out an ad. For a director of operations. Manage people. Run the paperwork through. Get permits. I want you to go work there. And I want you to tell me what you find."

"I don't know anything about real estate. Why would they hire me?"

"You managed a seventy-person agency. You know a half-dozen city commissioners. You know every block of this city. I'm sure you will manage to sell yourself to them."

"They'll figure me out."

"No, they won't, Leonard. You're too good for that. You brought down an entire criminal operation within the NYPD. You solved a murder while the department was hunting you as a suspect. We couldn't catch you then. Eleanor Hill won't catch you now."

"Am I going to be working for the NYPD, then? Am I undercover?"

"They'll pay you plenty if you get the job. Your arrangement with me will be informal. Harder to trace. You help me on this one, then when it's over, we'll see what sort of special investigator position might be open on this squad."

Leonard stared at the paper Mulino had handed him. Mulino could see him checking off the qualifications. Manage large organizations. Handle detailed analytics. Paperwork. City government. So what if it was putting up buildings rather than dragging down cops? Recognition set in across Leonard's face. Mulino could see what he was thinking: he could do this.

"All right, Detective. I'll put together a resume. I'll send it in."

"We put your resume together for you already. We already sent it in. Your interview is this afternoon." Mulino reached out to shake Leonard's hand. It was thin, and still a little cold. The guy really should start to wear an overcoat. Mulino let go of Leonard's hand and spoke.

"Good luck."

As soon as Leonard Mitchell was out the door, Detective Mulino slumped into his chair and propped his bad knee back up into the air. A small comfort at last.

CHAPTER SIX

Leonard could barely recognize the block. He had seen his own neighborhood change quickly enough. He had seen the new condos rise, and seen the old brownstones lathered in scaffolding and reborn as urban luxury. But there was never any need to go to downtown Brooklyn. After all, it was filled with odd shops selling used tires, stolen jewelry, and day-old chicken wings. At least that was how he remembered it.

It was as though an entire neighborhood had been plowed under and replanted with glass and steel. One thirty-story building after another anchored the avenue. A bank where the pawn shop used to be. A national chain selling dull jewelry where the Moroccan guy used to roast lamb skewers. It couldn't have all been built in the six months that Leonard was away.

He found what he was looking for soon enough. At twenty-five stories or so, the glass monolith was one of the more modest on the block. He double-checked the address and went inside.

The lobby was tight. More room to squeeze a juice bar on one side and a watch store on the other. The guard at the desk was indistinguishable from his brethren across the river. He looked down at Leonard's cheap suit and worn shoes. When Leonard had been at

DIMAC, this would be the moment that he would pull out his badge. When he would metamorphose from a dumpy underdressed visitor into a law enforcement official. But he couldn't do that anymore. A little card saying that you are the spokesman for the Parks Department does not impress thick men guarding elevators.

"Leonard Mitchell. I'm here for Eleanor Hill."

The guard nodded. He looked down at his list. Leonard was now just an ordinary man looking for a job, and if he wanted to go inside, he was going to have to be invited. And it would stay that way if they hired him. Even at the Parks Department, he could barely get his old contacts to return his calls. Tony Licata of the *Daily News* had been almost a drinking buddy when Leonard was at DIMAC. Now, unless Leonard was calling about a body, Tony wouldn't even pick up the phone. If Leonard went to work for Eleanor Hill and there was no scandal for him to report back to Ralph Mulino, he would have transformed himself into just another working stiff.

Lost in thought, Leonard didn't notice when the guard nodded at him and sent him through the elevator. He didn't see that the elevator was pre-programmed to take him to the proper floor. He barely took in the sweet young man who offered him coffee, and didn't see the view when he reached the offices of Hill and Associates. Only when he had been ushered past the bright glass walls, peering out across the river at lower Manhattan and its own brand-new glass tower, and was seated across from Eleanor Hill herself did he snap back into the present.

He was slumped into a designer stainless chair strapped with cream leather, struggling to bring himself up. Eleanor Hill looked down at him. Her chair was higher, maybe, or perhaps her entire desk was on a pedestal. She was holding a sheet of paper at a distance with her left hand, barely glancing at it as she drilled into him.

"Twenty years in city government. Investigating the police. Press secretary for DIMAC. Deputy Commissioner. Acting Commissioner. And over to the Parks Department. You have never worked in the private sector a day in your life. What made you wake up one day and decide you wanted to work in real estate? What makes you think you're remotely qualified for this?"

That wasn't a good start. Leonard pushed himself up from the chair a little, but slipped uncontrollably back down. It was a losing battle. But Eleanor Hill was a powerful woman. Her time was valuable. She wouldn't have scheduled an interview with him just to humiliate him. He might as well answer.

"I've supervised a staff of sixty investigators. I've worked with sensitive information. I've put dirty cops in jail. I figured to run your operations you'd need someone with a spine. You have accountants to work out your rent rolls and your depreciation."

Eleanor put the paper down. At least he had her attention. "What it looks like to me is that you made your city pension and you're looking to cash out."

In some ways that was true. It had been a long struggle working for the city. As soon as he left, he would be guaranteed 75 percent of his salary just for staying away. It wouldn't kick in for a few years, and he couldn't get it if he had another job with the city, but other than that it would be waiting for him. If he could find a nice quiet job behind a desk making a good deal more than he did at DIMAC, then seven years from now, the pension would be a healthy raise. He would never be rich by New York standards, but he could sure move out of the Ebbets Field Apartments. Still, he was smart enough to know that admitting it wasn't the right answer.

"I enjoyed DIMAC. I was working on justice. I was bringing down the corrupt. I was fighting the good fight. It doesn't seem the same at the Parks Department. I want to make a difference, and real estate seems to be—well, that's what's making a difference in this city now."

"In this borough, anyway. Look around you, Leonard. Look behind you."

Leonard turned over his shoulder. He had lived in Brooklyn for twenty years. He remembered the night that Amy Watkins was stabbed for her handbag, walking home from the subway on Park Place. The townhouse that she died in front of sold last year for $3.2 million. He remembered Shoot the Freak and the rickety roller coasters at Coney Island, dismantled and replaced with bright blue-and-orange rides that came pre-packaged from a factory in Kansas. He remembered when Gavin Cato was mowed down while fixing his bicycle on President Street. And he remembered the riots that followed. Now those streets too were lined with unadulterated luxury homes.

Out the floor-to-ceiling window, following Eleanor's gesture, he could count six new residential towers, each over fifty stories tall, not to mention the arena, the shopping center, the parking garage. No one had bothered to repaint the insides of the courtrooms at Brooklyn State Supreme in fifty years, but any sliver of land that could fit an apartment building had become fair game.

"Do you see that, Leonard? It's progress. Thirty years ago this borough was a wasteland. Crime. Poverty. Corruption. You know something about corruption. Remind me how hard it was to bribe a state senator from Canarsie in 1976?"

Leonard didn't say anything. They both knew the answer. Eleanor went on.

"And now look around you. New stores. New restaurants. New housing. Everyone in the world wants to come and live in Brooklyn. They make television shows about the place. And we have provided that. Through hard work. Through taking a burnt-out building, rebuilding it, and finding someone who will take the risk to move into it. And then doing it again, and again, and again. Until the whole place is transformed."

"I understand." The best thing to do when someone is giving a speech is let her talk. Pretty soon you'll understand what she's really saying. She probably wasn't going to say that everything she was taking credit for was made possible by fat tax credits. Or by ending subway crime, so rich people felt safe enough to shuttle home from a Times Square office to a Crown Heights condo. Bernie Goetz was only thirty years ago, after all.

"And what credit do we get? For transforming this borough into the jewel of the city? Do they thank us? No. Look at the papers. Who are always the easy villains? Developers, builders, creators. I was at a community board meeting last night and it was shut down by protesters. Did you hear about the community board meeting?"

Leonard had done his research. He had dug up the controversy, read about the vote, seen the proposal for the new building that Hill and Associates wanted to splay along Empire. Mulino wasn't the only one who could do legwork. "I heard."

"And why? Because I want to bring more housing to their neighborhood—affordable housing. They'd rather keep the junk shops. I grew up in Flatbush. My father runs a church in Flatbush. And there was a reason that people who were living in Flatbush in 1982 joined his church. There was nothing else on offer in this city. Now I offer more. With new buildings come opportunities. Sanitation comes by twice a week instead of once. The Department of Transportation builds out the crosswalks. Express buses, more subway cars. Because there are new buildings. But no matter what we do to improve lives, I'm still the bad guy."

The speech sounded familiar to Leonard. But he couldn't place why. "It sounds like you need a press secretary. I can do that too."

"Leonard. I need everything. I need someone who can go to a building site and make sure I don't have union guys taking two-hour lunches and harassing the girls on the street. I need someone to call the *Daily News* when a bunch of yahoos wants to shut me down. I need someone who can walk into the Department of Buildings and get me a permit before my so-called 'expeditor' can. I don't need another office manager."

"I understand. I know some people at DOB, the *Daily News*. I earned a lot of favors that I haven't called in yet." There had always been a few DIMAC investigators who made their way over to Buildings. The rap was that the work wasn't as hard, and if you missed an investigation or six, there were no real consequences. A place you could go to kick back. The whispers were that the whole agency was on the take.

"Good. Let me tell you what I need this week. I have an open house on Sunday. It's a small job. We just bought the building. We're selling it as-is. A bring-your-architect listing. I don't like paying three and a half percent to a broker when I already pay a staff. I could go out and show the place to people myself, but I don't work on Sundays."

"I don't have a brokers' license."

"We have licensed staff to close the deal. You'll just be a representative of Hill and Associates. Here is the listing. And here are the keys."

The folder and the key chain felt as though they had come flying over the desk. It had all happened so fast. A slick printout of a brick townhouse. Prospect Heights. One of the last four-stories to be converted from apartments to a single family house in the neighborhood.

"So I have the job?"

"You have this job. You run the open house. Get a sign-in sheet. The place is a wreck. Don't pretend otherwise. We won't vouch for even a light switch. If another developer takes it off our hands, even better. All you have to do is make sure no one coming to the open house steals something."

"What is there to steal?"

"There are still a couple of renters in the building. It's bad enough they'll have to leave. We want to safeguard their property."

"I understand." The distasteful side of the whole thing. Of course there would be renters in place. That's the reason to flip the property quickly. Evicting people wouldn't be good for Eleanor Hill's corporate profile.

"Thank you, Leonard."

"I'll let you know how it goes."

"Come back on Monday for that."

It was a start. But he hadn't learned anything that would explain why anyone wanted to kill Wade Valiant. One step at a time. He shoved the keys in his pocket and left her office.

As he drifted down, he remembered why Eleanor's speech about being targeted despite doing so much good for the world sounded familiar. It was a cop's speech. With only a few words different, it was a speech about how the thin blue line protects the population from gangbangers and villains, and how the population's response is to be angry at those very cops. How if anyone understood all the sacrifice made by police officers, they would put down their picket signs and pray that patrols on the streets would double, that thousands more would be stopped and frisked. It was a speech, Leonard also remembered, that was usually given by the chief of the officers' union. And it was usually given a few days before jury selection in the manslaughter trial for a couple of cops who had shot another unarmed black teenager. Anything to get an advantage.

Leonard tucked the open house materials into his bag, swept past the doorman, and made his way into the first frost of an early winter.

CHAPTER SEVEN

Mulino stared across his desk at Detective Bruder. The kid actually had his cell phone out. If the Chief of Patrol wasn't best friends with the guy's dad, Mulino would have whipped around the desk and yanked it out of his hand. Meanwhile, Detective Peralta was sitting upright like a petulant sixth grader hoping the teacher would call on her, notebook at the ready. Mulino wondered what he had gotten himself into by becoming a supervisor.

Bruder pretended that the text on his phone was about the case. "TARU tells us they are still trying to find something." Mulino knew better.

Peralta made a quick jot in her memo book. *You don't need to take notes when he doesn't say anything useful,* Detective Mulino wanted to tell her. But you criticize a young detective and suddenly you're a mean boss. Or maybe the subject of an EEO complaint. Best to ask questions. Act like these two were the ones getting investigated. Speak slowly; wait for answers; keep calm.

"So what, exactly, did you ask them? And what, precisely, did they say?"

Bruder held up his finger. Reading from his phone. That kind of reaction would have merited a Command Discipline on the spot in Mulino's day. He wanted to smack the kid. But then he thought again about Bruder's family and held off. A week before, when Bruder had been in the field, Mulino had stopped at the kid's desk and seen what he was reading all the time. It was a pro-police online message board. The kind of place where every cop in the country who guns someone down is a hero, where every crowd of protesters is made up only of savages. It was a big red flag, that kind of thing. Usually most of the people trolling through those sites were retired—a bunch of Archie Bunkers who could yell together without getting out of their recliners.

When a young cop was reading that, it meant that the message of the new NYPD was not getting through. Mulino had his own problems with the new messaging, with the white-glove treatment you had to use sometimes nowadays. But he understood the reasons for it. There were plenty of past sins to be made up for. And more than anything, he understood that if the Commissioner tells the command officers how things are going to be, then that was the way they were going to be. You want to work somewhere where every employee can publicly bitch about his boss with no recrimination, then go get a job teaching college.

Mulino was done with Bruder. Even the kid's father would understand if Mulino took some action now. "Detective. You can finish with your cell phone later. What did you ask TARU, and what did they tell you?"

Bruder's glossy eyes showed he hadn't heard the question. Even the second time. Peralta flipped back a page in her memo book and started to read from it. *Nice to have someone to bail you out of a jam*, Mulino thought.

Bruder settled into his chair. Mulino could tell he wasn't used to being talked to like that. He would have to get used to it. Peralta read the details. "We did provide the cell number, email address, and pedigree information to the Technical Assistance Response Unit at eleven hundred twenty-six hours yesterday. Having received no answer from them this morning, we called at oh-nine-hundred forty-four hours. The lieutenant there told us he had no new information to report."

Peralta had made the report, but Mulino was still talking to Bruder. "No new information like, Manny hasn't used his cell phone and he hasn't checked his email? Or no new information like, we haven't even bothered to check yet?"

Bruder stewed. "The lieutenant didn't say."

"And did you ask?"

Peralta looked back down to her memo book. She flipped another page. She wasn't going to find the answer there. Bruder was going to have to come up with his own excuse.

"So those guys. They are really busy. They've got the Thanksgiving parade coming up. Gotta make sure there isn't any terrorist chatter, people getting ready to attack the parade. There is just tons of data they have to sift through. So, you know, we can keep asking, but you know . . ."

At least Bruder had put away the cell phone. Mulino wondered what TARU would find if they got their hands on that. How many text messages that were not strictly work-related, sent during work hours? During the supervisor's training, Mulino had been told about an LA County investigation where a cop had been fired for sexting on a department-issued cell phone. They had to spend a year in court to prove it was okay for the department to check his cell records. And that was when the department had issued the phone and paid the bill.

Bruder's phone was his own. Asking for those records would mean not just the kid's dad, and the kid's dad's friends, but a wall of union lawyers talking about the Fourth Amendment. As though they thought about that when they were kicking down doors. Used to be, they could always find a way to fire you if they really wanted to.

Mulino at least had their attention now. He looked from one to the other and spoke very slowly. "Detectives, here is what we are going to do. You're going to tell me what you have done to find Mr. Reeves. You're going to tell me what you have found out about Mr. Valiant. I presume you spoke to some friends? Some coworkers, during the course of the whole afternoon yesterday?"

Peralta nodded. Bruder was bursting to speak. A bit lip; he knew just enough to hold off on interrupting for now.

"Then you are going to call back TARU. You are going to ask the lieutenant what devices they have tracked, what requests or subpoenas have been issued, and to which carriers. And if they tell you they haven't run anything yet, then you'll tell me that so I can call them up and rip their heads off. But if they tell you that they have run all the data, and Reeves's cell phone isn't pinging, then you're going to tell me that too. Because that would tell me something, wouldn't it?"

Bruder couldn't help himself. "They're going to find him soon enough. And it's pretty clear that he killed the guy. So what are we spinning our wheels for? Why do we have to talk to every guy that knew them? It's a waste of time."

Mulino steamed. It was a struggle to keep calm. Someone had taught him back when he was a hothead, so he had to teach these two now. "If you keep up the way you have, Detective Bruder, I have no confidence whatsoever that you are going to find Mr. Reeves. And even if you do, with nothing more than we have right now, the DA will not be able to convict him. They have these people called criminal defense attorneys in this country. And if you don't have a motive, they can come up with all sorts of stories. Mr. Reeves had some sort of seizure. Mr. Reeves lost control of the machine. Mr. Reeves was trying to lower Mr. Valiant, and the machine malfunctioned. And then they say to the jury that you know they're right because they haven't heard the prosecutor give any reason at all that Mr. Reeves would want to kill someone. And what exactly do you propose the prosecutor should do then?"

Bruder slouched back. "That's the lawyer's job. We're just supposed to get the bad guys."

Mulino looked to Peralta. Bruder was turning into a lost cause. Untouchable based on his family, but incompetent and proud of it.

Peralta was going to have to do all the heavy lifting on the case, only to have Bruder boast to his friends at the bar that he'd cracked a homicide. Only to have him whine that she shouldn't be a detective at all, to think that the Department had made a special exception for her, when really it had made one for him. She was going through the memo book again.

"We spoke to the other workers on site. There were no beefs between the two men. Everyone liked Wade. Most people liked Manny. They seemed to like each other. Not best friends, but no one was sleeping with anyone else's wife or anything. No public fights."

"Who didn't like Manny?"

"A couple of newer guys thought he was sort of a pain in the ass. Talking about how long he'd been at it and how he could have done their jobs better than they did. He had some sort of injury that put him in the cab instead of on the scaffolding. The new guys thought he rubbed it in their face a little."

"But not Wade."

"Wade wasn't a new guy."

Mulino nodded. This was expected. The first time you ask, no one wants to come out and accuse someone of anything. But you dig a little, listen a lot, give people a chance to open up, and you'll hear it then. When Peralta went back to those guys who didn't like Manny all that much, they would think of something that kind of pissed them off one time or another. Something a little petty or a little mean. That would be the start.

"And when you checked with the employer?"

"There was no one at the office of Hill and Associates in the evening when we stopped by. We couldn't reach the CEO, Eleanor Hill. We've put in a request for HR records for both men. They're going to tell us by the end of the day whether they will comply without a subpoena."

"And if they won't?"

"Then we'll get a subpoena."

"Call the DA's office today. Get the subpoena out to Hill and Associates today. Don't wait for them to decide whether they are cooperating."

"Okay."

Bruder was back now. He had blown off whatever steam he had needed with his outburst. "And don't forget the father."

"What?" Mulino asked.

Peralta looked to Bruder, then back to her book. "Yeah. When there was no one home at the office, Timmy said maybe we should go call on the father. See what's going on with him. Maybe thought he would know something."

"You went to McArthur Hill's church?"

"It was Timmy's idea."

Bruder was looking at the floor now. As much as Mulino thought it was a bad idea for his detectives to burst in on a politically connected pastor without paving the way first, he didn't like one of them throwing the other under the bus for it either. That was the kind of behavior that would get Peralta's locker glued shut. Or worse.

"And what happened?"

"He yelled at us. He told us we were profiling his entire congregation. He told us that we thought . . ." She had to look this part up. "That we thought not only the sins of the father flowed to the son, but that the sins of the daughter's employee flowed back to the father. He was pretty upset."

Bruder steamed again. "He was trying to hide something. That's what all the yelling and the calling us racists was about. He's got something going on that he didn't want the police looking into."

Mulino waited for the pair to quiet down. "Okay, detectives. You call TARU. You ask them what I told you to ask them. You get specific information. How often they pinged the phone. Activity on the email. And then you get back to me. You let me deal with McArthur Hill. Stay away from that place. If you are going to go to a church, a church where they feed on dressing down the NYPD, you have to play it very slowly. So don't try that again."

"Okay."

"Now get out there and get TARU to track down our only suspect."

The two of them stood and pivoted out of Mulino's office. They weren't rocket scientists, but they would have to do. Mulino would have to get Bruder off of his cell phone. He kept his own cell phone inside a desk drawer when he had a meeting. Old habit. He pulled open the drawer and saw that, while he'd been grilling the detectives, he had received a two-word text message of his own. It was from Leonard Mitchell, and it made him smile.

I'm in.

CHAPTER EIGHT

Leonard walked along Empire Boulevard, the subway behind him and the glum tower of Ebbets Field ahead of him. It had almost been too easy with Eleanor Hill. He had the job, but he didn't know anything yet. And he wasn't sure how he could find anything out. Showing townhouses wasn't going to help him discover what secrets Hill and Associates had to hide. But he wouldn't get any further into the organization if he didn't show the house. So he jingled the keys and thought about what he might tell the prospective buyers on Sunday. *Sure, the place is a shithole, but it's right around the corner from that new Korean place everyone is talking about.*

At Washington Avenue, he stopped. He was two blocks from home, but a block and a half in the other direction stood a house he'd been meaning to visit for a while. Last year, while he had been investigating Ralph Mulino, his old boss, Christine Davenport, had been murdered. It turns out she had found out just enough about the dirty cops to get killed, and had left behind just enough information so Leonard could crack the case. Her husband and son had left for New Jersey. Once he got out of Moriah Shock, Leonard had tried to find them, but there was no trace. Their names didn't show up in any databases—not the public ones and not the ones you can get access to through the city. Leonard figured they had changed their names, stayed in New Jersey or gone even further afield. They had every right to be afraid. Christine had been killed, and her husband had never learned the whole story. Anyone would worry that someone dangerous was still out there.

Leonard eventually gave up looking for Adam and his son. But he still periodically searched for the name, and just two weeks ago he found a hit. Adam had bought a house not four blocks from Ebbets Field. He had switched jobs and joined the community board. The same community board where Eleanor Hill had tried to pitch her latest project. Adam likely would have been there, would have seen her and the protesters, both. Now he taught at Brooklyn College, only a short subway ride away. He was living on Guilder Street, a tidy row of townhouses where the lawns all backed up to Empire Boulevard. Leonard had been meaning to go by every night for the last two weeks. Now was as good a time as any.

Leonard rang the doorbell. There was still contractor's paper over the small window in the door. The house was nice, a pretty little limestone with bay windows. Those still had contractor's paper on them too. He hadn't even bought blinds yet. After a moment, Leonard could hear movement, and the paper over the window jiggled aside. Behind the window was a face Leonard had seen only a few times, at a company party and maybe once in the office. Adam Davenport looked a little heavier now, and as though much more than a year had passed.

Adam opened the door. Leonard still couldn't tell if the man recognized him. He could hear shuffling in the background, someone coming down a flight of stairs, maybe.

Adam looked tired. "Yes."

"Mr. Davenport."

"Yes."

"My name is Leonard Mitchell. I worked with Christine."

Adam looked over his shoulder, as though maybe he would say something to whoever was inside. Then he turned back to Leonard.

"You're the one that got arrested."

So Adam knew that part. Someone had told him something. Leonard wondered how much he knew. He wondered if Adam knew how much the city owed Christine. How much she had found out. And how she had stashed away the fruits of her investigation on a flash drive posing as a refrigerator magnet, hiding a trove of data in plain sight.

"Yeah. They arrested me. I was trying to find out who killed Christine, you know."

Adam considered. Maybe he would open the door and let Leonard in. But instead, he spoke. Quietly, flat, as though he were accepting a delayed apology. "Okay." Maybe Adam was angry at Leonard. Maybe he thought Leonard should have done more. Or maybe he was afraid of him. Or maybe, at some point, there stops being a difference between anger and fear.

"It's cold out here."

"Maybe you should have worn an overcoat."

Noise again. Another look over the shoulder. It would be the son. Henry. He wouldn't be used to a house yet. Leonard had been to Davenport's apartment in Manhattan once. The boy had slept in what was essentially an oversized closet. But he had been only five then. Or maybe six.

"Mr. Davenport, I did everything I could. I don't know how much Christine told you. She found out some very bad things. She wasn't afraid."

"And look where that got her."

"I just mean when you think of her, you should be proud of what she did."

Adam nodded. There was puzzlement now, in addition to anger and fear. They wouldn't have wanted to tell him everything, whichever detectives had briefed him after the case. They would have said that her killers had been killed, which was true. They would have said she had uncovered some dirty cops, which was also true. But they would never have told him the scope of the conspiracy. It would only have frightened him.

"I'm very proud of her. Thank you."

"You just moved to the neighborhood?"

"I got a new job. I was with my family, for a while."

"I couldn't find you. And I spent a good part of my life finding people for a living."

"We didn't want to be found. I figured after a year, if no one had found us, they weren't looking anymore." So it was true. They had been hiding. Using fake names, maybe, or staying with friends, never using a credit card. Never signing a lease. It gets hard, after a while. Leonard could understand why Adam was back.

Leonard held out his hand. "Welcome to the neighborhood, Adam. I live in Ebbets Field. You can probably see it out your window."

Again, there was a quiet distance in Adam's answer. Just the facts. *Don't think we are friends now or anything.* "Okay. Yes, I can."

Leonard thought to go. He had made his introduction. But there was something still he could learn from this man. "Adam. If you don't mind. I want to talk to you about the community board. About the meeting this week."

"Yeah. I was there. I just wanted to do my part. I'm new in the neighborhood. I want to help."

There was more clamor back in the house. Leonard saw a flash of movement. Behind Adam was another door into the house that was only half open. Someone had run past it at full speed. And now was coming closer.

Leonard figured he might as well try to learn something. Adam hadn't exactly kicked him out yet. "Were you there for the protests? For Eleanor Hill?"

Adam waited to answer again. Measuring what Leonard might really be asking, what he was driving at. "She never gave her presentation. The protesters shut down the meeting. I read her packet online. She had emailed us all. It looked . . . well, I'm sure you can find a copy to read. Are you investigating real estate developers nowadays instead of cops?"

The door behind him opened, and there was the boy. Short, dark hair, with his mother's narrow features, and a devious child's smile. He was wearing plain blue pajamas. Seven, Leonard guessed. Just old enough to have decided that pajamas with stars or dinosaurs or race cars were for babies. He looked up at his father.

"Dad? Can I have some screen time?"

Adam looked like he had aged another five years since answering the door. He turned and spoke to the boy.

"Ten minutes of screen time, Henry. Then brush your teeth, then read and go to bed."

"Only ten?"

And a look came over Adam. The look that every parent has now and again. *I could keep this up, but what is the point, really?* He relented. "Okay. Twenty minutes."

And the boy scurried back up the stairs. Leonard took out his personal card. No office. Just his name and phone number.

"You know there was an accident on the construction site, Adam. I'm just trying to figure a few things out."

Adam took the card, looked at it. Leonard could see him wonder. Trying to figure if Leonard was a cop now. Or looking for a lawsuit. And then feeling too tired to try to figure it out.

"Okay."

"You go ahead and put your son to bed."

"Thanks. I will." Adam Davenport shut the door and retreated to his lonely house. Leonard turned down the three front steps and onto the lovely manicured street. As he walked back toward his own apartment, he figured that the encounter with Adam went about as well as he could have expected.

CHAPTER NINE

Detective Peralta thought the houses were doing their best to look like one another. The same red vinyl awnings. The same white window sashes. The same shape: boxy brick below to make you think the place was bigger than it was, and a peaked roof to make you think you were anywhere but Queens. Detective Peralta looked down the uniform block. The homes of white people who have lived in the city for fifty years. Instead of running off to Ronkonkoma or Baldwin, they just tried to make Elmhurst look as suburban as possible. Even the street names were subtle reminders of an older, settled power: Hampton, Ithaca, Judge. As though no one in Elmhurst wanted to be reminded that they lived in New York City at all.

Peralta herself had grown up in Nutley, New Jersey, raised by parents who never had to flee the city because they had never gone there to begin with. Solid Victorian houses dotted a neatly trimmed town square, all of it close enough to Manhattan for the occasional daring teenage excursion. Her parents had been as afraid of the city as all the white parents, and she had been just as eager to get out of the suburbs and hit New York as all the other kids. But instead of moving to the Lower East Side and sharing an apartment with six kids who all thought they would be discovered as dancers or sculptors or fashion designers, she had taken the NYPD exam, moved to Hoboken, and hit patrol with glee.

Her parents had threatened to disown her. They hadn't put her through Rutgers so she could walk the slums and maybe get shot. She didn't care what they thought. She had the bug. The city, to Aurelia Peralta, did not mean the latest kimchi shop or the most inscrutable piece of performance art or the doughnut you had to wait in the longest line to buy. It meant the street deals and the knives and now and again the guns, the vicious pulse of never-ending action, most of which was action that was not strictly permitted under the law. The only way to get in on that action was to become a criminal, a cop, or a social worker. Peralta's parents hadn't raised her to be a criminal. But she was no social worker.

The fact that the other cops made boneheaded assumptions based on her name and complexion didn't bother her. They asked if she was from Washington Heights or from Highbridge, expected her to speak Spanish to the guy behind the counter of every bodega, to walk the streets with an extra swagger. Good thing they didn't notice, as the guy behind the bodega counter always did, that her Spanish was of the suburban-high-school variety. And good thing she had never lacked in swagger. Finding out that other recruits couldn't tell the difference between someone from the barrio and someone from Essex County was a worthwhile lesson in and of itself. Playing like she was from the street at least kept guys from grabbing her ass. Sometimes.

Detective Bruder was the kind of cop she could control. Convinced of his own merit, insulated from the world by friends and family who had always been cops, and dumber than a sack of hair, he couldn't even tell when she was playing him. The first thing he asked her when they got assigned together was what her score had been on the entry exam. This after six years on the force and a promotion to detective. She'd made up a number that sounded low enough so that he would think she was a charity case. She liked being underestimated.

So when Detective Bruder was driving her down a quiet street in Elmhurst, looking for a blue, late-model Impala with the license plate number she had scribbled on an index card, Peralta knew she would be doing all the legwork. Bruder thought that driving made him a big shot, but the truth was that it took every ounce of his brainpower to keep from running over a pedestrian. Aside from checking out the houses, she checked the models and license plates of every parked car, front and back.

That's all they had, after all. Manny Reeves hadn't driven to the job site that day. Wade Valiant had picked him up on the way into the city. And TARU hadn't come through with any pings from the cell phone. Bruder hadn't pressed them, like Detective Mulino asked him to. He'd just nodded to Peralta after putting in another call. "I guess they'll get to it."

So they had Reeves's address. But the uniforms had been in there already. Nothing unusual. The guy hadn't been back after Valiant had died. And they had his plate number. So Detective Peralta was sitting shotgun on a Sunday morning casing the license plates in Elmhurst. The car would have to be parked close enough to the residence that Reeves could walk home. Elmhurst wasn't like downtown Brooklyn. You could still usually find a parking spot on your own street, or at worst the next one. But it turns out there are a lot of Impalas in Elmhurst. Either that or everything looks like an Impala nowadays.

Bruder was cruising down the street too quickly for Peralta to catch every car. She tapped his shoulder as she spoke. "Slow down."

Bruder pulled their Crown Vic up to another parked car. This one was boxed in so Peralta had to lean out to look at the plate. She checked her index card. Not a match.

"Okay, keep going."

Bruder started the car back up. "You know, if we just wait till tomorrow, traffic might find it when they give out the alternate side tickets."

That had been their first hope, that the car would have been cited on Thursday when the traffic division came down the street to give a citation to every car parked on the left shoulder so the street sweepers could come through. But Thursday morning was when it had all happened. So most likely, Reeves had parked his car where it wouldn't get a ticket until Monday. And that was tomorrow.

Peralta kept watching the plates as they went by. "Yeah, no hurry or anything tracking the guy down. It isn't as though someone's dead or anything."

"I'm only saying."

Peralta thought of the TARU guys. Either they really were sitting around playing pinochle instead of running the numbers, or Manny Reeves had not used his phone in three days. Or logged on to his email. Posted a picture of his breakfast on Twitter. That was a sign that he knew people were looking for him and he didn't want to be found.

Or maybe that he was dead too.

It was dull work, making your way up and down the street. Looking for a car that might not tell you anything about who killed Wade Valiant, even if you find it. But Peralta was working a homicide. Her first one. There was no way on to the Homicide Division itself; there hadn't been for years. There simply weren't enough people getting killed. The department had decided to shut down any new hires or transfers into the Division until it shrank to a reasonable size. There had been lots of detectives sitting around as murders had gone below eight hundred a year, five hundred, down to three hundred and eighteen. But when they started back up again, the department had not been ready. They didn't even have an exam to dust off. With Homicide suddenly understaffed, investigations of merely-somewhat-suspicious deaths were getting picked up by other bureaus. So Detective Aurelia Peralta, technically in OCCB, suddenly had the chance to work what looked like a murder to her.

She saw another car, the last one on the block before Elmhurst Avenue. "That one, Timmy."

Bruder stopped the car and Peralta leaned out. She double-checked the index card. "Detective," she smiled, "we have a match."

Bruder turned off the car and stepped out. Peralta circled the Impala. It wasn't as though she thought she was going to find a bloody handprint on it. But hopefully there would be something. It was locked, of course. If it hadn't been, it would have already been gone. Inside, it was a mess. Fast food wrappers. Coffee cups. Maybe underneath the piles of garbage there would be an address book. A name of a friend. A piece of mail. Something to help them keep looking.

"You ready?" Bruder had brought his heavy-duty knife, a tiny hexagonal stud at the hilt. The window punch could spiderweb a car window in an instant. They already had the warrant ready, if Mr. Reeves were to do anything so dumb as come back. They were in plainclothes but both had their shields out on chains around their necks. It wasn't like anyone would think they were stealing the car. And at least Bruder had the right tool. Peralta wouldn't have been surprised if he'd simply shot the window out.

He heaved back and smacked the window punch into the driver's side with a powerful *thwack*. The window splintered but held its shape. Bruder pressed with his hand and the pebbles dribbled away. He reached in and opened the door. Within minutes the two of them had emptied the car of trash. But other than trash—candy wrappers, used Kleenex, a week-old *Daily News*, a box from White Castle—there was really nothing else. An ATM receipt was the closest thing to evidence in the car.

Bruder was kneeling by the front passenger seat; he leaned over to his partner. "You want I should pop open the glove compartment?"

"Sure." Peralta stood back from the car. Bruder was probably going to do this with his knife, and could easily cut his thumb off in the process.

Bruder took out the knife. As he jammed it into the locked glove box, his cell phone went off. He stopped, wriggled out of the car, and answered.

"Yeah? Where? Okay." His eyes widened. He hung up and turned back toward the car. "Let's go."

"We're gonna leave the car unlocked?"

"We can call patrol along the way."

"Along the way to where?"

"Brookdale Hospital. That was TARU. They just picked up a ping from this guy's phone."

CHAPTER TEN

"From the book of Matthew, the parable of the tenants."

Eleanor Hill looked up as her father plied his trade from the pulpit. His voice was low, no louder than a man saying grace at his family dinner table. McArthur Hill had no need to shout. He would woo the arena-sized room unamplified. His authority was so secure, his audience so enraptured, that the eight hundred congregants would lean in close to hear even a whisper. Eleanor remembered the voice lessons he had sent her to as a child. Breathe with your gut. Relax your throat. So the voice carries even if it isn't loud.

So many careers to choose from when you give up on acting: lawyer, salesman, pastor. Projecting your voice is a learned skill. Volume has nothing to do with it. In his trim, gray pinstripe suit, a royal blue stole tucked around his once-athletic shoulders, McArthur Hill would own nearly any room he was in. But this room, more than any other, was his to own. He went on, quietly captivating the packed church.

"Chapter twenty-one. Verse thirty-three. 'There was a landowner who planted a vineyard, and put a wall around it, and dug a wine press in it, and built a tower, and rented it out to vine-growers and went on a journey.'"

He paused and surveyed the crowd. To Eleanor, tucked quietly ten or twelve rows back, it seemed that he was looking just over her head, making eye contact with someone just a few rows behind. But this she knew was another actor's skill. Look between faces, make it seem as though you are meeting sets of eyes. It is alarming to be actually met with the gaze of the man behind the podium, and comforting to think he is looking at your neighbor. So you look just between them. Her father's soft, controlled voice went on.

"We rarely look to the beginning of the parable of the tenants. We always speak about the end. But I want us to think for a moment of the landlord. He builds the vineyard. He builds the hedges. And then he leaves on a journey. He makes demands of his tenants. But he makes no peace with them. He does not know them." She had heard her father on this parable a dozen times. But this part was new. This blaming of the landlord, with its implicit undertone: *What did he think was going to happen?*

"Verse thirty-four. 'When the harvest time approached, he sent his slaves to the vine-growers to receive his produce. The vine-growers took his slaves and beat one, and killed another, and stoned a third. Again he sent another group of slaves larger than the first; and they did the same thing to them. But afterward he sent his son to them, saying, 'They will respect my son.' But when the vine-growers saw the son, they said among themselves, 'This is the heir; come, let us kill him and seize his inheritance.' They took him, and threw him out of the vineyard and killed him.'"

Hill stopped again and looked over the rapt crowd. Slaves. Beatings. Murder. Eleanor knew they had heard this all before. That too often their own weekly lives had been intruded upon by violence. Maybe not like twenty years ago. Maybe not even like ten years ago. But everyone in the congregation would know at least someone whose cousin, or whose cousin's friend, had been beaten. Had been knifed. Or knew someone who had. You put your trust in people, and that's when they come after you with the clubs.

"Imagine for a moment this landlord. He owns slaves. His tenants are his slaves in another way. They are not free to use the land on which they live as they see fit. He cannot even show his face to his own tenants, to collect his rents in person. And we ask, what sort of landlord will not enter his own vineyard?"

Eleanor's mind began to drift. Her father the magician. The man who could command the stage at any rally, who could draw praise from electricians, cab drivers, and brakemen, who could win favors from mayors, commissioners, and even the governor once. The first thing anyone had asked her, her whole life, was whether she was this man's daughter. And it was always asked with a sense of awe. A man who had always done so much good for so many. Others always seemed to envy her.

But those others who envied her never had been judged by her father, never had been held to his standards. She had lived with decades of it. The questions that carried a hint of accusation. Why did she feel she needed to see her friends on a day she had a piano lesson? Why was she too sick to go to church but not too sick to go to the park? Had she considered where the tenants in that building she was buying were going to live now? But this was new. He would not give an entire sermon about evil landlords just to point her out. Instead she thought about their call two nights before. When she had pulled into her home just after the community board meeting and returned his frantic messages.

––––––––––

"Something terrible has happened. Something truly terrible."

"Dad, what is it?"

"The police are here. At the door of my church. Your doings have brought them here."

She had sped to the church as fast as she could, knowing it would be another late night. Her father told her only that the detectives had knocked, and that he had politely but firmly told them they had no business in a holy house.

But Eleanor knew he wouldn't have stopped there. He would have no doubt lectured them on *Mapp* and *Terry* and a host of Supreme Court cases that they probably don't teach to patrol officers. He would have reminded them that he didn't intend to end up like Tamir Rice or Freddy Gray or Michael Brown or Sean Bell or Ousmane Zongo or Timothy Stansbury or Khiel Coppin or Patrick Dorismond or Amadou Diallo or Anthony Baez or Eleanor Bumpurs or a hundred others who had been killed before either of these two had been born. They were just a couple of lugheads following leads, and someone had told them that McArthur Hill had something to do with Hill and Associates. But no one had told them what. And then he would have shut the door and called Eleanor to demand that she sort the whole thing out. And here she was.

When Eleanor got out of the car, the two cops were standing on the sidewalk in front of the church. One of them was a typical white Staten Island cop, the kind of guy who couldn't get a job anywhere except on the NYPD or behind the bar at McSorley's. The other was Hispanic, but didn't sound quite like she was from the city, with the kind of trumped-up toughness that people who grew up soft tend to have. Maybe from California or something. Maybe they had been thinking about getting a warrant. Maybe they were waiting for a supervisor. Or maybe they had been killing time until their shift ended.

"What can I do for you, Detectives?" Eleanor had never had her father's fear or anger toward the police. Toward any authority figures, really. She had always been able to bend people to her will. She could talk her way out of a traffic ticket and make the cop feel bad he had ever pulled her over. She had learned just enough about how to seduce people from her father's sermons. She had learned enough about the tough, mean world of the streets around her to know that cops are just another bunch of civil servants to manipulate.

The white one spoke. He probably thought he was in charge. Eleanor could tell that neither one of them was in charge. There would be a lieutenant pulling the strings. But the white guy always would think he was in charge of something. "You're Eleanor Hill?"

"That's right."

"Man died on your worksite today."

"I'm well aware of it. I think my foreman spoke to one of you on the scene. Or both of you."

The Hispanic one now took out a memo book and a pen. Well trained, this one—get everything down on paper. She paged through her notes from the day of interviews. "Your foreman. That's Rex Harper?"

"Sure."

"He didn't have much to say."

"He was there, at least. I'm going to have even less to say than him. And I can't imagine what you think my father would have to say."

The detective flipped through a few pages. "We're looking for the guy who may have been in the cab. Manuel Reeves."

"I met him once. I'm sure Mr. Harper had his address. His phone number. All the paperwork he gave us when he signed on."

The white detective was growing defensive now. It's what happens. As soon as they realize you aren't going to cower and defer to them, they get weak. They keep trying to justify themselves. *It looked so much like a gun. He was moving his arms in a furtive manner.* "We were just looking to follow up on everything we could. Every lead we had."

"Well, no lead should have led you to my father's church."

The Hispanic one wasn't done. "But Mr. Hill, he is an owner in your business, right? He has a stake of"—she turned another page to look this up—"20 percent."

Eleanor walked up to the detective, close. Over the detective's shoulder, the light inside the church had been shut off. Her father would be downstairs, writing, rehearsing for Sunday. Eleanor put a hand on the detective's shoulder. When you carry yourself a certain way, when you wear the right suit and stand just so, the cops will forget, for a moment, that you are a black woman in Brooklyn and will instead realize that you hold all the power, maintain all the influence, and have all the friends. The detective didn't try to take her hand off and didn't try to step away. The girl was really afraid of her. Good.

"Detective, I'm not sure how much you know about corporate governance. My father gave me some money when I started my business. He invested in it. And now that business has done well and his investment has paid off. But he doesn't look at payroll. He doesn't know the names of our employees. He works for his congregation, and his congregation does not have a happy history with the NYPD. He may have told you that."

"He did."

"So why don't you go back and type up all the interviews you did tonight? Tomorrow you can ask your supervisor to call me. Or you can have his supervisor call me. Because while you may have thought you were doing the right thing by coming out here tonight, I can assure you that you were not."

With that, her hand came gently off the detective's shoulder. The two of them slunk back into their cruiser and slithered away. Her father was still downstairs writing. She knew better than to disturb him while he was working, even to tell him that she had sent the detectives away. She was going to have to wait until Sunday to hear what he had to say to her in public.

———

The parable had continued while she thought of the visit. "Verse forty-five: 'And when the chief priests and the Pharisees heard His parables, they understood that He was speaking about them.'"

He nodded, silent. Light from a follow-spot in the rafters shone off his nearly bald head. Eleanor could see a bit of sweat on his forehead. After almost an hour, only a single drop. He stood to his full height, his arms out to his sides, thumbs touching his index fingers, and went on.

"Of course, Jesus was telling the Pharisees that they had been poor tenants of the church. But the parable is not merely a story of evil tenants. For we are all owners as well as tenants—owners of this church, of our neighborhood, of our village. And if we are poor landlords, then evil may befall us. Otherwise, we too may be subject to vengeance."

By now, he was looking right at Eleanor. He was making eye contact, giving her that sinister feeling that you have been singled out in the crowd. She understood that he was speaking about her, and she had to break away.

Ten minutes later the crowd filtered out of the church to an uplifting hymn, and Eleanor quickly escaped. There were friends, family, well-wishers to be avoided. She didn't feel like talking much to anyone right now. Which is why she was so upset when a heavyset white man in a sport coat that didn't match his pants looked up at her just as she started to open her car door.

"Eleanor Hill?"

This was not a cop you could talk your way around. Eleanor knew that in some circumstances, the less you said the better. The man gestured to a blue sunburst badge on his waist.

"I'm Detective Ralph Mulino. If you wouldn't mind, I'd like you to come with me."

CHAPTER ELEVEN

Leonard stood in front of the house, keys jingling in his pocket and brochures tucked under his arm. The place must have been nice once. Brick. Four stories. It was the third of four adjoining townhouses, all of them now sagging from age and wear. Next door stood a twelve-story tower, sleek balconies speckling its glass hide with cement. Down toward the Underhill side, there was another one. Behind Leonard, toward the arena, the developments had metastasized to twenty, thirty, forty stories.

Leonard opened the gate and walked toward the ground floor door. Some enterprising architect would surely build a stoop and keep the lower entrance for an apartment. Leonard cranked open the heavy steel gate and the double-bolted door underneath. Those would go too. They were signals of an earlier, more fearful time. Some new owner would have much more to steal than whoever lived there now, but would take away the protection, convinced that Brooklyn had been tamed.

Inside, it was worse. Stained and peeling carpet in the hallway. A door to the right, halfway off its hinges. The same thick green carpet, speckled dark along the whole front wall. Water had leaked through the window cracks and festered into mold in the carpet. In the back, the plastic tiles slipped out from under Leonard's feet in the kitchen.

The stove had been yanked out from the wall, the copper piping salvaged for scrap.

None of it mattered. With these houses, being uninhabitable was almost a selling point. If there was nothing worth saving, it spurred buyers into full renovation. They would polish a grand staircase, install integrated lighting, plaster over any remnants of historic details, and make the interior feel as much as possible like the condos next door.

Leonard set down the glossy pamphlets that Eleanor had given him on the busted stove. There wasn't a table. He marveled at the price atop them: two-point-three million. And that's before the demolition, the renovation, the permits, the time sitting on the mortgage. Leonard turned and walked up the stairs to inspect the other three apartments.

The next two units were pretty much as he expected. Torn carpet, busted doors, kitchen cabinets that looked as though they would fall off if you tried to open them. He turned up the stairs toward the top-floor apartment. Whoever bought the place would still have a hike to get up to the fourth floor, no matter how the renovation went. Putting in an elevator was out of the question even for the newest Brooklyn gentry.

The crumbling stairs topped out at a cheap plywood door. It was locked. The key would be somewhere in the collection that Eleanor had given him. He was fumbling with the key chain when he heard a voice behind the door.

"What is it?" A woman's voice. Afraid.

Eleanor had said there was a tenant in place. But she didn't say anyone would be there during the showing.

"Uh. I'm Leonard Mitchell. I'm from Hill and Associates."

"We don't want anything. Go away."

Leonard had found the key. Better to try to talk your way in.

"Ma'am, I'm not selling anything. We own the building. We are having people by today to look at it."

"Go away."

Leonard slipped the key into the door. "Ma'am, I'm going to come in to talk to you."

"I'm calling the landlord. I'm calling the police. You can't come breaking into people's homes."

The lock turned and the door opened. Leonard stepped in. "Ma'am. I am with the landlord. We are selling the building. People are coming to look at the building. They are coming right now."

He had been speaking as he opened the door and hadn't had a moment to look around. When he finished, he saw the woman. Younger than he was, but not by as much as he would have thought. Black, pretty, a narrow face and distrustful eyes. She was dressed in a long skirt and a short-sleeve shirt. Glasses. The door had opened directly to the kitchen. She was sitting at the kitchen table, sipping a cup of coffee. If someone had burst into Leonard's apartment while he was shouting at them, he would have looked much more surprised than this woman. There was an envelope on the table in front of her.

"Well." She took a sip of her coffee.

The apartment looked nothing like the ones below. The kitchen tiles were in place. The shelves were neat. Leonard looked through the doorway on his right to see the living room. The carpet was clean, and a sofa and coffee table sat nestled in place. A stack of magazines fanned out along the coffee table. He turned back to the woman, at the kitchen table that was squeezed between the refrigerator and the door. On the refrigerator, bright magnet letters were jumbled and crisscrossed, never quite making a word.

"I'm Leonard Mitchell."

"And I'm you-don't-even-know-my-name." She pulled a letter out of the envelope. "This came one week ago. The last apartment cleared out eight months ago. We are the only tenants left. And one week ago I get a letter saying that the place is going to be sold so can I please be out of my apartment from one until three on Sunday."

She took a sip of coffee. She crumpled up the letter. She threw it at Leonard and it fell at his feet.

"Ma'am. I'm just here to show the building."

"Of course you are. Because the people who are in charge would never actually show their faces to me. They will send you and throw up their arms and say that there is nothing to be done. Well, there is something to be done."

She sighed and called, sweetly, to the living room. "Sammy!" Leonard stood still, watching her gaze and waiting. A boy, maybe nine, maybe ten, hair cut nearly to his scalp and wearing a Lionel Messi jersey, skipped into the kitchen. He sat gleefully on his mother's lap, a wide toothy smile.

The woman held her son while she stared at Leonard and spoke. "Mr. Mitchell, I live here. And I am not going to get out of my home to make it easy for you or anyone else to sell this building and kick me to the street. So I am going to sit here with my son for the next two hours and every time someone walks into this room I am going to weep. And I am going to wail. And I am going to tell them please not to kick me out."

The doorbell downstairs rang. They were already here.

"I think I'm going to just keep your apartment locked."

"I will hear them on the stairs. I will call out."

Leonard had spent most of his career working on behalf of those who had been abused. Reading the medical records of those who had been beaten by police officers. Sitting across from them and hearing their stories. Working to bring a little justice to the world. But now here he was, the enforcer. The bad guy. The white man bringing people by who were going to kick a black woman and her son out of their apartment. But he had signed on to work for Hill and Associates. And if he quit because he couldn't bear even the above-board part of the job, he would never learn what was going on behind the scenes. He would never get Mulino anything. He nodded to the woman and subdued the knot in his stomach. He walked down the stairs to open the front door.

There they were, a crowd of them already. Bearded white men in skinny jeans with skinnier wives, each wide-eyed at the idea of a real Brooklyn townhouse. Leonard opened the door and smiled. They started to filter past, an indistinguishable mass of recently acquired wealth.

"As you'll see, the place needs a lot of work. But the location is perfect. And the bones are in great shape."

They filtered past him, the men pretending they knew the first thing about beams or soffits or LED lighting. There was chatter about tankless water heaters, ductless air conditioners, and other expensive amenities. The men talked about building a passive house, the women noted the obvious water damage, and none of them ventured into the overgrown backyard. Leonard nodded and smiled and handed out brochures. He did his best to answer the concerns of each couple. But he knew that as soon as they went upstairs, the happy buyers would come face to face with a problem much bigger than picking out new appliances.

CHAPTER TWELVE

Doing it the right way would have taken too long. Detective Peralta couldn't wait for the hospital intake coordinator to send a fax to OCCB, where it might sit in an inbox for a day or two before a PAA decided to hand it to a sergeant, who might or might not initial it and fax it back. Flashing the badges and saying they were investigating a murder would have to do. Peralta had asked Bruder to watch the door in case a nosy administrator got ideas. At least he was good for something.

Peralta couldn't stand these big hospitals. The wide halls never seemed as clean as you hoped; the strong smell of bleach masked the faint whiff of urine. Peralta couldn't read the codes that were sent by a different set of scrubs or a different length of lab coat: who was a nurse or an orderly or a doctor or an intern was lost on her. She could tell you whether the bars above a sergeant's shield meant that he had saved a life or merely aced the firing range, but the uniforms of the city hospital were incomprehensible.

But she would have recognized a lawyer. A lawyer would be wearing a suit. And a lawyer would not be happy if two detectives had bluffed their way past the front desk, asked where Manny Reeves was being held, and taken outposts inside the room. He would have quoted New York State privacy statutes, and HIPPA, and reminded the detectives that they were supposed to have provided the intake coordinator with an initialed fax from their command. Maybe even a warrant. Peralta had asked Bruder to guard the door because she didn't have time for lawyers. Bruder thought that guarding the door was the important job.

Manny Reeves was alone in the room, in the window-side bed. The bed was thin, with a cheap aluminum railing. There was no budget for tricked-out hospital beds in this place. The window itself was smeared with dirt from the outside and bolted shut. Whether to prevent jumpers from getting out or dealers from sneaking in was anyone's guess. Through the window, Peralta could barely make out the grim traffic along Flatbush and the bare trees looking more dead than hibernating. Manny Reeves was unconscious. Both legs were bound, bandaged. His torso was elevated with a pillow but not in full traction. The right arm was in a cast, but the left arm and the head were clear. He was intubated and on an IV. There was no bandage on his head. They were probably keeping him under so he wouldn't scratch at the casts. He was white, around thirty, scraggly brown hair already thinning, with a wispy beard—maybe trying to look like the new craftsmen with their thick manes, and failing at it.

Peralta pulled the chart from the railing at the foot of the bed. Most of the codes were the same that the department used, a circled L for left and a circled R for right and "time and place of occurrence" condensed to "tpo." The true medical jargon she could look up later. She took out her cell phone and snapped photos of the four pages, in case she had to get out of here in a hurry. The hospital lawyers would love that. Once she had the photos, she started to walk through the chart herself.

Manny Reeves had been picked up in the bottom of a ventilation shaft about six blocks from where Wade Valiant had died. He had broken both legs, an arm, and his right hip. Peralta figured the dressing on the hip was under the covers. He had been brought in unconscious and kept under for the past few days. Peralta couldn't make out if the chart gave a reason why. They had gotten his name from somewhere, his address. Most likely someone went through his possessions.

Peralta looked around the room. There was a cupboard on the wall between the bed and the bathroom. Reeves wouldn't have been able to get up and use it yet. One of the tubes running under his covers was probably a catheter. The clothes and wallet would be in the cupboard. Next to the bed was a small table; on it, a cell phone. It explained the ping. Some helpful nurse had plugged in the phone this morning. That meant that they thought he might be waking up soon. There was no indication he had ever been awake long enough to talk to anyone. That was good. She would get to him first. Maybe it was worth sending that fax after all.

"Detective Peralta?"

Bruder at the door. Peralta slipped the chart back into the slot at the foot of the bed and took a step away. She pulled up her best police posture. If it was a nurse it wouldn't matter. If it was a doctor she could flash her badge. And it probably wasn't a lawyer.

"Yes, Bruder."

Peralta looked up as soon as her hand was off the chart. There were two of them, and Bruder hadn't kept them from making their way inside already. Neither one of them was a doctor. Instead it was Detective Mulino with a thin woman in a Sunday suit. Caramel skin, hair pulled tight behind her head in bun; her fingernails had been done professionally and tastefully. The woman who had dressed her down in front of the church, Eleanor Hill. Detective Peralta hoped the woman wouldn't remember her. Maybe she thought all Hispanic female cops looked alike.

"Detective Mulino, I was just . . . I was checking on the patient. We heard from TARU about the cell phone ping."

"Peralta, this is Eleanor Hill. She runs the company that was putting up the building."

No look of recognition. That was a relief. Or maybe she was faking it. Peralta relaxed a little as she shook the woman's hand. Mulino spoke.

"What have you got for us?"

"Well, we just got here."

Mulino cocked his head. "Detective Peralta, I notified intake and there are two hospital administrators on their way here now. You and I both know that once they are here, it will be six hours before they give us their records. So I hope you were a good detective and got a peek at that chart and can tell us something useful to act on during those six hours. Or you can spend those six hours here watching him."

Some rules were made to be broken. Mulino could give you a hard time, but when push comes to shove, he was an old-school detective after all. "He was found at the bottom of an air shaft."

The woman in the suit took a breath. "Where?"

"At 80 Smithdale Street. A few blocks from the accident."

Mulino this time. "I think we can stop calling it an accident."

Eleanor Hill was already reaching for her cell phone. "That's David Verringer's building."

"You know him."

"Everyone knows him. He's—well, you can go run the records on the building yourself. He gets money from the city to house people on their way out of shelters. The city pays him more than any market tenant would. The place is a dump. The heat is never on, there's mold. The building is so bad that the neighbors complain."

"An old friend of yours, this guy?"

"That's what your affordable housing gets you in this city. Taxpayers making someone rich to keep his tenants in misery."

"And any reason, Ms. Hill, that your employee would be in this guy's building? Especially right after trashing your crane and getting another one of your employees killed?"

Peralta watched the woman as she considered. Detective Mulino never stopped conducting an investigation. He didn't sit out at a table and swing a light over you. But when he asked you what time it was, the question was loaded. Asking you where your employees might have gone is an interrogation. Always with that chipper tone. He would ask you for a cup of sugar and slam you over the head with it. As the woman bit her lip, waiting to answer, Peralta marveled. Maybe, after all, these developers were all in it together, somehow. As Mulino always had told her, finding out the what is easy. But you have to work to figure out the why.

"No, detective. I have no idea. We want to help in any way we can. I don't have much contact, usually, with the men on the sites."

Mulino nodded. Peralta was already putting together theories. The slumlord was sabotaging Hill's building. Or Hill had set it up to make it look that way. She had wanted to cash in an insurance policy, maybe. She had wanted to drive a stake through her competitor. Get David Verringer out of the way so she could make his building into a glass condo too. And after all, maybe he didn't put in Bosch washing machines and Sub-Zero fridges, but he was providing housing for actual poor people. Peralta knew that when someone like Eleanor Hill talks about affordable housing, she means something that you could never afford on an NYPD salary, even if you make detective early.

They were interrupted by Bruder again. With two men in suits at the door. They were white, with neatly cut dark hair, and they wore indistinguishable suits. If one of them hadn't had a mustache, she wouldn't have been able to tell them apart. They brushed past Bruder and spoke only to Mulino. It was as though the rest of them were not even in the room.

"Detective, we understand you want to have some information on the patient." The first one did the talking. The second one held the paperwork. "You're going to have to fill out a few forms. You can fax them to your squad and when they come back we can give you access to Mr. Reeves's files. You understand we have privacy laws here, and we just want to be compliant."

"I understand." The men hadn't introduced themselves. The one holding the clipboard slipped around to the foot of the bed and fished out Manny Reeves's chart. Very clever. Because three NYPD detectives might not actually know where you keep it.

"Only one question, guys. You have any sense when this guy is planning to wake up? You know, we'd like to talk to him."

"You'll have to talk to the doctors for that."

"But I can't talk to the doctors till we get the forms done?"

"That's right."

Peralta realized that she had been in the room close to an hour now. She hadn't seen a doctor come in. No nurse, no attendant, no nothing. The big-city hospital. Somewhere in the bowels of the building there were some very expensive machines, but the ordinary suffering patients were left to wait it out.

Mulino looked to his detectives and spoke. "Bruder, I want you to stay on this door. You call us if anyone comes and tries to talk to him. You call us if he wakes up. He's an NYPD detective, he's allowed to stand at the door, isn't he?"

The lawyer without the clipboard looked at Bruder. Then to Mulino. Peralta figured he wasn't actually sure. Better to go along than admit it. "Yeah. He can stand there."

"I'm going to go and fill out this paperwork. Detective Peralta, could you go look into that other matter that we were talking about? The Housing and Preservation Department question? Look up those violations. We have a few hours before this will pick up."

That other matter. To throw off the administrators. Peralta nodded. He meant the building at Smithdale Street, where Peralta had found out that Reeves had fallen. But if he said that, the suits would be on to them. As the two suits led Mulino out through the hall, Peralta turned back toward the stairway to the hospital entrance. He had mentioned HPD violations, and Eleanor Hill had said the building was a dump. She could look up the violations in ten minutes. But that was just the start of it. She knew what Mulino had really asked her to do. He had just given her license to do real legwork.

CHAPTER THIRTEEN

From the roof, all Peralta could see was a heap of accumulated scraps. Looking over the edge of the air shaft at 80 Smithdale Street, she thought that the residents threw their garbage straight out here instead of bothering to walk to the kitchen. It was a long way down. Not as far as Wade Valiant had fallen. But Detective Peralta was at least a little surprised that Manny Reeves was still alive. Speckled along the inside walls were a series of small, smudged windows. They were where the garbage had come from. And they were the only reason that the air shaft was there.

You can't call a room a bedroom in New York unless it has an exterior window. By building an air shaft that was eight feet square, the original builder could put a window in a little room in the back of each apartment. That window made the room a bedroom, and that bedroom made the unit a two-bedroom apartment. Never mind that the window was about eighteen inches tall and only twelve across. Never mind that unless you were on the top floor you didn't get any light, and even then only for a few hours in the middle of the day. Or that you kept the window closed all the time with a shade pulled because otherwise someone only eight feet away could look in at you. And that all you really used it for was to throw garbage out into the heap at the bottom of the air shaft. It was a bedroom, and that meant they could jack up the rent.

Or they could have at one point. Because from what Detective Peralta could tell on her way into the building, there was no one living there who could pay any rent at all. Or who would want to. The front door not only hadn't been locked, it had long ago been busted with a crowbar and barely hitched back on its hinges. What otherwise would have been called the interior lobby was crowded with broken tiles, piles of trash, and mail strewn on the floor because the mailbox keys had been lost or stolen long ago.

She hadn't seen any people on the way up. With the building not secure, most of them probably just kept their doors locked and hoped no one was coming to bang them down. What she had noticed were the cables. On every floor, big orange extension cables ran across the hall, snaking out from under the door of one apartment to its neighbor. The paint on the walls was so old, it had given up on peeling and begun to sag like drapes.

There was no railing over the ledge of the air shaft. That was probably some kind of violation as well. It wasn't listed on the 194 violations she found on the HPD website when she looked up the building just after leaving the hospital. Inspectors can't catch everything. The tar roof was in decent-enough shape, with less trash than there was in the bottom of the shaft. Peralta stood and looked around. The building felt large if you looked east, down the row of barrel-front limestone townhouses. If you looked west, toward the avenue, where the new steel giants cut off views and access to the park, it felt weak and small, about to crumble under its own weight.

Someone had to have called 911. Someone had to have turned in the body. The building was four stories, twelve units each; that was big enough that there ought to be a building manager, a super, something. It was back to good old-fashioned legwork, banging on doors and showing her badge. Aurelia Peralta headed down from the roof and into the unforgiving corridor, crisscrossed with extension cords.

She knocked politely at first. No answer. She stepped over the orange cable and went to the next one. Knocking harder. Banging. Nothing. She was hesitant to identify herself. Most likely someone in every one of these units had some sort of problem with the police, or knew someone who did. She wasn't serving warrants, but if someone saw her and ran away, she would have to give chase, if only to save face. And she was investigating a murder; she didn't want to spend all night processing paperwork on some skell who had skipped arraignment after getting picked up selling a dime bag. Patrol officers can pride themselves on the sheer number of collars they pick up. Peralta wasn't in the volume business anymore.

But after a whole hallway of silence, after banging on the doors hard enough that she was afraid she might knock one down by accident, she knew she needed another strategy. The place wasn't empty. Whoever was in these units knew someone was out there. The doors were thin enough that they could hear her from one hallway to the other. She could pull the fire alarm, but panic wasn't what she was looking for either. She walked back down the hallway past the extension cords and turned for the floor below.

The extension cords. The HPD report had said that up to 40 percent of the units didn't have any working power outlets. The residents were running power across the hallway so they could keep their lights on and run their televisions. Never mind the fire hazard. Never mind that the HPD citation was from four years before and no one seems to have sent an electrician. People will do what they need to do to survive. If they were surviving on the power from one unit to the next, then it was at least one way to get their attention. And the cords were lying out in the hallway. She wasn't breaking into an apartment or anything.

Peralta reached into her belt and took out a utility knife. She knelt by the bright orange cable and started to saw at it. She was worried that the metal on metal would send a shock once she was through the orange casing, but it sliced through the cord quickly and simply. The cable cut, Peralta stood in the hallway and waited.

Behind the door on her right there was a sudden commotion. Chairs being turned over, maybe. Dishes headed to the floor. Peralta stood facing the door so she'd be ready. Whoever was about to open it would not be happy.

The door flung open to a very small man, maybe in his early seventies. He couldn't have been much over five feet, thin, and he wore reading glasses. He had a full head of white hair clipped tight, standing out against his dark skin. His nose and ears seemed too large, or maybe as he had aged, the rest of his features had simply receded. Before he said anything, Peralta spoke.

"I'm here about the man in the air shaft."

He saw the badge. He saw the knife, still in her hand. She could see fear wash over him in an instant. "I didn't see anything."

"He fell three days ago. Someone saw it. Someone called 911."

"You came here to cut off my power? I take oxygen."

"I came here to talk about the man in the air shaft. There's a hardware store on Flatbush, and I'll buy you another cable. You didn't see him fall, but you heard the ambulance come. You saw the commotion."

"I was in my room. I'm in my room most days. I didn't hear anything before the ambulance. I looked out my window and I saw them take him away."

"Anyone see him come in? Anyone see who he was talking to? What was his business in the building?"

"I need my oxygen to get working again."

Maybe he was in trouble. Maybe he did need his oxygen. But maybe, too, that was a little leverage. "You got a super in this building? You got a landlord?"

"Look around you. Landlord never comes by except to turn things off. There's no super. We do the best we can. I didn't have heat all last winter. If you want to go find people to lock up, why not start with our landlord?"

"I'll get you that extension cord." But then something else occurred to Detective Peralta. Every building is like a neighborhood. And every neighborhood has its neighborhood watch. Whether it is a leafy street in Nutley or a slum in Flatbush, there is always someone who is the eyes and ears. "But before I do, can you help me? Is there someone in this building who will know? Someone who always knows what's going on? When you want to know something about what is happening, who do you talk to?"

"You want to see Evangeline."

Fifteen minutes later, sending the man back upstairs with his extension cord, Detective Peralta was accepting a cup of tea from a plump woman in a bright dress. The apartment was spotless: the tablecloth edges were folded neatly, the counters were scrubbed, and the windows had been freshly cleaned from both sides somehow. In a place so prim, Detective Peralta could forget about the violations in the building, the man without his oxygen, the pile of cigarette butts and needles in the bottom of the air shaft.

"I called emergency afterward. I could see out the back window he was hurt. I wasn't about to go poke my nose out and see what happened. We have professionals for that."

"Did you see him come in?"

"I heard him come in. You can hear everything here. I heard them both come in."

"Both?"

Evangeline lifted her mug of tea to her lips and smiled. Peralta reached for her memo book. She was going to have to start taking notes.

CHAPTER FOURTEEN

Each time her company had grown—from a pet project run out of a conference room in her father's church, to an apartment in a building she sold six months after she bought it, to the top floor of a glass tower in the new downtown—Eleanor Hill had thought that she could delegate the paper. But it never worked. Every time she did a new deal, there was always paper. And each time, somehow, she had to walk through it herself. She had thought that leases could be signed by subordinates. She had hoped that wire transfers could replace handing off checks. Pretty soon all she would need to do, she had imagined, was scout buildings, give a thumbs-up, and collect the money.

And yet here she was, on a Sunday night, in her office, with stacks and stacks of paper to look over. Not just look over. Read. There would always be paper, and never enough people to hand it over to. A big building means hundreds of apartments. And the language in every lease might be the same, but someone has to read through it, even just once. Eleanor had lawyers draft it for her, but she knew she'd have to read the final copy herself. In the end, you can never really trust anyone. Plus the permit applications. The talking points the lobbyist was going to use. Her own presentation to give to the community board and the City Council. Owning her own development firm didn't feel like being the boss of anything at all. It felt like being a high school English teacher, grading everyone else's papers while they were at home drinking beer and watching the game.

She felt as though she was always working while everyone else got the credit and the money. Her father most of all. He'd never turned down a check from her, that's for sure. But he let her know, with all the subtlety of that morning's sermon, just what he thought of her. He was a good man, an honest man, and a pillar of the city. But there was no pleasing him. You try to impress your parents, but whatever choice you make is the wrong one. If you make it financially, they wish you had been a social worker. If you tend to the sick, they will be put off that you never made any money. And heaven forbid you become an artist.

Eleanor had a brother who had moved to Los Angeles to be an actor. The profession her father had first loved. Twice a year they heard that he would be playing a drug dealer on a cop show or a gunshot victim on a hospital show. So twice a year there was something that Eleanor knew her father would not be caught dead watching. It was easier, knowing that there really was no pleasing the man. She turned back to the lease, puzzling over what the difference was when the lawyer used the word "shall" instead of "will."

There was a ding in the hallway. The elevator. Maybe her father had come by to apologize. Or maybe the community board had come in on its knees to beg her to build the apartments. Or maybe her brother had just won an Oscar, and was coming to show it to her. A girl can dream.

She looked up from the leases, ready for just about anything. Through the glass hallway, silhouetted by the newly lit skyline, she saw a thin man in a cheap suit, bringing back a stack of brochures. She leaned back in her chair and smiled.

"How did it go, Leonard?"

Leonard Mitchell seemed worn out. He had started out a little bit worn out. But a day showing a gut renovation project to Brooklyn buyers could suck the life out of anyone. The buyers were demanding and ignorant. They would ask for a hard number on the costs to fix up the house. And they wouldn't know a contractor, barely could tell you two brands of dishwashers, and weren't even really sure what they wanted the place to look like when they were done. Plus, the house that Leonard had shown that afternoon had its own unique challenge.

Leonard staggered into her office and sat in the comfortable chair across her desk. Last time, he had looked as though he was trying to hold himself up. This time he fell right into it.

"You told me there was a tenant. You didn't tell me she would be there."

"Margaret was there?"

"Is that her name?"

"You didn't ask her name?"

"She told me that if we showed the house she would cry and she would wail and she would tell people she would fight them in court if they tried to evict her. And she did that. People walked through the first two stories and then got upstairs and ran out of the house like they'd been shot at."

"Did they, now?"

Leonard was growing excited. "And she had a little boy with her, and he was crying too."

"Sammy. The boy is named Sammy."

"Well, Sammy has a set of lungs on him."

Eleanor set down the lease. She reached to another pile. Picked up another stack of paper. "Margaret is a very smart woman, and she's in a bind. She's doing what she needs to do. In the end she knows she'll have to go. She figures she can hold off eviction for a year, eighteen months. And she knows exactly what eighteen months is worth to a buyer looking to redo the house. So when she gets her number, she'll leave."

"It's not an act, Eleanor. She is really being kicked out."

"She is really being kicked out. But it is also an act. Why was she able to sit and tell you calmly what she was going to do if she was so distraught? She knows exactly what game she's playing. And she's good at it. That's why I'm not redoing the house myself. She's going to get her number, and whatever her number is, it isn't worth it to me."

"So that's what we do around here? We kick people out of their homes? Figure out what they can be bribed with and drop the hammer?"

"If it makes you feel bad you can go talk to the original seller. He could have kept on running a low-rent apartment building for the rest of his life. He was making more than he was paying. But pretty soon the building would get assessed higher. And his property taxes would go up. And he's watching up and down the street and seeing how much he can sell for. So you can blame him if you want to find someone who isn't charitable. Or blame the city. They drove down crime and now people with more money want to come and live in neighborhoods they didn't want to live in before. Or blame the people moving in. They could stay in Manhattan or Wichita or Seattle if they wanted to. But if I hadn't bought the house, someone else would have. And I'm only selling it because it doesn't work out for me to kick out Margaret personally. And I'm not in the business of holding on to property while the price drops. Or trying to play the next crash. No one wants to catch a falling knife. I am in the slow and steady game. Ever upward. Just a little bit at a time."

Leonard picked up the papers and straightened himself out.

"No one wants to catch what?"

"This business is boom and bust, Leonard. I've lived in Brooklyn all my life and I have seen my share of booms, but I have seen bubbles pop too. And when a bubble pops, everyone is hoping to get in at the bottom. To buy low and be ready for the next boom." She took out a pencil and tossed it in the air. "A dropping price is like a falling knife. If you get it by the handle, if you find the bottom, great." Her hand snapped onto the pencil, a sharp confident *thwack*. "But if you are too early, or too late, and you buy in the middle of the fall, you're left holding the knife the wrong way. In fact, it's more like it's holding you."

"Okay. Well, I don't know what you were sending me out there for anyway. It seemed like a waste."

"Not at all." Eleanor took the stack of paper from across her desk. "We got six offers on that house this afternoon. People are willing to take the leap. People think they can handle Margaret. God bless them. You did a good job."

The man looked a little stunned. He reached across the desk and took the stack of papers. They had come in by fax. Another antiquity roaming around her office. She worked in an industry where people still sent faxes.

"You need to write those up," Eleanor said. "There is a form on the system. And you made a sign-in at the open house? Put them in the database. It's busywork for now. But I trust you'll be able to handle bigger things. You can take the office at the end of the hall. Your credentials are printed out. On the paper on the desk."

Leonard stood up and straightened the stack of papers. He mumbled something and walked down the hallway toward his new office. Eleanor smiled. She was comfortable with this one. She had been burnt once before, by someone she had been unable to control. Who had turned on her. This guy was soft, maybe already broken by his last job or the stint upstate, or just too eager for the money to do anything but serve. She wouldn't have anything to worry about from him at all.

She sighed deeply and went back to her paperwork, red pen in hand. A teacher's work is never done.

CHAPTER FIFTEEN

Leonard could tell from the smell that the DIMAC offices had not changed a bit. The carpet runs were still patched with electrical tape. The walls were still smudged with decades-old handprints. And there was still that smell: some rough combination of sweat, blood, and fear. Leonard hadn't been to his old workplace, the Department to Investigate Misconduct and Corruption, in well over a year. Since then, the mayor had installed an outsider to run the agency. Barry Schaeffer wore a shock of white hair and bespoke suits; he didn't care what the other city bureaucrats thought of him because he could always fall back on his private-sector fortune if he needed.

Schaeffer had gotten to work issuing press releases crowing over every arrest that DIMAC made. Cops who faked their overtime or firefighters who pulled family jewels out of the ashes and put them up on eBay. But Leonard had followed the cases and seen that they weren't going to trial. The evidence was always a little thin, or hadn't been obtained by the book. The investigations were pure show now; quick and shoddy and made for the cameras instead of a jury. In Leonard's day, they caught just as many miscreants. But they had closed their cases tight and won at trial. Other than the press releases, not much had really changed. As Leonard could attest by the smell.

It was going to be a quick visit. Leonard had some paperwork to collect; he would dash in, dash out, and get back to Mulino in an hour or so. There was plenty to tell the detective after the night he had spent at Hill and Associates. It took Leonard only half an hour to enter the data on the offers that came in on the townhouse and to add the sign-in sheet to the database. Six offers. Four of them were from other developers, two were from people planning to buy the place and rehab it themselves.

The individual buyers were probably out of luck. They thought they would be able to cope with Margaret and Sammy. They thought they would begin an eviction proceeding, or buy her out, or make her life miserable enough to make her want to move. But they didn't know how to do the first, they didn't know how much the second would cost, and they didn't have the money for the third. It was why Eleanor was unloading the house, after all. She knew the woman's name. She knew the son's name. She had probably been dealing with them for six months and figured it was time for them to be some other developer's problem.

Which happened more often than Leonard would guess. Because after he entered the buyers' information in the database, he started combing through the digital files of Hill and Associates. And the information showed that Eleanor Hill had sold off a number of properties just as they were on their way to becoming sour.

He had been worried, scrolling through company transactions that weren't strictly part of his job assignment. But minimal security meant they probably weren't tracing where Leonard was going either. Even if someone found out what he had been looking at, he had a ready excuse. He was an eager new employee, after all, just trying to familiarize himself with the business.

He had gone through most of the documentation surrounding fifteen transactions. While Hill and Associates did put up its share of buildings, what it mainly did was buy property from one developer and sell to another. One parcel Leonard tracked had been sold five times, each time for up to half a million dollars more than the last. One company bought and sold it twice within three years. It had finally been bought by a Chinese public pension fund, run by a consortium of investors in Singapore. Leonard looked up the parcel itself on a map and had seen that it was still raw dirt. It was that way on all of the deals—Hill and Associates would buy land, sell it to another developer, that one would sell it to a third, and finally a foreign hedge fund or multinational investment platform would buy it. And no one would buy it from them.

The developers were getting rich off of a game of hot potato speculation. It wasn't even clear to Leonard that Hill and Associates was making much money off the properties where it actually built anything. In those buildings, there were bills to pay: raw materials, labor costs, payments to workers' comp, insurance, and hordes of intermediaries delivering wiring and pipe and appliances and glass. In the end, a couple of the condo buildings had sold for big gains, but most broke about even. A few more seemed to be in the red. The real money was in driving up the price of land and then leaving it in the hands of people in another country who had heard the words "Brooklyn Real Estate" and thought they were getting a steal at any price.

Whatever holding company laid out the big bucks on the final deal thought the value of whatever plot it had bought would double every few years, just as it had for the last few years. Maybe it wasn't worried that it couldn't sell the land now. It could always sell it later for more. Or so everyone thought. *To catch a falling knife indeed*, Leonard thought. Maybe it wasn't a swindle exactly, and maybe the Eastern European conglomerate wouldn't really notice that it had paid twenty-two million for land that really was worth closer to eight. But it was the kind of scheme where you could make an enemy.

And if Hill and Associates was making enemies, that gave Leonard a couple of theories about Wade Valiant. Maybe Valiant had found out what was going on and was demanding a cut to keep from telling the dupes. Maybe someone who had been left holding the bag thought that causing industrial accidents was a good way to get back at Eleanor Hill, and Valiant just happened to be in the way. If you crossed someone in Uzbekistan, there was no telling exactly how he might take it out on you.

Leonard had made a list of the buyers that were last in line. Some of them might not even know that they had overpaid yet. He would take the list to Mulino this afternoon. Digging up information on the companies themselves was NYPD business. They would be able to run databases and search visa records and maybe that would get them somewhere.

But until then, Leonard had to keep up his cover. Which meant that he had to pretend he was going to Hill and Associates to work, on the up and up. And to do that he would have to collect his pension papers from all the city agencies where he'd ever worked. He'd already been by the Parks Department that morning. His commissioner wasn't thrilled with him leaving after less than a year on the job and pulling out of city service just after hitting his twenty, but there wasn't much he could do about it. And Leonard couldn't exactly tell him the truth.

Here at DIMAC, Leonard just wanted to get his papers and get out. He didn't need to talk to Schaeffer about anything. He just had to get the human resources people to run his social into the system, hit print, and give him what came out. In city government, that would ordinarily take about forty minutes. Leonard walked up to the reception desk, where the civilians filing complaints and the city employees waiting for interviews get filtered into their separate waiting rooms. He didn't know the man at the window. They changed pretty often.

"I'm Leonard Mitchell. I used to work here. I just need to duck into HR for a minute."

If it had been someone he'd known, he could have nodded past, but this guy made him sign in, show an ID, go through the whole routine.

Leonard could play patient with the best of them. He had spent over a decade in these halls and knew that rushing a municipal administrator is a good way to get stuck where you are for hours. He complied, got his pass, and hurried into the office.

Head down, hoping not to be seen by his former employees and most of all not by the new commissioner, Leonard ducked left and trekked to the end of a long hallway. He turned the corner and saw a familiar face.

"Carol."

Well past pension age herself, Carol looked up from the game of solitaire she was playing on her computer. At DIMAC, employees are not given desktop Internet access. They haven't been since the last mayor walked past someone who was reading the news at his desk and had him fired. So the bureaucrats with little to do pass their time with antique hobbies. Minesweeper. Solitaire. Some of them don't even turn their computer on and just spend most of their day surfing the web on their cell phones.

"Hi, Leonard." A faraway voice. A woman who had ground her life into a thin meaningless powder alone at this desk, doing nothing for years.

"Carol. I'm leaving city government. I'm leaving the Parks Department. Can you run my pension papers so I can take them over to DCAS?"

The Department of Citywide Administrative Services. It would be his last stop before seeing Mulino. The city agency whose job it is to be the bureaucracy for all the other city agencies. Payrolls, report printing, water, sewer, power, contracts with outside vendors, technical support, all of it went through DCAS. Every year Leonard had drafted a request for sixty thousand dollars—out of a city budget of eighty billion—to get digital voice recorders instead of the 1970s cassette players that his investigators used. And every year DCAS had said no.

"Sure, Leonard. I'll start that up." Carol clicked at her computer. She was going to finish her solitaire game first, it seemed. Leonard stepped inside the doorway. The room had no windows, no other cubicles, no place to sit. Carol was the lonely little HR department in a lonely little corner of the government. Leonard leaned against the wall while Carol tried to play a red eight on a red nine.

"Leonard. They told me you'd dropped by."

And with that, his plans had been foiled. Barry Schaeffer, his lion's mane of white hair tousled almost down to his shoulders and his suit softer and more luxurious than any that a city employee would normally wear, was holding out a stout red hand for Leonard to shake. Leonard was in no position to turn him down.

"Hello, Commissioner."

"So you came by to learn how to do things right around here? Figure out what it was that kept you down all those years?"

"I'm getting my papers printed. I'm leaving city government."

"You won't get the actual pension for almost ten years."

"I know how it all works, thanks." Leonard didn't care much to be lectured on the subtleties of his pension by Barry Schaeffer, who lived on the sixty-third floor of a skyscraper on Fifth Avenue, and owned houses on Nantucket and in Vail. As Leonard looked at Schaeffer in person, the Commissioner looked older and fatter than he always appeared from a distance. Sort of like your uncle dressed up for a wedding before he's plowed into the Scotch. But you can see it coming.

"Carol, you mind giving us a few minutes?"

"Sure, Commissioner."

Leonard chimed in. "I really needed to get this done as soon as I can."

"She can finish when she comes back. I'd really like to talk to you."

There was nothing to say. Leonard looked at the floor as Carol slunk out. Schaeffer closed the door, boxing them in to what wasn't much more than a very bright closet.

"Look, Leonard."

"Commissioner. I don't want to hear about everything I did wrong. I'm out. You can run this place like you want."

Schaeffer cocked his head. He looked softer all of a sudden. He wasn't playing the tough hero any more. Now he was your uncle at bedtime, when you were a kid, that time you stayed with them for the summer and got talked to about breaking the neighbor's window with the baseball. "You didn't do anything wrong, Leonard. You got a raw deal. Everyone knows that."

"I'm not looking for any sympathy."

"I'm not offering. I just wanted to thank you. You had to take the hit for what happened. Someone had to take the hit a little. There were people that died. But you did good work. We appreciate that."

Leonard nodded. "So what is with all the press conferences? Why are you in the papers every two weeks telling people how incompetent we were?"

"People like to be told stories, Leonard. When I was a trial lawyer, that's all I did was tell people stories. There is a kind of filter you can use in a swimming pool drain that costs fifteen cents. And a little girl died because that filter wasn't on a drain and her bathing suit got caught in it. And I told the story about how cheap that company was that they didn't spend fifteen cents on that filter, and it cost them millions of dollars. Of course I didn't tell the story of how that company offers the filter, but when the girl's parents bought the pool they didn't want the deluxe drainage system. It's not my job to tell the whole story. I just tell one part of it."

"But it isn't true."

"Of course it's true. It might not be complete. But it's true. We are arresting cops. We are arresting motormen. We got a corrections officer. If the DA can't convict them, that's not my problem. This crane that came down in Brooklyn, we're going to lock up the building inspector."

Leonard could see Schaeffer watching him. He had caught something in Leonard's expression. Leonard had flinched at the mention of the crane. The wide red face looked down into Leonard's. "What?"

"The crane didn't fall because it hadn't been inspected. The crane was fine."

"That may be true. But the inspector didn't inspect it. So we have a culprit."

"What if you have more than a culprit, Barry? What about when you have a conspiracy? When you have what I had?"

Schaeffer smiled. "Of course. That's the whole truth, isn't it? We keep the lid from blowing off, Leonard. That's all. The truth is, you need a little misconduct and corruption to keep the city running. We'll arrest a cop when there is cell phone video showing him roughing up someone in Manhattan. But we can't make the police department tell its officers to stop roughing up any kids anywhere. There are Columbia professors gladly sending their fifty dollars a year to the ACLU, happy to point fingers at whatever cop they think ought to get arrested this week. But if every cop thought he could lose his job for throwing anyone against the wall, they would stop doing it. And if no one ever got thrown up against the wall, no one would be afraid. And pretty soon, someone who isn't afraid would like the look of that professor's laptop as it's hanging out of his satchel. And after that your professor is voting Republican.

"We can't stop everything. We are in the business of making people believe that everything is okay. Because if we actually tried to go after it all at once—well, we'd end up out of a job, or in jail. Wouldn't we?"

Leonard looked up at the broad, bright face of hypocrisy. Don't try too hard, Schaeffer was saying. Don't go chasing the real demons, hunting down the true conspiracies. Because then you'll end up broke and beaten and imprisoned. Just like Leonard Mitchell had been. Schaeffer opened the door and nodded.

"All I wanted to say was thank you. For all that you did. It really meant a lot to us."

And with that, he was gone. Leonard looked out into the hallway. Carol was nowhere to be found. Leonard leaned his head against the wall and waited for her to come back and print a piece of paper that would help him see a little bit of money in about ten years' time.

CHAPTER SIXTEEN

Eleanor Hill knew who it was when she heard the footsteps. Anyone else would have been stopped at security downstairs. Anyone else and she would have been called and notified. But the security desk on the ground floor knew that there was one person you did not ask for identification. Ditto with the person at the upstairs kiosk, or the few employees who buzzed about on a Monday morning after a busy working weekend. Eleanor knew the purpose was to surprise her, to keep her on her toes. No matter how much authority you accumulate, no matter how many successes you pile one atop the other, no matter how much money you make, there are some people who will always tower over you. There are some people who will never allow you to feel superior, but the very fact that the visit was unannounced meant it could be only one person. Eleanor Hill looked up from her paperwork at the broad man silhouetted against the bright skyline of a newborn city.

"Hello, Dad."

McArthur Hill took two steps forward, away from the window. A gentleman of the last generation, his hat was already off, and his bright pate reflected the overhead lights as he stepped out of the glow from outside. "Eleanor."

She stacked the papers and put them to the side. "Please have a seat." She didn't stand up herself. Maybe he would see this as a slight. Eleanor had been slighted enough by him over the years. He could swallow his chivalry for half an hour, at least. Her father folded his overcoat and draped it over one chair, set his hat down on it, and settled into the other.

She looked down at him from her raised desk and spoke. "I'm sorry I couldn't stay after the service. Sundays are busy in this business."

"Of course."

Was she supposed to acknowledge that he had been trashing her in front of his congregation? Half of the members of the community board that stalled her projects, and almost all of the demonstrators, went to his church. He had not been subtle. It was the usual routine; she was a landlord, and to McArthur Hill's congregation, landlords were the villains. She had dared to succeed, to build a business, to make money.

"Was there something in particular today?"

He shuffled in the chair. She would make him bring up the sermon, make him ask her if she had understood. It would be a blow to his ego to think that he had not been clear. "I came to talk to you about the police officers who came to my church."

"I took care of that. I spoke to them. There was a death on a construction site on Thursday. They are trying to figure out why it happened. They saw that you were an owner and they wanted to talk. They were only doing their jobs."

"Police officers only doing their jobs have caused my congregation no end of trouble over the years, Eleanor. I have been on too many marches against police officers just doing their jobs to take that as an excuse."

"I spoke to them. They won't bother you. They probably spent the weekend getting chewed out by a lieutenant." No need to mention that she had just seen the two officers at the hospital, guarding the chief suspect in the murder. She had pretended not to recognize them. Maybe they were dumb enough to think she actually hadn't.

Her father shook his head. "I'm sorry. But that's not good enough for me anymore. I don't know why it is that your business seems to attract attention. But I'm not interested in being a part of it anymore."

This was another subtle dig. Last summer her father had been more upset than anyone when they found out about the employee, about everything that had gone wrong. A few hundred thousand dollars out the door, and if you tell the police about it, then that makes your business look weak and unsecure. If you sue the employee, that puts it in the press. So you do what you can to keep it quiet, and you suffer the loss on your own.

The lawyers had assured her that the best play was to call it an employment dispute. And hopefully she wouldn't have to worry about employment disputes any more. After all, Leonard Mitchell was stuck with her; it wasn't as though he could go back to city government if things went sour.

But when you run a business and someone steals a quarter of a million dollars, at the very least you have to issue a statement to the investors—her father and three others. The lawyers had told her that disclosure was the best option, and she had bit her lip and clenched her fists and gone through with it. Even as she promised they had taken care of the problem. Promised they had cleaned house. They had a carefully worded report from the lawyers telling them that there was no cause to alert the regulatory authorities. But she couldn't keep the news from the passive investors, and that had meant that she couldn't keep the news from her father.

"Are you here to offer a word of sympathy? About the worker who died?" She motioned to the papers she had stacked aside when he came in. "What I'm working on here are his funeral arrangements. I was going to ask if you'd host the service but he lived on Long Island."

"He has his own people."

"And the police officers have left you alone, Dad, but they haven't left me alone. They haven't stopped asking whether we had some arrangement with the Department of Buildings or whether we had the proper safety protocols in place or if maybe something even worse is going on around here."

"And that's why you have insurance."

He was right about that last part. She had tendered the claim. She shuddered to think about the blow to the rates—they were high enough already—but it was the right thing to do. The police, after all, were investigating an accident. The word had leaked about the building inspector but that only confirmed that the crane had been faulty and had broken and Eleanor didn't have to worry about anything more serious than that.

Because she couldn't take another scare. You start to run a business, you hire people that you know and trust off the bat, but once you have ten, fifty, two hundred employees, you end up hiring strangers. And when you hire strangers, you just never know. As she had learned. She hoped, looking back into her father's unforgiving stare, that Leonard Mitchell would work out. He had seemed soft enough, desperate enough for the money that he would put up with anything. He had made it through a pretty rough day no worse the wear. After the last one, trust would be long in coming, but maybe he was a step in the right direction. Maybe a few weeks from now she could even tell him why it was so important to right the ship.

Eleanor had been up late working all weekend, and here was something more being asked of her. "So you want out."

"You have done very well, Eleanor. I was happy to help you when you started. And I appreciate that you gave me a stake. Some people think their parents are just giving them money as an early inheritance. But I don't want a stake in what you do anymore. I don't want to worry about what I'm involved with. I don't know who will be knocking on my door the next time."

So it was about what had happened. About the theft. Deep down, she couldn't blame him. How was he to believe for certain that it would never happen again? He was gracious enough not to mention it. But it also meant that she couldn't change his mind.

"It's going to take a little time. To get the paperwork in order. To figure out the value, to raise the money. Everything is in the buildings. We don't have 20 percent of this company lying around just to hand out."

He had brought a briefcase. He reached into it and tugged out a packet of about twenty pages. Eleanor recognized it. The operating agreement they had put together about ten years ago. With her father and the three others. The lawyers had been telling her it was time to revise it. Now it was too late.

"I looked through this. It says a shareholder wishing to transfer his shares to the corporation may do so upon thirty days' notice. The value is to be calculated as five years trailing EBITDA. That won't take too much time. This is your thirty days' notice."

That was the thing about her father. He could preach to the poor; he could understand them and tend to them and offer them comfort. But he understood the ways of the rich as well. No one had to spell out Earnings Before Interest, Taxes, Depreciation, and Amortization to him. And no one had to tell him that in a big leveraged real estate company, Interest and Amortization would be very high. So if you calculate the earnings before you take them out, the company will seem like it is worth a lot more than it is.

She was going to need to get a loan. Float a bond, find another investor maybe. Whatever number the accountant came back with when she phoned him with this request was going to be huge. The company was doing fine, but couldn't just cough up three or five million dollars at the drop of a hat. And the latest project was stalled. The towers along Empire had just been squashed by the community board. Or if not squashed, at least delayed. If that one had been going forward she could have wrestled the money up somehow. Now she'd have to look to other alternatives. And her father wasn't going to make it easy on her.

But buying him out would make some things easy on her. She wouldn't have to get his signature on the annual unanimous consent filed in lieu of a board meeting. She wouldn't have to listen to him chide her even as she mailed him a monthly check. And she could have the satisfaction of knowing that however he invested his windfall, he wouldn't make it work for him the way it would have if it stayed with her. If he poured it into the church, he could save on the taxes anyway.

He was holding out the paperwork as though maybe she would like to confirm what it said. She nodded to him and waved him off. He slipped it back into his bag and smiled.

"Okay, Dad, I hear you. I'll call the accountant today and we'll get you a number. And then we'll figure out how to raise it." Her mind was already racing ahead, putting together a plan. In trying times you resort to whatever you need.

"I'm sure you will figure something out." And the hat, the overcoat, the briefcase were all being shuffled away as he turned back toward the wall of windows and disappeared into the light.

"I'm sure I will too."

CHAPTER SEVENTEEN

Detective Mulino leaned back in his chair as Peralta paged through her memo book. She had written everything down, at least. A witness had said Manny Reeves had come into the building with someone else. But Peralta wasn't offering anything more. She needed a little prodding.

"So what did this other guy look like?"

She kept paging through the memo book. Mulino looked over his desk. The paperwork had started to come in over the weekend, and it was getting out of hand. Filings from the real estate company with the Department of Housing Preservation and Development, the witness reports Peralta and Bruder had compiled on the day of the incident, and background reports on both Valiant and Reeves. All of it had made its way to Mulino's office and collected itself into small mountains across his desk. He would get to it this afternoon. He would have to make a phone call to Chief Travis once he had taken it all in.

He was torn about that. If the guy in the hospital were to die, then the case starts looking an awful lot like a double murder. And while OCCB might be able to investigate an accident and hang on to it once it looks intentional, the Homicide Division doesn't much care for other people investigating multiples. But as long as Bruder hadn't called from the hospital, Mulino had to assume that either Reeves was alive and unconscious or Bruder had fallen asleep himself. Either was a possibility. Mulino watched as Peralta paged carefully through her memo book. She had found her notes about the witness description.

"She said he was an older guy. White. Maybe sixty. A little stooped. Seemed very buddy-buddy with Reeves on the way up. Nothing about how he was dressed."

"Did you ask?"

Peralta turned another page in the memo book without saying anything. She would make an okay detective someday. But it was going to take a little work. She looked back up at Mulino, all of a sudden the teenager who got caught taking her father's car out for the night.

"No."

"You only get one chance to get a witness's first impression. You gotta get everything you can from your first five minutes."

"I understand. I didn't want to intrude too long. It's not a lot of fun for any of those people to live in that building."

"He's squeezing them out so that he can flip the building."

Peralta looked up. "No, I don't think so. That's not what Evangeline said. She said the building is full. It stays full. Always new people coming in. They get vouchers from Homeless Services and are supposed to get housed there instead of shelters. There are only a dozen or so permanent tenants. The rest are in and out every few months."

That would make the owner worse than even your typical slum lord. Instead of trying to push people out by keeping the place in disrepair, he was profiting on a steady state of misery. Collect rent from the city and skimp on everything. The tenants won't even protest; they'll be out soon enough. You have to keep it worse than a shelter or when their number comes up, they won't want to leave.

"So we've got Reeves coming in with a man who was in his sixties, white, anything else? Guy have a beard? The two of them say anything?"

"They were talking to each other. They sounded like they knew each other. But she couldn't make out the words."

And to be fair to Peralta, this tenant wouldn't have seen much more, hunched at her peephole, trying to keep tabs on the comings and goings like a typical neighborhood snoop.

"This woman know the owner of the building? She would have recognized the owner if she'd seen him?"

"Neither of the guys was someone she'd seen before."

"But that's not the same question, is it, Detective?"

Peralta's nose was back in her memo book, trying to find the answers to questions she hadn't asked. It was better than Bruder, though. He would have come back with a marijuana collar and no intel on Reeves at all, and thought he'd done a great job.

There was a knock at the office door. Mulino looked up through the narrow glass partition to see Leonard Mitchell. He tilted his chin to Peralta. "Can you let him in?"

Mulino could see Peralta's worry as she stood and opened the door. Talking PD business in front of a civilian was frowned upon. Discussing an open investigation was unacceptable. She would probably steam over and explode if he didn't explain to her what was actually going on. She opened the door and Mitchell, looking thinner than usual, in the same dull suit as always, nodded to her and stepped in.

"Have a seat, Leonard." Peralta wasn't even looking at him. She'd closed the memo book, as though maybe he'd look over her shoulder like he was cheating on a high school math test. Mitchell settled into the other chair across from Mulino's desk, the shoulders of his suit folding upward as he did so. He had a thick envelope of paperwork under his arm. Mulino hoped it wasn't going to be added to the piles on his desk.

"Detective Peralta, I want to explain something to you and I expect you to understand it is in confidence. For your safety, for mine, and for the integrity of the investigation. Do you understand?"

"Yes, Detective, I understand." Peralta was a good soldier and if Mulino gave her a direct order it would stick. He went on.

"I have engaged Mr. Mitchell as a civilian investigator in the Valiant case. He has infiltrated Hill and Associates. They think of him as their chief of operations. I have my suspicions about Eleanor Hill. But I don't roll up to her father's church with my gun out. We go about this the right way. So when you talk to Mr. Mitchell, what you tell him is in confidence and what he tells you is in confidence. And that means more to him than it does to you. He's the one who is in potential danger. Do you get that?"

Peralta looked Leonard over. Mulino could tell what she was seeing. Just another guy who spent most of his work life sitting at a desk looking at a computer screen. To most detectives, the only real investigations are the ones that take place on the street; there is no need to respect the guys that go through the paperwork. Forensic accountants, fraud investigators, personnel officers: they are all basically support staff. So Peralta was trying to figure out, Mulino could tell, whether or not this guy was worthy of her respect, or just another paper pusher. Plus he had been at DIMAC. Whatever Mulino told her, whatever she told him, she would eventually make up her own mind.

"I get it."

"So, Leonard, is that thick envelope another report for me? You go through and pull their tax returns?"

"You're off the hook, Detective. This is my paperwork. I'm headed to DCAS after this to put in my papers."

"Working for us doesn't count as continuation of city service?"

"Technically, I think this is freelancing. And it doesn't matter anyway. I made my twenty and I'm not under the illusion you're going to pay me enough to move my number."

"Fair enough. So what did you find?"

Leonard looked over to Peralta. He was sizing her up too. No wonder, given what happened to him last year. Once he had learned about Davenport's death, the ring of cops that killed her had turned its sights on him. And they almost succeeded. It was understandable that he would be wary. Peralta was green, but she was as clean as they come. Mulino followed Leonard's gaze to the other detective and nodded.

"She's on the team, Leonard. You can say whatever you're going to say."

"Okay. So I spent most of last night on their servers. Reading about their old transactions. You'd think they'd make most of their money on the buildings that they put up, but that isn't true. They make a lot more buying and selling undeveloped land. Some developer will buy a plot for two million. Then Hill will buy it for two and a half. Then sell it to someone else for three. They just pass it back and forth. And by the time someone pays six for it—usually someone overseas—there is nothing they can build to make it back. Sometimes Hill makes the last sale. Sometimes one of the other developers does. Either way, it's the overseas buyer who gets screwed."

It wouldn't surprise Mulino. It looked simple enough to make a killing putting up condos in Brooklyn from the outside, but business is business, after all. And anyone in business needs to have an edge. Given even the above-board prices in Brooklyn nowadays, no one would ever stop and ask if you were in fact playing the pump-and-dump instead.

"You see anything else? Anything from city agencies? Federal? HUD or anyone else?"

"I was only there one day. They had me host an open house yesterday. With a tenant in place who the buyer is going to have to kick out."

"At least they let you hit the ground running."

"I suppose so."

"And you've got a list, I suppose, of the buyers who are at the end of the chain in all this? The ones holding the land after it's finally bid up too high?"

Leonard slipped out a single sheet of paper from his envelope. "Of course. These are the names of the entities, the managing agents, the countries of incorporation. I figure you guys could run it down from here."

Mulino took the paper and gestured to Peralta. *You see?* Her eyes were dull. Maybe she wouldn't even pick up the lesson. Mulino had to give it all the same. Don't talk to the boss until you have something actionable to show.

"Thanks, Leonard. Detective, could you run this down? See if we know anything more about any of these groups? Try the warrants database, call someone in the Fraud Division and see if they can help you out."

She nodded. Mulino hoped she'd have better luck with Frauds than Bruder did with TARU. It was tough, teaching these kids what to do. They thought they had made detective because they were good investigators. But they had been promoted only because they had the potential to learn. They didn't actually know anything yet. Peralta stared hard at the paper.

Mulino picked up the filings from his own desk and set them in front of Leonard. "Leonard, I've got a present right back for you. This is all the paperwork from HPD, DOB, Finance, anywhere we could find something on your friends at Hill and Associates. Let's see if there is anything more we need to track down."

"Okay." Mulino could tell Leonard was disappointed. No one wants to be the guy with the stack of papers to wade through. But he wasn't about to protest, now that he had quit his job. And he would know that it made sense for him to do the background on Hill, to synch it up with what he was doing there. As Leonard sized up the stacks in front of him, Mulino's phone went off. He looked down at it. It was Detective Bruder. This ought to be interesting.

"Hello, Detective. How are things at the hospital?"

"I just figured I should call you. The guy that fell down the air shaft. Mr. Reeves? He just woke up."

CHAPTER EIGHTEEN

Adam Davenport was out of breath. He had run two blocks down Underhill after double-parking. Normally Adam picked Henry up from the afterschool program at five, or even six. But today he was getting him right when school let out, at two-forty. Today they were both going to talk to the woman that Henry called "that nice lady." Because Adam hadn't taught his seven-year-old the words "grief counsellor" yet. And right at two-forty, the school was mobbed. You couldn't get a space in front of the school, and Adam realized that he had put on enough weight that running even a block and a half left him winded.

That nice lady. Sessions with the counselor were the only times Henry would even mention his mother. The counselor had told Adam to take it slow, to not impose a timetable on the boy. He will come around when he comes around. So once a week they sat in the office and Henry would say very sweet things about how he missed his mom, and Adam would hold his son's arm, and the boy sometimes would cry. And the rest of the week Henry would bite his nails, pick at the green plastic wristband his mother had given him, or wake up at two in the morning screaming.

By the time Adam reached the school, the noise came from all directions. Kids were pouring out of the building from the front and side, and swarming over the playground behind. Parents of kindergartners gingerly guided their precious ones down the front steps as the middle-school kids zoomed past, hoping to be the first ones to buy a pack of Skittles at the bodega down the street. The traffic was nearly at a standstill in both directions. A line of cars was double-parked up St. Marks, and most of the way along Underhill as well.

Henry's class let out on a side entrance, along St. Marks. The teacher would open the door and the kids would stream out toward a crowd of parents huddled behind an iron fence. When Adam got there, the crowd was thinning. The teacher stood still, guarding the three or four remaining students. The bulk of the parents and babysitters were shuffling away with kids who were issuing practiced whines for ice cream and cupcakes. Adam stood at the entrance to the gate and scanned the last four kids' faces. He knew them: Amelia, Compson, Lillian, Clyde. Antique names had been trending across the tonier parts of Brooklyn for years. But his son wasn't there. He looked up at the teacher.

"Is Henry here?"

A blank look. The teacher looked down, counting the boys again. She looked up at Adam. "He was here. Did he go to the playground?"

The school's playground was a flat concrete yard that had been repaved and repainted as soon as white people started moving to the neighborhood. Now it had two basketball courts, bright outlines of a soccer field, and surrounding it all, dark red lanes for an eighth-of-a-mile track. After school, some parents would hover by the fences and stare at their phones while their children wore themselves out for an easy bedtime. Henry was allowed to hit the playground without his father. Most kids weren't. But Adam had never been a hoverer. And the grief counselor had said that a little independence would be good for the boy.

Adam nodded. The yard was louder than the school. There was a soccer game going on. Festooned in kits from European clubs, the six-, seven-, and eight-year-olds swarmed and dove, unafraid of the pavement below. They were still mobbing the ball; no one had taught them how to play the game properly, what separated it from tag. But they were having great fun.

Adam slipped past the lower exit to the school and turned into the playground toward the soccer game. He made out a couple of Henry's friends. Leander. Hopper. He didn't see Henry, but it was a big crowd still. Up the steps and toward the yelping fray of children. He stopped at the edge of the game. He counted through the bodies. He didn't see his son. For the first time, he had a hint of worry. He looked over the rest of the playground. There were older kids playing basketball, girls playing hopscotch, kindergartners swarming the unbreakable play structure. It felt suddenly much colder than it was outside. For a moment he thought he would go back and ask the teacher again. Leander scored a goal. Adam walked up to him and put his hand on the boy's arm.

"Leander, did Henry come play with you? Is Henry here?"

The boy looked up with wide empty eyes, a bit of sweat creeping into his broad blonde mop of hair.

"Henry. Henry was here. He was playing with us."

"Where is he? Did he get hurt? Is he at the nurse's office?"

The boy cocked his head in thought.

"He was playing. Someone came to talk to him. He came and called out his name. Henry went with him. I thought it was his dad."

"I'm his dad, Leander, you know me."

And nothing from the boy. Why would there be? If Henry had gone to speak to some grownup, the other children wouldn't question it. The children are always being picked up by babysitters, uncles, and stepparents. Some have two dads. Some have two sets of parents. They are not each other's keepers. Leander was tugging away from Adam, trying to get back to his game. If Adam kept holding him, the boy's own mother might come scold him, if she could look up from her tablet long enough. Adam released the boy into the marauding crowd. He tried to think who could have come by to get the boy for him. What a stranger could have told Henry to make him come along. Nothing. And again nothing. And then a flash of what happened to Christine, why they had spent a year with his parents in New Jersey. How he had convinced himself that it was wrong to be afraid and that he ought to come back to the city and out of hiding. And now this. And what this might mean was suddenly too horrible to imagine.

He stopped and turned to look back toward the school. A heavy, brick complex, three stories, walled with makeshift air conditioners and metal bars added to the windows sometime in the 1970s. A building that had gone up as a symbol of efficiency and utility, and like most of the city that it had lived through, had sunk slowly into fear.

He could barely hear the buzz of the sport around him. The parents huddled by the edge of the playground were, like he had been fifteen minutes before, oblivious to the danger of the world. They were happy in their bubbles. Adam, already living with the greatest loss he thought he would ever know, felt as though his whole life was suddenly a scab that had been ripped off and had started to bleed. Someone had come for his family, again. He fell to his knees on the cement playground. There was no noise, no crowd, no comfort that could slow his collapse. He moaned as he dropped, and barely had the energy to raise his arms to break his fall as he faded from consciousness and smacked the ground.

CHAPTER NINETEEN

Mulino beat Peralta and Leonard to the hospital door. Maybe they were younger, and Peralta was certainly in better shape, but Mulino could still turn it on when he had to. They were rounding the last corner of the hallway when he reached the door to Reeves's room.

There was someone standing guard, but not who Mulino expected. It was a uniform officer, from patrol, one step removed from traffic enforcement. Small, white, meek, the guy couldn't have been more than twenty-six years old. Mulino looked at the collar brass—the patrol cop was from the six-seven. He was not even technically out of the local precinct; Brookdale was on the edge of the seven-oh. The six-seven was just across Bedford, near enough to bring in a body just about every week, so the guy wasn't too far out of his sector. But there wasn't supposed to be a uniform watching the door at all. There was supposed to be Mulino's detective, Timothy Bruder. Mulino didn't remember telling his direct report that he could kick off. He moved in very close to the little cop.

"And who are you?"

"I'm PO Reggie Shay. I'm in the six-seven."

"I can read your collar brass, officer. I can read your nameplate too. That's not what I mean when I ask who you are."

"Timmy—Detective Bruder said his tour was over and he had maxed out on overtime for the month already. He called me up and asked if I could watch the door until you got here. No one's come in or out. I mean, except for the doctors and the nurses."

You can promote someone to detective because he passes a test and has a lot of collars under his belt and because (let's face it) his dad knows a lot of guys at One P.P. But you can't make someone think like management if he doesn't want to. Timmy Bruder would spend his whole career calculating to the penny how much his pension was going to be worth. And he'd put in his papers the first day he was eligible. He would not do a lick of work if he couldn't add it to his time sheet, and monthly caps on overtime meant a monthly cap on how many hours Detective Bruder would serve the people of New York. If Mulino didn't like it, he could call up the union rep. But Mulino liked talking to the union reps even less than he liked talking to Reggie Shay.

"And I suppose you wrote down the names of each doctor that came in, and each nurse, and each orderly, so that I can go up to personnel and make sure people with those names actually work at this hospital?"

The uniform kid didn't say anything.

"And you checked them all for hospital ID. You told them that PD needed a secure room and you were very polite and apologetic but you did need to check their ID to make sure they weren't some co-conspirator coming in to give Reeves a story. Or a friend of the guy who pushed him off a building coming by to finish the job. You did all of that, right, Police Officer Shay of the six-seven?"

The kid looked at his shoes. Mulino thought maybe he was going to cry. He was worried he was laying it on a little thick. Then again, this was someone the city trusted to run around with a gun and a pair of handcuffs, so giving him a tongue-lashing to teach him how important it is to take care on the job might not be the end of the world.

"I just watched the door, Detective. Timmy just told me to spell him for a little while watching the door. I did my best."

Mulino put a hand on the recruit's shoulder. They sure did raise them soft nowadays.

"Okay, Officer. Head back to your precinct. I'll talk to Detective Bruder."

The kid slunk away. Mulino checked over his shoulder, making sure that Leonard and Detective Peralta had caught up with him. Leonard was out of breath, but Peralta already had her memo book out. Good for her. Mulino pushed down the handle and swung into the room.

The odor was better than he had remembered it from the day before. The sharp antiseptic hospital smell lingered, but the stink of rot and muck and who knows what else was gone. Once someone wakes up, he can call to have the bandages changed, his bedpan emptied. The unconscious in a big-city hospital are treated only marginally better than the corpses in a morgue.

And Reeves wasn't as far from the morgue as all that. He looked pretty much like he had the day before: bandaged, bound, and weak. His eyes were fluttering open a little and he had a tube in his left hand with a button at the end of it. That would be the morphine. Mulino had seen plenty of gunshot victims given the opiate drip as they came out of it. Reeves would be able to give himself a very small dose with the button, and then it would lock up and deny him a hit for half an hour to ward off addiction. Sixty seconds after he squeezed, he would lunge at the button again, desperate for another. Then he'd writhe in pain for twenty-nine hopeless minutes, a junkie in the making.

Mulino walked up to the right side of the bed and stood by the man's bandaged arm. Leonard had taken a place at the foot of the bed and Peralta was on the man's other side, by the morphine. They could look at the chart all they wanted now, but they had to be careful talking to Reeves. Witnesses have rights, after all. And Detective Mulino had just enough of a soft spot to make sure he honored them.

"You there, Manny?"

The eyelids fluttered. Mulino's voice brought him back just enough from whatever happy place he had been in. His left thumb started madly pumping the button. Maybe a little more morphine would help. But a little more morphine wouldn't come in for about twenty-six minutes.

"You are Manny Reeves, right?"

The man turned his head slightly toward Detective Mulino. His beard was so thin it looked as though you could brush it off his face. His hair was wispy and hadn't been washed in days. His whole body had the limp look of failure, the feel of a man who had given up trying to do much of anything. If Mulino hadn't read Manuel Reeves's personnel file, he would have thought he was twenty years older than he actually was.

The man strained his neck and craned it down again. Mulino figured it was safe to read the gesture as a nod.

"Mr. Reeves, I'm Detective Ralph Mulino. I'm with the NYPD. Do you understand me?"

The same weak gesture. Mulino nodded along with him, if only to give him confidence. To show him he was being understood.

"Mr. Reeves, you fell down an air shaft. Do you remember falling down the air shaft?"

And this time a little moan. A faint whistle, like wind through the chimney. The man was trying to talk. Mulino leaned in. He put his ear right up against the man's face. Reeves's eyes were closed but he was doing his best to make out words.

"Didn't. Fall. Pushed."

Mulino looked up at Peralta. "Detective, please note that Mr. Reeves claims he didn't fall down the air shaft. He claims he was pushed."

Peralta jotted in the memo book. Mulino looked down to the foot of the bed. Leonard was watching the broken man, silent. Mulino remembered how Leonard had almost thrown up when he had seen Christine Davenport's body for the first time. And it hadn't even been a particularly gruesome corpse. Or maybe Leonard wasn't silent because he was sick. He was staring at the man's eyes. He had done his share of interviews, after all, and anyone who interviews people for a living has a personal system for figuring out when a witness is lying. Maybe Leonard was trying to judge Manny Reeves, even in his semi-conscious state. Maybe Leonard was trying to figure out if this guy had himself put together enough to lie to a detective on his way out of the coma.

"Do you know who it was that pushed you, Mr. Reeves?"

This time Reeves's head turned toward Mulino. Reeves opened his lids a little wider. The deep-set eyes looked up at Mulino's face, then down at the shield hanging around his neck. The eyes were conscious now, more than they had been. Reeves turned his head back level. He looked straight up at the ceiling. Then he squinted his eyes shut, hard, firm.

"That wasn't a nod, Mr. Reeves, but it didn't look like you said no either. Can I try this again? You went to 80 Smithdale a few days ago with another man. Older than you. Gray hair. Wearing an overcoat, we're told, even though it might not have been cold enough for it. You went to the roof with this man. And the next thing anyone knows is, you are in the bottom of the air shaft almost dead. You want to tell me who this guy was?"

The eyes stayed squinted. The thumb squeezed for another hit. It wasn't coming.

Peralta leaned in on Reeves's other side. She put her hand on his arm. Gentle, coaxing. She spoke quietly and firmly.

"We want to help you, Mr. Reeves. We want to find out who did this to you. Anything else, anything that might have happened before you went to that building, we can figure that out later. But you have to know, you help us out on who it was tossed you over the edge, and we will remember it. Because once we are done finding the guy that did this to you, we are going to have other questions. You have to understand that."

Mulino grimaced. It was too soon. Their best hope had been to get the guy to spill something while he was still in a morphine haze. Before he could process the kind of trouble he was in. Asking someone to horse trade, to make deals, was for later. When he was conscious and clear and could weigh his options. Right now, the guy could probably barely figure out where he was, let alone what he had done to get himself nearly killed. All Peralta had done was remind him. And once he was reminded, he would start worrying. And worried witnesses are unlikely to be much help at all.

The man started moaning again. He gestured to Peralta. She knelt close and put her ear to his mouth. Mulino knew already what the guy was going to say, so the frown on Peralta's face didn't surprise him at all. He barely noticed that his cell phone was going off, vibrating in his pocket. At least he had remembered to turn the ringer off in the hospital. Peralta had stood up and was writing in her memo book when Mulino pulled out the phone and saw that it was Chief Travis from OCCB calling. He looked to Peralta as she finished her note.

"So what did he say, Detective?"

She finished scribbling. "He wants a lawyer."

Mulino shoved off from the bed. Maybe Peralta took good notes, but she hadn't figured out how to talk to a witness yet without scaring the life out of him. Mulino started wondering what kind of menial task he could assign Peralta, to peg her down a notch. He looked back at the barely living man and spoke.

"Well, then, I guess we're about done here."

His phone started ringing again, and this time he answered. "Mulino."

"Detective, it's Chief Travis."

"Hello, Chief. I'm here at the hospital with the second victim. He just came out of consciousness this afternoon."

"Okay, Detective. Your team has done a good job so far. But based on what you've picked up, this case is going to the Homicide Division. You know as well as I do, this wasn't an accident. They've got more guys to do the kind of legwork it's going to need."

"Whatever you say, Chief. Frankly, I kind of figured." Mulino was a supervisor now, but wouldn't have the chance to work his own case to the close. But you can't let them see you're disappointed.

"Can you spare someone from your team to work with them? Get them up to speed?"

Mulino looked across the hospital bed at Detective Peralta. She was still writing in her memo book. She wouldn't even realize he was punishing her. "Yeah. I think I can manage that."

"Good. Because I have something else for you now. I need you to come to OCCB headquarters right away. Not that the murder isn't important. But this is more urgent. We need you down here now."

"You want to tell me why?"

"I'll tell you that when you get here."

"Then I guess I'm on my way." Mulino shot a glance to Peralta on his way out the door. She was looking up with a sad pair of forgive-me eyes. At least she knew she had dropped the ball. That was some kind of progress, anyway. So Ralph Mulino, still dutiful, packed up his phone and wound his team out of the hospital.

CHAPTER TWENTY

Leonard didn't know exactly what was done in these circumstances, only that when he and Ralph Mulino came in to see Adam Davenport, the man looked like he'd been wrung through a piece of heavy machinery and then softly petted back to life again. The niceties were already over. Adam had a cup of coffee. He had had his cry and his scream and maybe he had gone somewhere and thrown up. There was a sandwich in front of him—baloney on white, it looked like. They don't spare any expense when they bring you in to give a statement about your missing son. Leonard wouldn't have wanted to eat anything if he had been in this guy's shoes either.

The room was nice. Nicer than anything that Leonard had used to interview witnesses at DIMAC. The place had a plush couch and a coffee table and a stack of magazines on the end table. Adam was being swallowed by the couch. The coffee and the sandwich were on the coffee table. There was a napkin, but the sandwich wasn't even on a plate. Across from Adam, there was a single plastic chair. The chair was the only thing that looked to Leonard like it came from the police department. Other than that, Leonard would have thought they were in a psychiatrist's waiting room.

They'd left Peralta with Reeves, for what good it would do. She had goaded him into asking for a lawyer and now she could wait for Legal Aid to log the case and find someone with a manageable caseload to send over. On the way in to OCCB, Mulino drove while a line detective told Leonard what had happened. Adam had gone to pick up his son from school. No son. No witnesses except for a seven-year-old boy. All the boy had said was that the person who picked up Henry had been a grownup, male, white, wearing dark clothes and a jacket. And clean-shaven: among elementary school parents in Brooklyn, this at least winnowed the field.

They'd called Mulino because Adam was Christine Davenport's husband. Mulino had asked Leonard to come along. Homicide would take over the murder. But Mulino had worked the Davenport case, and Leonard had known her. So it only made sense that they would talk to Adam.

The machinery of the NYPD had already been deployed to try to find the boy. An intake detective had taken down the details: time and place of occurrence, names of possible witnesses. There were uniforms now probably speaking to any school employee who could possibly know anything or have seen anything: the teacher, the janitor, other parents who had not really been watching as their kids kicked a soccer ball around a cement yard. The boy who had spoken to Adam was probably holed up somewhere being forced to tell his story fifteen or twenty times, his terrified mother sitting next to him, worried that this could happen to her someday.

But the machinery of the NYPD had only been deployed to find out the what. To maybe track the boy himself. Mulino and Leonard were in this plush little room to find out the why. Adam Davenport was sitting staring at his phone. Hoping maybe that someone would send him a text, call him with a ransom. Even Leonard knew that things didn't work that way. But he wasn't in the hope-dashing business today.

Adam spoke without looking up. "I told the other guys everything that happened. I don't know why I can't leave. Maybe he'll come home. Someone should be at home."

Mulino took the lead, making his way to the chair across from Adam. "Someone's at your house, Adam. The chief thought that maybe you should talk to the two of us a little."

Adam looked up from his phone. First at Mulino. Leonard couldn't tell if it was relief or surprise that shone in the man's face when he recognized the detective. But when Adam turned and looked up at him, Leonard could see that he was filled with anger. Anger and fear. Adam turned back to Mulino.

"What's he doing here? He isn't a police officer."

Mulino spoke slowly. Leonard knew better than to try to defend himself. "Leonard's working with us. He was working with us when Christine died. He was extremely helpful."

"He went to jail."

"Leonard stepped over a couple of lines. But he's paid for that. And we wanted him on board here. He knows a lot about what happened to Christine."

"More than I do, I think. No one ever told me what happened."

Leonard saw his opening. "Mr. Davenport, I came by to tell you. That night I was at your house. I told you to call me. I want to help you. I did everything I could for Christine, and I did everything I could to find out who killed her after. She found out some very dangerous truths. If anyone didn't tell you everything she found out, it was to protect you."

"Some job they did." And the phone was back up again. He was looking back into it like a child placated in a restaurant by his stressed parents.

Mulino settled into the chair. He held his hand up to Adam and guided the phone down. "Mr. Davenport. Adam. We need to talk to you. There are people out there looking for your son now. There are people at your house. But someone did this to you. And we need to walk through some things. I know you gave a description of the boy to the intake guys. But I'm going to ask you to do it again."

Adam stammered out his description. "White, he's got straight brown hair, just past his ears."

Mulino was taking his own notes now. "Height?"

"Not quite four feet. Forty-seven inches? Tall enough to get on the roller coaster at Coney Island."

"Clothes?"

"He is wearing a soccer jersey. It's white, has the name Ronaldo on the back."

Mulino wrote it down. Soccer jerseys nowadays. They all looked the same to him.

"He have a school bag? A lunchbox?"

"A green backpack. It's too big for him, it has wheels on the bottom like a roller bag. They give them so much to bring home now, the bags are too heavy for them."

"Does he have any jewelry? A chain? A watch?"

"He wears a green plastic wristband. His mother gave it to him. Like those cancer survivor things, but thicker. It snaps together, but he never takes it off. He's always picking at it."

"Shoes?"

"Blue sneakers."

"Any scars? Any birthmarks?"

"No." And what seven-year-old kid, after all, looks all that much different from any other one?

Then Mulino straightened up in his chair. He got a little more serious. He leaned in. "Now, Mr. Davenport, we need to talk about anyone who might have wanted to harm you. Because that can help us find him too. If anyone wants something from you, you will know. But we don't want to wait for that. The best way you can help us is to tell us anything that's happened. Anything out of the ordinary. Any conflict. Any argument you had with anyone at work. Just to help us get started."

"But what if it's just some random stranger? What if some madman just whisked him off the street? He could be anywhere. He could be doing anything to him."

Mulino set his hand on the man's knee. Leonard had never seen this side of the detective: slow, calm, building confidence. Offering support and comfort. And at the same time, building trust. It was a good way to get the attention of a victim, to get him to feel comfortable enough to open up. But it was probably a good way to talk to suspects too. You don't bring them into the precinct and smack them over the head with the radio anymore. You put them at ease. You let them talk. Because then they tell you something. And after all, Leonard knew, in a situation like this, there is no such thing as a surprise. Anyone can turn out to have done something horrible. And Adam himself was a white grownup with dark clothes and a jacket. And clean-shaven too.

"Adam, we are going to do our best. There are guys hitting the apartments of anyone in Brooklyn who could be a suspect for this. We keep lists nowadays and there are people out looking as we speak. But most of these are not random. Most of the time when a kid is taken, it's by someone they know. That's why they go with them. Your son probably wouldn't walk away with someone he had never met, would he?"

Adam started to bite his lip. He was looking at the floor. He set the phone on the table and grabbed his knees. He was going to have trouble talking. But Mulino had opened him up and he was, at least, going to talk.

"We just moved. With the money from the insurance, we bought a place. The house hasn't come together. We let the contractor go. Maybe he's mad at us. I joined the community board. I thought I was going to do my part, was going to help out. Everyone yells at each other all the time. People come into the meeting with signs and pickets. They clear the hall. Maybe one of them is mad at me. Maybe I said something at the community board. There haven't been any fights at work. I'm a professor. I just go in and teach my classes and leave. Students complain about grades. Someone on the faculty might think I'm not pulling my weight. But I couldn't imagine anyone who would do this."

The community board. So he had been there when Eleanor Hill had given her presentation. From a few blocks north in the Ebbets Field Apartments, how could he not? The whole stretch of Empire was filled with a gas station, fast food joints, storage units, a methadone clinic. A big, valuable chunk of real estate was being frittered away on low-end commerce. It was close to the park, it was close to the subway, and there were plenty of people who wanted a piece of it. Eleanor Hill had a big piece already, and was trying to cash in. Leonard had seen the plans for the condos that would go up on Empire once they bought, rezoned, and knocked down a block and a half of buildings. The people on Guilder Street didn't want their own views blocked, their privacy compromised by new arrivals, Juliet balconies, and cigarette butts tossed from fifteen stories up. But the people on Guilder Street owned their houses. They weren't renters fighting off displacement like Margaret. It was one set of rich people fighting with another.

"Have you been working on the zoning, on the community board?"

"We only had one vote. There were people who came in and protested the vote."

"Anyone threaten you at the board meeting? Anyone say anything they would do?"

For the first time Adam reached for the cup of coffee. It was probably cold by now.

"I knew some of the people in the protest. I just thought I had moved to the neighborhood and I should do my share. But it's very . . ."

He didn't have to say it. Leonard's mind was already turning. If you get Adam Davenport to move out of the neighborhood, if you get news of a kidnapping or a murder even, then who is going to want to build a block of condos? Stomping around inside a community board meeting can slow the process down. But if you really want to stop people from building housing in your neighborhood, the best way to do it is to make sure that new arrivals don't want to live there. And new arrivals want to live everywhere in Brooklyn, except where it isn't safe. If you really want to kill the value of a plot of land, put the precinct at the top of the crime stats. Talk about a falling knife.

Leonard was already thinking ahead. The kidnapping was sure to make the papers. Someone from PD was crafting a short, meaningless statement and putting out a tip line. Leonard knew that as soon as he was done talking to Adam Davenport, he was going to make a call himself. To his old friend, Tony Licata. He had information once again, and that meant that Tony would be willing to talk to him. If there was a neighborhood angle on the kidnapping, Tony would be able to dig into it too. Leonard spoke.

"Adam. We'd like the names of whoever is on the community board. And the people behind the protests."

Mulino looked up at Leonard. Leonard could see just a twinge from the detective, just a sense that he was muscling in on Mulino's investigation. Not showing the proper deference. He stepped back a bit and looked at Mulino as he spoke to Adam. "The detective and I will look into it. I'll be taking direction from him. It's Detective Mulino's case."

Mulino seemed placated. He turned back toward Adam. "And that contractor, too. You never know."

"Yeah. Sure."

"And we need to get you a place to stay. Your home isn't safe."

"I thought you said you had police there."

"We do. But in case anyone comes there. Tries to do anything. We don't want you around to be in the middle of it. It could get dangerous."

"Okay. Where will I stay?"

Leonard already had an idea on that front. But he would wait until he could run it by Mulino. Instead he stepped back and let Mulino offer his consolation as he pulled out his own notebook.

"We'll find somewhere. Now why don't you start giving me those names?"

CHAPTER TWENTY-ONE

She always got lost in here. Detective Peralta had figured her way around the meaner parts of Brooklyn and the suspiciously quiet corners of Queens. She had even tagged along with enough of her fellow cops on nights out after long tours to tell the difference between Tottenville and St. George on Staten Island. But Manhattan, aside from the blocks around the old academy on East 14th Street, was still something of a mystery. And the depths of One Police Plaza were a deeper mystery still.

The flat, red brick plaza was just big enough to make sure that no one wandered into police headquarters by accident. The mean, burgundy cube was fourteen stories tall, fourteen stories deep, and fourteen stories across. It was almost the opposite of a prison, it seemed to Detective Peralta every time she approached: its very architecture was designed to keep everyone out. Peralta herself, a detective even, had shuddered each of the half-dozen times she had gone inside. No mean and crumbling housing project was half as scary as the monolith that controlled every aspect of her job.

And inside, it was no easier. Everyone knew that the Commissioner was on the fourteenth floor and the Deputy Commissioner for Public Information was on the thirteenth. Other than that you were on your own. There was no directory. There was no concierge. After you flash your badge and get by the metal detector, you can climb up the single broad staircase to the second floor or you can take an elevator. If you don't know where you're going and you open the wrong door, you might just lose your job.

No wonder that Bruder had called TARU rather than coming down himself. Peralta didn't have that luxury. The homicide detectives who had stolen the case told her to go to Frauds in person, probably just to get her out of the way. There were four of them: each white, each older than Detective Mulino. If they could put four detectives on a single case, Peralta thought, maybe the murder rate wasn't quite going as far through the roof as the tabloids were saying.

The four of them had sat very politely with her in a secure room in the hospital. They had brought PO Shays back to guard the door again. Apparently they didn't have Detective Mulino's misgivings about his attentiveness. She went over every memo book, every entry she made in the last four days. The body in the street. The engineer's report on the crane. She told them about scouting out Reeves's car, the visit to 80 Smithdale, and the interview with Evangeline. And finally she told them about Reeves himself waking up, saying he was pushed, asking for a lawyer.

She left out the part about Leonard Mitchell and the real estate company. She figured Mulino wouldn't want them knowing he was hiring his confidential investigators from DIMAC. She told them Mulino's theory in broad strokes—Hill and Associates might have screwed over a couple of counterparties, mainly overseas. Mulino had asked her to run down any questionable transactions by those companies. She had been about to call the Frauds unit when they'd been brought to the hospital.

The tall one stopped her at this. "What are you saying exactly? Some pension fund has decided to get back at the developer by taking out a hit on one of its employees?"

"I'm just saying we wanted to look into it. You never know what someone who bears a grudge might do."

One of the detectives seemed to be chuckling at this. A squat one, with an extra layer of fat around his chin. He looked up to the tall one and shrugged. "You never know. They have a point."

The tall one looked back at Peralta. "You know what. That's not a bad idea. But don't call Frauds. They'll take forever. You gotta go there in person. You know where they are?"

She had said she didn't; he had written something down for her. It meant a trip to Manhattan and to One PP. Mulino had already taken the car, so she would be riding the subway in. While the train was cruising over the Manhattan Bridge it occurred to her that the homicide detectives hadn't believed her. They had one way of solving murders: find each person that knew the victim personally, lock them in an interview room, and shout at them until one of them either confesses or rats out another one. Foreign speculators paying off hit men doesn't enter into their mindset all that often.

They probably hadn't asked for her help to begin with; Travis had forced her on them. She felt like such a sucker. Maybe they hadn't even given her the right room number. It would be just like a pack of old-school detectives to pull a prank on her like that, give her the address of some secret undercover operation where she could get suspended just for seeing an officer's face.

Seventh floor. She turned down one corridor and crossed another. And then down a long hallway. The room numbers lining the halls had not gone in order. Seven nineteen was followed by seven thirty-four, then seven-oh-six. Par for the course at the PD. At the end of the last corridor, she found the number that the tall detective had given her. And a nameplate on the door: Fraud Investigations Unit. At least it wasn't a prank.

Peralta knocked at the door. There was no answer. It was the middle of the afternoon on a Monday. She knocked again. She tried the door. It was locked. She wasn't about to turn back. She pulled back her fist and whaled on the door a couple of times. No harm in really trying to get someone's attention. She stood back from the door, breathing heavy. She was just about to reach her fist out and pound it again when it opened.

The detective behind the door was under thirty, lean, black, bookish. Hair cut very short and wire-rimmed glasses. He wore civilian slacks and a white button-up shirt but had his shield out on his belt. Detective Peralta held up her fist just before she would have hit him in the face. He spoke calmly and slowly.

"You gotta give us a few minutes to answer the door, Detective. We've got things to do back here. You aren't serving a search warrant."

"I'm sorry, Detective."

"Simmons." He held out his hand and she shook it.

"Aurelia Peralta." It felt like she was shaking the hand of an accountant. A gentle, indoor hand. Simmons turned and Peralta followed him in, realizing she was talking now with a detective who might not have been on patrol for even a year before getting a job behind a computer. The NYPD needed these guys too, she figured. You can't outsource everything.

"You're here to follow up on a request?"

"I'm here to put one in."

Simmons looked her over. She could tell he was calculating how long she'd been on the force. How much she already knew and how much she had left to learn. He wasn't much older than she was, but he had the smug look of a man who was about to tell you how little you understood. Or maybe, she thought, it was just this guy's way of checking her out.

"Detective, you have to put in a request by phone, by fax, or by email. We have to get it in the queue. You can't just come on in here and burst your way in line. We have a lot of research to do here."

"It's urgent."

"What is it, someone in Brooklyn Heights had her credit card stolen? Worried that the nanny is going to start running up charges at Barneys?"

Peralta took out the sheet of paper that Leonard Mitchell had handed Mulino. She had folded it into quarters. She didn't want it to look crumpled. After how it had gone with the homicide guys, she was going to have to play it extra-cool to convince this guy to do much of anything for her.

"This is a list of overseas investment companies. Each of these companies bought a plot of land from Hill and Associates, a Brooklyn development firm. Each of those plots of land had been bid up to well above market value before the sale. We are trying to see if any of these companies has made any recent significant payouts in the United States. Or if their principals or officers have recently traveled to the United States." Peralta could tell that she had Simmons's attention. She wasn't just some larceny detective hunting down credit card thieves after all.

"Detective Peralta, what bureau are you with?"

"I'm with OCCB."

"And why is OCCB requesting these records?"

"I'm working on a homicide. This request should be treated as though it's coming from Homicide. I'd really hate to have to walk downstairs and fax it to you. Seeing as I am standing right here."

Simmons held out his hand and Peralta handed him the paper. For the first time since Thursday morning she felt the rush of authority, the glow of real power. First Mulino had been telling her what to do, and then the homicide detectives. The fact that she could play Bruder didn't count for much. But now, in a dim little office with a tinted window offering a view into the empty plaza, she was the one in charge.

Simmons sat down at his terminal. "There are a dozen companies on here. It's not going to be done right away."

Peralta could feel she was still in charge; she might as well press her advantage. "That's why you have to start it right away. Here's my card. Call me when you find anything out. Anything at all."

And Simmons nodded as he buried himself in the computer. Peralta felt her whole posture change as she turned back out into the hallway. Her shoulders were relaxed and rolled back, just as they had been after a fierce high school soccer game against West Morris or Verona. She turned down the corridor and toward the elevator. The place didn't feel like a maze at all to her anymore. She felt like she was at home for the first time.

CHAPTER TWENTY-TWO

"I don't know, Len. I've got a clean statement from the DCPI on this. I'm not sure I want to muddy the relationship."

Tony Licata leaned back in his swivel chair. Leonard waited for him to tilt forward. What he had to say, he wanted to say up close. Licata almost lost his balance, then swung forward to catch himself. Leonard, planted in a folding chair, now had his face inches away from his old friend's.

"There is more to this one than the DCPI is letting on, Tony." The Deputy Commissioner for Public Information, the NYPD's chief spokesman, was famous for doling out just enough information at just the right times to keep the daily print reporters totally dependent on him. He was famous for being vindictive, too. Use a source that wasn't approved, and you'd get a call that one of the dogs from the Westminster Kennel Club show had been electrocuted by a live manhole cover on Rector Street. Just to make you run downtown and wander around a construction site looking for a dead animal that didn't exist. Report too aggressively on a police shooting, and you would be locked out of the room when the officers give a press conference celebrating their inevitable acquittal.

The press needed the DCPI to give it the daily river of blood, fires, and betrayal that made up the bulk of a tabloid paper. But get too close, try too hard to get the story underneath, and the DCPI would turn on you in a heartbeat. It was like an abusive marriage, and the tabloid guys were every day on the wrong end of it.

Tony Licata closed his eyes. Leonard was sitting across from him in the tiny sheet-rock office the *Daily News* got to use inside One Police Plaza. One of a dozen identical cubes connected by a hallway so narrow you couldn't squeeze two people past each other in it. The Shack, they called it—a tiny warren where each paper and a couple of radio stations got a desk, a computer, and a phone in thirty-six square feet. So that they could already be in the building when the DCPI wanted to give an announcement on the thirteenth floor. Or so they could be close to a subway to the outer boroughs if there was new mayhem to report.

But the NYPD wasn't so generous as to give reporters easy access just for kicks. Housing all the police reporters essentially in one room together was a good way to keep tabs on them. The department could make sure that no detective could come tip them off. There was a good reason that, even though the department gave each office in the Shack a dedicated phone line, all the reporters made all of their calls on their cell phones.

Leonard didn't have to worry about being seen walking into the Shack. When he had worked at DIMAC, he had been in here every week, dropping a story to Tony at the *Daily News* or one of the guys at the *Post*, or the *Times* if he could interest them, about some piece of petty corruption or another. And as far as the guys watching the comings and goings knew, Leonard worked for the Parks Department now. Maybe he was just catching up with an old friend. There was no way he could be coming in suggesting that the afternoon's kidnapping—sure to be on the cover of both tabloids and the front of the Metro section to boot—might not be the work of a random stranger. Random-stranger kidnappings sell papers because they feed fear. If the kidnapping was the work of angry protesters, or maybe the work of a developer trying to scare people off of serving on the community board. . . .

"Look, Len. It's conspiratorial. You want me to say what, exactly? 'Sources are looking at the community board?' Hill and Associates is so desperate to put up condos that they have stooped to kidnapping the children of those who oppose them? And this is Hill and Associates, run by the daughter of McArthur Hill? You want me to go to my editor with that?"

Tony had always been a realist, an old-school tabloid gumshoe. Someone who got inside the hangar where they were reconstructing the airplane to write about where the hole in the fuselage really was. Who snuck into the morgue and counted the number of bullet holes in the body before comparing them to the autopsy. He wasn't afraid to call out power. He wasn't ashamed that his main goal was to put his own name on the front page. But he wasn't naïve either. He wouldn't just take Leonard Mitchell's word for anything. They had done each other their share of favors. But there is a line that can't be crossed, and Leonard knew it.

"Just mention in the article that Adam Davenport is on the community board. Play up that angle while you're talking about who he is. You want to make him look prominent. Make it seem like he's some kind of activist, fending off the developers."

"You must have mistaken this office for the *Times* next door. I get eight hundred words. I don't get to do a think piece on the victim's politics."

"You can fit it in. Look, Tony. Ralph Mulino has this case. The DCPI can feed you all he wants about what Missing Persons is doing. I'm sure they are knocking down doors. But the interview with Adam this afternoon was at OCCB. And it was done by Ralph Mulino. So you want to be the one who gets the call when there is going to be a handoff? When someone touches base and they are going to meet in the park and leave the boy and fifty officers are going to be hiding in the bushes to jump the offender? Then give us something now. We want to see if it gets any traction. If the person we are looking at blinks."

It was a small lie, throwing that "we" out there, as though Ralph Mulino agreed with Leonard. As though Mulino even knew he was out here, bargaining with a reporter, promising he would be there when they caught a bad guy someday in exchange for a few inches of ink tomorrow.

But this was Tony Licata's language, and his currency. You give a little to get a little. You slip a few lines into the story that don't technically need to be there, and three days later you're the one with the scoop on how it all went down. Every word in a tabloid story is there for a reason. They are written so close to the bone that there is no room for excess. So anything that seems like excess is in fact a favor that someone negotiated. Leonard knew that Tony gave and received favors with the best of them.

"And how is Ralph, nowadays?"

It was Leonard's turn to be patient. "He's good, Tony. He got his own squad. He made SDS. He supervises a couple of detectives. He was on the crane accident until Homicide concluded it had to be a murder and yanked it away from him."

"Still playing second fiddle to someone else, then. Still can't finish his own cases."

"Well, he's on this one now. And I think he's going to finish it. Maybe if you throw him something that will help him close it out. Just a sentence or two. Where everyone else goes on about how his wife was the DIMAC commissioner, and how she was murdered, you put in who he is. What he's been doing. Because what he's been doing may be what got him in trouble."

"You kill me, Leonard. I've got a very clean statement from the DCPI."

"We'll remember you." Leonard patted Tony's knee and stood up. He knew better than to think he would get a firm answer from Tony one way or the other. He had put in his pitch and he could open the paper tomorrow like everyone else to see what came of it. He wheeled out through the tiny hallway and onto the landing of the second floor of One Police Plaza, the broad staircase leading to the lobby ahead of him.

He saw a familiar figure coming out of the elevators. Detective Peralta. She had followed the Valiant case to Homicide. It had been only a few hours, but she looked different, like a weight had been lifted off her shoulders. He noticed for the first time how attractive she was too, her high cheeks and thin lips suddenly visible, as she owned the room. He couldn't help but stare at her from above as she turned past the bored cop at reception and out onto the dull plaza.

Mulino had told her to call Frauds. Likely the Homicide team had told her to come in person. The team would be canvassing now, doing things the old-fashioned way, looking for an angry friend hot-headed enough to kill Wade Valiant. Whatever she had found, she was proud of it. Leonard had to get back out to Brooklyn himself. He hurried down the stairs and trailed the detective, his head down just far enough that he would be able to deny seeing her if she spun around.

CHAPTER TWENTY-THREE

It was a lovely little house. Detective Mulino stood on the sidewalk of Guilder Street and surveyed a whole street of lovely little houses. Stoop on the left, bay window on the right. There would be a short stairway underneath to a finished basement or a rental apartment. Before hitting the street, Mulino had looked up the property records. Forty houses had been put up over the course of twelve months in 1911, back when this part of Brooklyn was just being captured from farmland. The shuttle train had been put in and could take commuters to the bustle of downtown Brooklyn in fifteen minutes. The subway would come later.

Now the row houses looked quiet and stately, protected by their age. But when they had been put up, they were just as much of an eyesore to the local farmers as the condos were now. Probably there were complaints then about newcomers staking out houses, ruining the agricultural character of the neighborhood. Change comes quickly to Brooklyn, but over the long haul the same stories are told over and over again. Now it was the homeowners' turn to complain.

Mulino double-checked his notebook. Stephanie Gray. Twenty-five Guilder Street. She was the leader of the group of protesters who was disrupting the community board meetings, someone who had no qualms about getting her own name in the paper. She had been gathering people to stand in the way of Eleanor Hill's bulldozers, should the bulldozers ever come. It was the same movie that had been played out in Prospect Heights, where protesters had complained and stammered about building an arena on top of the old rail yard. The enormous Barclay's Center, with two full blocks of thirty-story condominiums spiraling north from it, was a testament to how the story ends.

Stephanie Gray was not going to be happy being visited by a detective. Mulino didn't have probable cause that any of the protesters, anyone on the community board, or anyone associated with Hill and Associates had anything to do with the disappearance of Adam Davenport's son. But if the community board protesters were involved, Stephanie Gray would know. And the only way to get probable cause was to go ask questions.

As he climbed the steps, Mulino's knee reminded him that it had been a long time since he had sat down with his leg propped up. His knee ached from a day of running from the hospital to OCCB and now back down here to Flatbush again. Since the promotion, he had been able to spend more time in the office. Not that he was lazy about it, but it was getting harder and harder to walk and run. He shook out the leg and rang the doorbell.

She opened it quickly. Mulino thought for a moment that she had been watching from the window. Stephanie Gray was a short woman in a broad African-print dress, graying hair tied back tight, her dark cheeks and chin soft and slightly plump. The softness of the skin made her look younger than she probably was. She had perfect posture and spoke slowly.

"What can I do for you, Detective?"

Mulino hadn't taken his badge out. If she had been watching from the window she would have seen him in the Crown Vic with the four extra antennas coming out the back. Then again, some people can just tell. And Detective Mulino wasn't under the illusion that he could fool anyone into thinking that he was anything but a cop.

"I'm Ralph Mulino. Can I come in?"

"Are you cold?"

Mulino didn't care much for the song-and-dance about getting into someone's house. You can't go in without probable cause unless they give you consent. But consent is a funny thing. Mulino once knew a traffic control officer who had stopped a guy for a broken taillight. The guy had been out of control, screaming that he was being racially profiled, that the cops thought he was buying drugs because he was a white guy driving through Harlem. He eventually shouted that, "You could take this car apart piece by piece and you won't find any drugs in it!" That sounded like consent to Mulino's friend, who proceeded to bring in a specialized team to take off the wheels, remove the seats, and lift out the radiator. It had taken them six hours in the end, and the guy was right: they hadn't found any drugs. But when he sued the department, a judge agreed with Mulino's friend that his angry outburst, on the face of it, consisted of consent to take the car apart. There was a moral there somewhere.

But this woman was too sly to accidentally give Mulino access to the house. So he had to play it carefully. "I'm a little cold, ma'am. But I just thought we'd both be more comfortable inside."

"I am inside. I'm plenty comfortable. You can stand where you are." She had opened the door wide enough to stand, but still had her hand on the handle. She could give up on him and close it at any moment. But closing the door could be suspicious. That could give him probable cause for something. He looked over her shoulder, hoping to see maybe a bong on a table or a gun on a dresser or a stolen Rembrandt on the wall so he could force his way in and sit down. Mainly he wanted to sit down because his knee was hurting.

"You heard about Adam Davenport?"

"The new guy? The professor with the kid? I know him."

"But you haven't heard anything."

"I know he joined the community board. I know they came to their senses and voted against the towers they are trying to put in. He hasn't bought his raffle tickets for the block party yet. But I don't think you're here about the block party."

Mulino watched her eyes. He thought he was pretty good at telling whether or not someone is lying. But then again, so does everyone. The woman didn't seem to be hiding anything. He'd play it slow just the same.

"You know he's on the community board?"

"We went in last week to talk some sense to them. To tell them that enough is enough. There are six new buildings on Flatbush. We don't need any more over here. Seems like eventually someone is going to listen. But they had us removed. They called the local precinct. Are you here investigating my complaint against the arresting officer who removed me from the community board meeting?"

"No ma'am. If you filed a complaint, you can talk to the investigator. Internal Affairs, DIMAC, wherever you went." Mulino was cautioning himself not to react. She had probably complained that the handcuffs were too tight. No one has ever been arrested and failed to complain that the handcuffs were too tight. When you're constantly yanking your arms while you're cuffed, they certainly seem that way.

"I know better than to complain to the city about a city police officer. I complained to the state. I filed with the Attorney General's office."

"Then I guess you'll have to follow up with them, ma'am." Always ma'am. Always polite. Don't give her a reason to accuse you of anything. It's too important to keep the conversation going.

"So then what are you doing here, Detective? If it isn't about my unjustified arrest last week."

Mulino hadn't seen an arrest when he had looked up Stephanie Gray. That meant that the precinct had voided it. They had removed her from the building and erased it from the system. They didn't even bother to give her a Desk Appearance Ticket, not even a summons. Cops usually like to keep a record, even if all you've done is pee on the sidewalk. The guys at the precinct were either great friends of hers or afraid of her. Or maybe both.

"Mr. Davenport's son went missing from school this afternoon. We're just trying to talk to anyone who might be able to help us out." That was the moment to keep his eyes on her. To see if there was any flash of recognition. To see if there was too much or too little of a reaction to the news. Stephanie Gray stared hard at the ground when she heard the news. She seemed to actually be distressed. But some people can fake that too.

"Oh, that's—" She pursed her lips. "That's awful."

"So I'm just trying to see if anyone has seen anything. If anyone knows anything. He lives just halfway down the block."

"Yes. Of course. I . . . I don't know anything." She was looking at her sandaled feet. Very still. Very quiet. Mulino thought he would wait her out. See if she offered anything before he pressed her. He took one step down from the stoop. To give her space, to give her the sense that he was about to leave her alone, even if he really wasn't.

She stopped as he took a step and looked up at him. Searching in her eyes now. "Why did you come to ask me?"

"We're talking to anyone we can."

The woman stepped forward from her door. She looked left and then right. Down the row of houses going either way. "No you aren't. I was in my window and saw. You came to my house the very first one. You could have canvassed the block. Why did you come to my house first?"

"We know there was some kind of incident at the community board meeting. I'm going to talk to everyone I can. I started here because we had heard there was some kind of conflict."

The woman turned and pulled the door half shut. Mulino couldn't see past her into the house anymore. "You came to talk to me because you think I might know something? You think that the fact that I want to protect my neighborhood and protect my house and keep developers from coming in here and sweeping away everything I have grown up with my whole life means I could harm a child? What is your theory? That I got arrested at the board meeting so I'm going to start kidnapping people's children? Is that what you think of me?"

"We know there was some kind of dispute. Maybe you saw something. Maybe you saw someone acting strangely."

"All of them on stage were acting strangely. Because they were preparing to destroy our neighborhood. I went in with my neighbors and we rallied for our rights and they had us arrested. And the handcuffs were too tight. You don't fool me for a second. If a boy was kidnapped in Westchester I bet you wouldn't go hassling the neighbors to intimidate them. To find some crime to arrest us for. This is reserved for the people of Flatbush, and don't think we don't know why."

Mulino stepped down again. He wasn't going to get any further with this woman. He happened to know a cop in Westchester who had investigated a kidnapping a few years ago. Three of the adjoining houses had in fact been searched basement to rafters, all of the owners white. But Mulino figured that telling that to Stephanie Gray wasn't going to make any difference now. Like Peralta and Bruder at McArthur Hill's church, Mulino had stepped into an immovable object.

At least, though, he kind of believed her. She hadn't seen anything. She hadn't done anything. He would continue up the block. He would talk to the other neighbors. He would check in with the officers who were guarding Davenport's house itself. But he knew that this afternoon would not give him anything of value. A few more people would yell at him. A few more doors would be slammed in his face. And he would have to take it and smile, and he would be no closer to finding Henry Davenport than he had been the moment the boy had vanished.

CHAPTER TWENTY-FOUR

Leonard stood in the lobby of his building and looked it over as though for the first time. It didn't seem so bad: new paint, new tile, the mailboxes were clean and secure. But Leonard knew that was for show, to lure in new renters. They always kept the lobby up to date. And whenever an apartment would turn over, it would look nice too: a crew would come in to yank out the kitchen, install a new stove, lay hex tile in the bathroom. It would be hard for a renter to tell that the new cabinets would start to droop in six months, and the stove would fail within a year. Leonard knew. Once upon a time his cabinets and his stove were new too. But that was life in the Ebbets Field Apartments.

Leonard had volunteered to look after Adam while the department hunted for his son. If someone really was after Adam, his house might be a target. Plus, the police had to keep the place secure to preserve evidence. Because—and they couldn't tell Adam—no one was yet sure that he was totally in the clear. You cover all your bases. Adam had packed an overnight bag while a patrol officer stood guard. A couple of pairs of underwear, a toothbrush, and a short walk into a different world across Empire Boulevard.

Leonard looked over at Adam. His foot was tapping. He was nervous, and probably thought he was in a housing project. The elevator finally arrived, and Leonard stepped inside. Adam stood tapping his foot in the lobby, distracted.

"You can come on in, Adam."

Or maybe Adam was tapping his foot because his son had vanished that afternoon. Leonard had to remind himself not to judge. Christine had seen something in the guy, after all. Leonard pushed the button for eleven.

"I'm sorry we have to do this. I know you'd feel more comfortable in your own home."

"I wouldn't feel comfortable anywhere. I want to go out and find him."

"They have officers doing that, Adam. They have people who are trained specialists. Where would you even start to look?"

Adam looked at his shoes. The right foot was tapping again. Harder now. His clothes were a mess. He wore a dress shirt that didn't fit him properly even when it was tucked in. His slacks were one shade of green and his tweed sport jacket was another. He had balled up his windbreaker and was kneading it in clenched fists, his fingernails digging into the hard fabric. His glasses were a little further down his nose than they were supposed to be and his hair was a disaster. That's what they cultivate at the universities, after all, Leonard figured. But in the elevator of the Ebbets Field Apartments, Adam Davenport didn't look like a college professor. He looked like the guy who challenges you to five-dollar chess games in the park. The elevator bell rang. They had reached their floor.

Leonard guided Adam down the hallway and into the apartment.

"This is home, Adam. You're welcome to it."

Seeing his place through the eyes of a visitor was always hard for Leonard. The place maxed out at about six hundred square feet, the single bedroom tucked off of the main room. There was nothing to it but a couch and a row of bookshelves. The couch was gray and old and Leonard would probably get rid of it and get a new one if he could ever figure out a way to get it downstairs by himself. The bookshelves were double-stacked, disordered. A life of sitting at home in this tiny space reading to himself, piled up against the wall, no room for a television.

A window looked out over the playground. They managed to clean it now and again. You could even see out of it.

"You can have the bed and I'll stay in here."

Adam was staring out the window, watching kids scrambling over a plastic play structure. Energy. Verve. You could almost hear them. "I can sleep out here. I won't be in your way."

"Whatever you want, Adam. Can I get you something? A glass of water? I have some beer in here somewhere."

Adam was still staring at the playground. His body still hung heavy, but his face seemed now so narrow, as though hunks of his cheeks had simply been carved away. He was too startled to cry.

"No. I'm fine. I'll manage."

"We're going to do our best, Adam. Detective Mulino will. I will. I know it's hard but there is nothing you can do right now. You should eat something. You should rest. You can heat up a frozen dinner. Whatever you want from the fridge." There wasn't much in the fridge. He guided Adam to the couch and sat him down. "I have to go out. I'm going to keep working on the case. Is your cell phone charged?"

"Yes."

"I will call you if I find anything. Everyone has your number. Detective Mulino, the Missing Persons guys. If anyone finds anything you will hear it."

"I know."

Leonard had sat the man down, but he couldn't pump him back to life. Adam Davenport was still a statue. And Leonard wasn't technically going out to work on the boy's disappearance. But he didn't need to tell Adam that. He was going back to Hill and Associates. There was much more to find out now. Leonard was a little worried about leaving Davenport alone, but the windows didn't open up wide enough to throw yourself out and the guy seemed maybe even a little afraid of going outside. It was the best thing for him. Leonard gave him a pat hard on the back, reminded him to make himself at home, and stole back out into his other life.

CHAPTER TWENTY-FIVE

Working late at Hill and Associates, looking across Brooklyn at the Manhattan skyline, felt somehow right to Leonard. Maybe he would stay. Maybe he could go full private sector: get paid well, pick up the pension in a few years, and manage Eleanor Hill's empire as it grew. Move out of Ebbets Field. Maybe buy a condo in one of her buildings. Wear nicer suits. Maybe he had already sold out, he thought, scrolling through another set of emails. He didn't have to give what he was handing over to Mulino. What would the detective do, after all? He hadn't signed a contract and he wasn't sure he was actually even being paid. He could call the detective the next day and tell him that he liked his new office, his new job. He had done his term serving the city and it was maybe time to serve himself for a change.

Then he remembered that there was one man dead and another in the hospital. That a seven-year-old boy had been snatched from the street. And that the only reason he was here, now, scrolling through the servers of Hill and Associates, was to find out if this place had anything to do with it. And if this place had something to do with murder and kidnapping, maybe he didn't want to work there after all. He had brought a flash drive this time. He pulled documents as quickly

as he could. He could always go over them later. He had seen most of
the transactions the last time around. There was nothing new there.

He had been given a generic login when he started, and a generic
password: 74Hill. Likely the year she was born. There had been no
security on the drives. He had been able to pull out every document
he wanted.

Hopefully, with the lax security, he would be able to get into the
email server as well. If he were in, he could read not only Hill's emails,
but anyone's. When 74Hill didn't work as her password, he tried
Hill74, then 74Eleanor, and finally got through with Eleanor74. His
boss was careful about a lot of things, but not so much digital security.
He searched for any documents with Wade Valiant's name and got the
usual claptrap: HR forms, tax receipts, payroll. All of which he'd already
seen; it was what the company had given over to the PD after the man
had died.

But when he searched the emails, he began to find more, all from
just over a year ago. Valiant had been emailing with someone in the
back office of Hill and Associates. Bob Armstrong. Leonard didn't
recognize the name. But it didn't make sense for a site worker to be
sending emails to someone in the office. They were all in Armstrong's
account; Valiant didn't have a company address. Valiant was updating
Armstrong on construction progress. What was ahead of schedule.
What was behind. Who was keeping up his hours and who was slacking
on the job. Maybe, at first, the sort of thing a foreman would report to
the back office.

But the emails back from Armstrong were stranger. It looked as
though Armstrong was ordering materials through Valiant: "Get me
two tons of one-thirty-second of an inch copper wire for Friday." Or
another: "Delivery at six a.m. Tuesday, glazing panels for four hundred
windows." There was no reason for the corporate office to be ordering
supplies from a construction worker. There was no way that Wade
Valiant could have procured two tons of copper wire.

Armstrong had been the chief of operations. Overseeing staff, managing budgets, pushing paper. The job that Leonard had just been hired to do. It had been vacant for over a year. There was a reason, then, that Leonard hadn't heard of him. But it was only when he searched the emails again, this time looking for anything with Armstrong's name in it instead of Valiant's, that he really found something.

About a year before, Hill and Associates' outside accountant had noticed a number of anomalies in the financials. The accountant had contacted Armstrong, who wrote back that the clerical errors would be corrected. Then the accountant emailed Eleanor Hill, forwarding Armstrong's response. Hill had written to a law firm, and that was where the emails got interesting.

Leonard recognized the name of the firm. It was where Christine Davenport had headed after leaving DIMAC. Where she had gone to conduct quiet internal investigations into the shenanigans of corporate clients. Find the bad apple and report it. Fire the person quickly so that no one has to tell the government. Of course, she had found much more than she had expected to. She had uncovered more than your typical pump-and-dump.

An investment banker named Veronica Dean had been placing big bets against companies. Gambling that the companies would fail. And the companies—a water taxi firm, a chemical plant, a string of restaurants—had each suffered a catastrophe just after the investor had placed the bet. Davenport had confronted the traders. She had been on her way to solving the whole conspiracy. But then she had been killed. And only Veronica Dean had gotten away.

Leonard turned back to the emails in front of him. There had been no grand conspiracy this time around. The law firm had run the numbers from the accountant. It had requested records; it had put its best minds to the problem. And it had figured out what the accountants had suggested from the very beginning. Robert Armstrong had been stealing from the company. The orders emailed to Valiant were fakes.

Also on the system were a series of dummy invoices: extra wiring, plumbing materials, steel, glass, and concrete. When you are putting up a forty-story condo building, an extra two tons of copper wiring is easy to miss. Armstrong had been paying the fake invoices with company money and collecting on the other end. Probably paid a cut to Valiant for being the beard. Maybe Valiant didn't even understand the scope of the scam. There are plenty of guys on the sites who will walk off with extra plaster for their home repairs, after all. It's the cost of doing business.

In all, Armstrong had walked about a quarter-million dollars out the door. A big hit, but not so much that the company would have to report it publicly. Just tell your investors why the dividend is going to be a little smaller this quarter. Make a claim on the insurance, pay the lawyers, and fire the guy quietly. Turning him in to the police would mean that he'd be charged. If he were charged, that would be public. And that kind of publicity is bad for business. So Eleanor Hill, Leonard pieced together, had swallowed her pride and done what was needed. Gotten rid of Armstrong and made it a clean slate. Valiant hadn't even been fired. But someone had spoken to him, surely. And Eleanor must have known who he was when he turned up dead. Another thing she should have told the police.

The emails back and forth to the law firm, however, were not from Christine Davenport. There was a different lawyer involved. It seemed from reading through the correspondence that it was just a coincidence. A run-of-the-mill case to a bunch of suits in a midtown tower. No police angle. No reason to notify the new hire that something unusual was going on.

Leonard looked out the narrow window, over the heap of downtown Brooklyn and across the river to the bright towers of Wall Street. It was late, but the lights were on in Lower Manhattan. Leonard figured that most of it was show. They kept the hallways and the offices lit for the janitorial services that came through at night, and to make the rest of the city think, when they looked up at the office buildings from their plates of gnocchi at the outdoor café, that the bankers must work really hard. They must really deserve their compensation. Leonard was alone in his building. No one else in this tower was working late—and Leonard realized that he wasn't even working at what was supposed to be his real job. He had found out some small scandal after all. There had been some real dirt inside Hill and Associates. Some theft. And maybe something Wade Valiant had done a year ago had come back to haunt him on the job site. But Leonard was tired. And from all appearances, the embezzler had been cleaned up and sent packing.

He had a thought before shutting down and logging out. He wanted to make sure that Christine Davenport hadn't been involved in the law firm's investigation after all. She hadn't shown up as sending any email from the firm, but there was no harm in running her name to see if anyone had mentioned her. He put in her full name; there were no emails on the server with a hit. Just to check, he tried Christine. There were a couple of hundred—he read the first two and realized they were about someone else. It would be too much of a slog. Maybe, though, just the last name. And when he tried that, he got a single hit.

It was a strange email. Short and to the point: "Robert. We have to be careful. There is a lawyer out there named Davenport. She has been investigating us. She has figured too much out already. Call me."

The first thing that was strange about the email was the fact that it mentioned Davenport even though she hadn't been investigating Armstrong at all. The second thing that was strange about the email was the fact that it meant Armstrong had been tipped off. It was sent a full week before he was fired, in the middle of August the year before. But neither of those were the strangest thing about the email. The strangest thing about the email was who it was from.

Because it was from Veronica Dean.

CHAPTER TWENTY-SIX

Ralph Mulino spread the papers over his desk. All six of them had the Davenport kid on the front page. Both tabloids, two free subway papers, the *Staten Island Advance*, and even the *Times*, though in that case, "front page" meant front page of the Metro section. Mulino noticed that the *Daily News* had a little more meat on Davenport himself: he worked on the community board, he had clashed with the protesters, he had clashed with the developers. That's the thing about being reasonable in a political fight. Both sides decide you're against them. If any of Adam Davenport's so-called enemies had taken it upon themselves to kidnap his son in retribution, they would be sweating a little now.

The long night before hadn't seemed to do any good. One homeowner after another had been just about like Ms. Gray. They liked Adam. They liked the boy. He was new, but he was welcome. That's the way it was on the townhouse blocks. They don't want any new buildings, but they don't have any grief with the people buying the ones that are already there. If people from Manhattan are driving up prices, that only means that there are better comps for their own places. Whether they plan to sell and use the proceeds to retire to Florida or hang on until they pass and leave the place to their kids doesn't matter. They all mentioned that he hadn't bought his raffle tickets for the block party yet. But none of them seemed worried to be visited by a detective. None of them gave any of the usual tells: cutting him off, trying to leave, acting too defensive or too outraged. The whole block had calmly condescended to him, recognizing that he was subtly accusing them without stooping to actually feeling accused.

Missing Persons had spared two uniforms for the hotline. It was ringing to OCCB, and the uniforms were madly jotting down every call that came in. Since it had been in the papers, they were ringing steadily all morning. One guy in Ocean Hill said he had taken the child and eaten him. Someone from Bedford Park promised she knew where he was—she'd had a vision, and the boy was being held in a log cabin somewhere outside of Poughkeepsie. The boy had been seen, apparently, in Coney Island, Highbridge, the American Museum of Natural History, Tottenville, Brownsville, and Phoenix. The general public was always eager to seem important, even if it meant confessing to a heinous crime or coming across as a full-fledged loony. The uniforms handed the tips to Mulino to review before phoning them to the detectives working the case. You had to work more of them than you wanted to, though, because if it turns out that the one you scrap is the real lead, and the boy ends up dead, you are an easy fall guy. But Mulino figured it was safe to hold off on sending anyone to Phoenix.

The two new uniforms at the cubicle only drove home the fact that he was without his own detectives. Peralta had been sent to work with the murder squad and hadn't so much as called in. Ambitious, that one. Maybe she would prove something to those guys and they'd take her on full time. But the homicide detectives were old, hardened, and most of them were at least a little bit racist. They'd take Peralta on because they were told to for this case, and because after all she had been working it. But Mulino figured she'd be back in a couple of days, with the murder solved or not. Bruder, he couldn't fathom. His overtime paperwork was on his desk, along with a note reminding Mulino that he was on an eight-days-on, two-days-off schedule. Today and tomorrow were his regular days off. And why would he put aside his personal time just because there is a missing child out there waiting to be found, hopefully still alive. Bruder acted as though he were working at the DMV.

"Did you see Licata in the *Daily News*?"

Leonard Mitchell was hovering in the doorway. Mulino gestured to the papers spread across his desk. "I saw all of them."

"It should get us some movement."

"I dunno, Len. I hit a lot of the activists yesterday. I don't like them for this. What would be the point? Guy's not going to change his vote because you scare him."

"He might move to New Jersey."

"Then you just get another new one in his house."

"Anything come in on the hotline? Anyone offering a ransom?"

"Only forty or fifty of them."

Leonard stepped inside the office. He closed the door behind him, gentle but secure. "I was at Hill and Associates last night. I've got to go in now, too. But I found some things out. I don't know how much it means to the kid being taken. But it has something to do with Valiant."

"I'm listening."

As Leonard spoke, it all started to come together for Mulino. Someone corrupt at the real estate firm. Lining his pockets, but at the same time working with Veronica Dean. Feeding her information on the bad deals, maybe. So she would know which pension funds were taking on risk. Small little bets for a speculator to make. Or he was helping her with the sabotage. Wasn't one of the little disasters from last summer a crane collapse too? Maybe this wasn't Robert Armstrong's first trip down the road.

Mulino still had questions. "So where is this guy now? They fired him, what's happened to him?"

"I don't know. I'm going to try to find out from Eleanor."

"See if you can do that without tipping her off."

"This guy has something to do with Valiant dying. Valiant was in on the fraud. Did Eleanor mention that the guy who died was helping her director of operations steal from the company all last year?"

"No. She didn't tell us much about him at all."

Leonard looked vindicated. "I didn't think so."

Mulino leaned back in his chair. Once you're in charge, any pushback feels like insubordination. "Look, Len. I'm working on the missing kid right now. Valiant is important, but tomorrow he is still going to be dead. If I have the chance to find Adam's boy, then tomorrow we have good news. So go in to work, do what you have to. Figure out anything you can. But when you figure it out, call Detective Peralta. She's on the murder. I don't mean to be a pain about it. But I've got four hundred tips to go through on the missing kid. And none of them look like they are any good to me, but it's all we have so I guess I've got to do that."

Mulino could tell that Leonard was sagging. He didn't like getting bad news any more than Mulino liked giving it. Leonard looked up at Mulino; he wasn't going to give up. "I let Christine down. She was working on this. She was working on this a year ago and none of us even knew it until she died. And the kid you're looking for is her kid. So if I owe something to her, I owe it to him too. This guy who used to work for Eleanor was in touch with Veronica Dean. She was telling him that Davenport had found her out. There is something more there."

"Maybe there is, Leonard."

"We found some of what Christine had found out. But what if there was more? What if Armstrong was still looking for something that we didn't find? Because I know Veronica Dean is still out there."

"You do what you have to do, Leonard. I have to try to bring this kid home."

Leonard nodded. He seemed a little disappointed, as though maybe Mulino would jump on board and carouse through the city with him on another adventure. But the truth of the matter was that Mulino's knee hurt and he had only had one cup of coffee so far. Hitting the streets wasn't his job anymore, and he finally felt worn out enough to be glad it wasn't. Since getting the promotion, actually, Mulino had felt tired all the time. Funny how you ache for something for twenty years, and finally you get it, and it feels kind of like a pain in the ass. It had led Mulino to do some thinking about the job, actually. But that could wait. For now, he would sit at his desk and sift through the leads. Leonard would be able to manage on his own.

"How's the father? He holding up okay?"

"He stayed at my place last night. He seemed okay this morning. I mean, under the circumstances. He's staring out the window a lot."

"You're doing a good thing looking after him."

"Thanks."

"Good luck, Leonard. Call up Peralta if it has to do with the murder. If you corner Hill and she confesses to taking the boy, give me a ring and I'll be there."

Leonard turned and shut the door. Maybe Mulino had been too curt with him. He was doing good work, after all. And if there was a connection between the real estate firm and Veronica Dean, that would be worth knowing. Mulino had been sore for a year about the fact that she had gotten away. They had locked up a deputy mayor, eventually, on a couple of federal charges. The prison was in Myrtle Beach or somewhere; the sentence had been knocked down to twenty-four months. Elected officials can always find good lawyers. And somehow they can always get back in the game. Mulino figured he would hear from that one again too someday. But the fact that Veronica Dean had bet on sabotage, and for a good while had won, and then managed to slip away, had gnawed at him. Maybe Leonard would find her. Mulino had other business.

But then he thought of something Leonard said. This Armstrong character. He hadn't just been in touch with Wade Valiant. He had been in touch with Veronica Dean. And that means he had made an enemy of Christine Davenport. And Christine Davenport's son was missing. So maybe there was something Christine had discovered that Armstrong needed, that he wanted to give to Veronica. He remembered that Leonard had said no one could find Adam all year. That he had been hiding out with his parents in New Jersey, no address, no phone, no credit card. And just a month ago he had shown up, out of the blue, in Brooklyn. Maybe Leonard hadn't been the only one looking for him. But that was no reason to abduct the seven-year-old. It's not as though a kid would have known anything.

The work at hand was just too pressing. Another uniform came in with another stack of tips. Mulino took them with a heavy hand and started to page through them. It was going to be a long day.

CHAPTER TWENTY-SEVEN

Leonard slipped into the office to see Eleanor Hill looking out the plate windows onto the low waterfront skyline. She was alone in the office. With all the action in her business on the weekends—showing units, taking bids, closing deals—Tuesday morning was quiet and still. Leonard had been worried he would be late after checking in with Mulino that morning, but aside from Eleanor herself, no one was around. He walked past his boss's office, gave a quick nod through the glass in case she turned to look at him, and slipped around the corner toward his own.

Today he was reviewing permits before they were sent to the expeditor. Eleanor had given up on hiding the obvious: the building on Flatbush, touted as occupancy-ready in the spring, was months behind schedule. Frost was coming, and you can't lay electrical and plumbing out in the cold and the snow. What everyone didn't know was that the permits hadn't even been filed. Ordinarily that would mean months of review by the Department of Buildings. But Hill and Associates, like every other developer, had a way around that.

The stacks in front of Leonard had been prepared first by architects, then by the electrician, plumber, and HVAC subcontractors. Each one was forty pages thick. Leonard had to confirm they had been properly put together, then hand them off to a professional expeditor. The expeditor would wait in line at the DOB just like everyone else. But unlike everyone else, after the expeditor got to the front of the line, he would walk out with permits in less than half an hour. Most expeditors would work for multiple clients, carrying stacks of up to twenty permit applications at a time, even though DOB rules forbid you from submitting more than four at once. DOB rules usually require months for approval too. DOB rules can be funny that way.

It was a strange job, being an expeditor. When the millionaires were in power, they wanted spires in Manhattan to house corporate headquarters or luxury apartments to be used as pieds-à-terre by kleptocrats and sultans. When the progressives took over, they wanted big apartment buildings rented out for as little as possible. The expeditor takes a professional fee, lays off a part of it as a reasonable bribe, and you get to break ground. When Leonard was at DIMAC, they had been specifically instructed not to bother investigating corruption between expeditors and permit officers at buildings. It could have taken over their whole office, and frankly, nobody cared.

So Leonard thought that before he could hand these off to the expeditor, he had to be sure that they were in good shape. No one else was really going to look at them. He wasn't an architect and he wasn't a contractor. But he understood paperwork, and he could read enough of a schematic and do enough math to figure out if the permits penciled out.

He had made it through the first one when he heard her at the door. Not that it mattered in an office where the walls were glass and the doors windowed. Eleanor Hill had a hint of agitation as she stood silhouetted by the morning light. Her body was still but her thumbs were tapping against her middle fingers: a quick repeated patter. Leonard set down his pencil and looked up.

Eleanor was still and cold and stared dead into his eyes. His heart sank. She had found him out. She knew he was working for Mulino. She knew he had been through the company emails. She knew he was a mole.

He started thinking of excuses, some way to buy time or explain what he had been up to. He was just trying to familiarize himself with the firm. He wanted to know as much as possible. He was only here to help.

"Can I talk to you, Leonard?"

Leonard could feel his heart reel out of control. He took a deep breath. *Keep your cool.* He looked up at her again. He prepared his list of excuses. *You haven't done anything wrong.* "Sure. Come in. Sit down. Or should I come to your office?"

Silent, she walked in and took the chair across from Leonard's desk. Harder, less pliant than those she kept in her own office. Not that a comfortable chair would have dulled her alertness.

"I have something I need to talk to you about."

Stay attentive. But stay calm. "Sure."

"The man who died last week. Wade Valiant."

"I read about it." She hadn't mentioned it when he interviewed. It had happened the day before. She hadn't spoken of it Sunday night. He reminded himself not to appear too familiar with it.

"The police tell me that the crane was faulty. That it hadn't been inspected."

Leonard nodded. The last thing he needed to do was correct her. If she found out that he knew anything about what the police thought, his game would be over.

"Okay."

"Leonard, we don't depend on the Department of Buildings to keep our cranes safe. I can't afford to rely on them for that."

"You're saying the crane wasn't weak? That the DOB didn't miss an inspection?"

"I don't know if they missed an inspection or not. But it didn't just fail. Someone did something to it."

Eleanor was staring him down, calm. Leonard had come in worried she was about to turn him in. But now he thought she had another motive.

"You think someone killed Wade Valiant? You should tell that to the police."

"Leonard, I think the police might not be telling me the whole story. I think they may believe he was murdered. And they might be right."

"Okay."

"And it isn't safe for my business that I am not being kept in the loop. I may have another employee who is a danger to others. I have worksites that offer too many opportunities for someone looking to do harm. If there is a suspect working for me, I need to know about it."

Leonard thought about Manny Reeves, in his hospital bed. Eleanor didn't even know that he hadn't come in to work. Let alone that Mulino liked him for murdering Valiant.

"So what am I supposed to do?"

She leaned close. "You used to work for the city. You have friends still. Some in the PD, I imagine."

"I investigated dirty cops. There aren't too many NYPD officers who think they are friends of mine."

"There must be some."

"You want me to spy for you."

"I want you to find out information. They aren't telling me anything. It's bad for my business. It's dangerous. If they think anyone at this business had anything to do with a crime, they should let me know."

Leonard could see the part she wasn't saying. The part she feared. The reason they wouldn't tell her about the suspect was that she was the suspect herself.

"Okay. I'm going to call on a few friends in the city. What do you want me to do about the permits?"

"You can give them to me. I'll hand them off to the expeditor."

She hadn't said anything about reviewing them first. Leonard didn't want to ask. He stood up and handed them to her. "I'll let you know what I find out."

And with that he was up, and after less than an hour in the office, he was out again. He couldn't help but feel bad telling Eleanor he was going to spy for her, when he had been spying on her all along. She had to know more than she was letting on. And he had to keep his guard up, after all. But all in all, he was beginning to like her.

———

Eleanor Hill looked over her shoulder as Leonard left. A little too quick, a little too eager. He almost leapt at the chance to go spy on his old friends. Something about that wasn't right. She would have to let him in on what happened last summer eventually. But now she had him out of the office, after all. He stayed a little too late, worked a little too hard. Maybe he was desperate, but maybe he was up to something. And getting him out of the office was worth it, even if she had to handle the applications herself. It was just another stack of paperwork. After what had happened in the past two days, Eleanor had much bigger problems than one dead construction worker. The clock was ticking, after all.

CHAPTER TWENTY-EIGHT

Detective Peralta put her feet up on the desk. She could get used to this. In the Homicide Bureau, everyone had an office. Even Detective Peralta, technically on loan from OCCB, had a door she could close and a desk of her own. It was the same gunship gray steel that was littered around almost every command in the department. But it was in an office. Not a cubicle like the one she had been sharing with Detective Bruder.

Outside of the office was a real lounge. Couches. A mini-fridge. A corkboard wall. A television set too, though she hadn't seen anyone turn it on yet. Probably used mainly for watching security camera footage. A coffee table. Peralta imagined joining in late-night sessions, photos of suspects pinned to the corkboard, the squad batting around ideas until someone hit on that stupendous moment where the whole thing suddenly became clear.

She had gotten in early, the only one there. The four middle-aged white guys were nowhere to be seen. She hadn't heard from them since being sent to One PP to run the names of the outside entities through Frauds. Still, they had her name on the door. It was written on an index card and taped up, but she belonged.

"Who is that? Anyone in there? Someone there?" Peralta recognized the tall one's voice through her door. He was out in the lounge. She swung down her feet and opened the door.

"It's me, Detective."

The tall one was standing with a cup of coffee in the middle of the lounge. The stocky one was sitting on the couch, a bagel in one hand and a coffee in the other. The low table was just far enough away from him, Peralta figured, that he couldn't set down one treat or the other without folding himself up too tight for it to be worthwhile. He looked up at her just as he chomped on the bagel, overstuffed with a double schmear. But it was the tall one who spoke.

"Oh, Detective . . ." he stammered for a moment. Peralta could almost see the list of Spanish names rolling before his eyes. She could sense him trying to figure out if it was better to just pick one and probably be wrong or to admit defeat. Ramirez, Muñoz, Sanchez maybe. In the end, it seemed, he was going to settle on just "Detective."

"Detective. What are you doing here?"

"I work here. I'm assigned to the squad for the Valiant case."

The tall one looked down at the stocky one on the couch.

"Nobody told you? We solved that case."

Since nobody could remember her name, it wasn't that surprising that nobody had told her. "What do you mean?"

"No, you see. We did a real canvas yesterday. Not an OCCB canvas. And we found the guy that killed Valiant."

Detective Peralta stood her ground, remembering what Mulino had always told her about the difference between the who and the why. "We know who killed him. Manny Reeves killed him. We were trying to figure out why."

A smirk from the tall one. As though now he was talking to someone who had to have things explained to her very slowly. "Nah. Manny Reeves didn't kill him. What you guys didn't know is that Wade

Valiant was dating the ex-wife of another worker on the site. What was the guy's name?"

The stocky one leaned his neck back and swallowed the hunk of bagel, a hyena throwing back a chunk of gazelle. He licked a smudge of cream cheese off his lip. "His name was Smyth. With a Y. But pronounced the same. Gabriel Smyth."

"That's right. You OCCB guys missed the whole thing."

Peralta knew that Wade Valiant had been dating Gabriel Smyth's ex-wife. She had interviewed whichever worker had told that to these detectives. She had it in her memo book somewhere if they wanted to challenge her. She also had found out that Gabriel Smyth and his wife had been divorced for ten years, that they weren't exactly on speaking terms, and Smyth himself was remarried. It was hard for her to believe the jealousy bug could steam for that long and one day erupt into murder. But more than that, she knew that Gabriel Smyth hadn't even been at work that day. He had stayed home with his sick son in Queens.

"I thought he had an alibi?"

"Alibi. You guys. What does someone who wants to murder someone do, first thing? What's the first thing you do when you are about to go kill someone, Douggie?"

So the stocky one was called Douggie. Peralta made a note. None of them had ever really introduced himself. "You get yourself a good solid alibi."

"That's right, Douggie. So, Detective." Again with the little pause. If he didn't know her name before, though, it wasn't going to suddenly come to him. "We went to talk to Mr. Smyth. After a couple of hours in the room, he admits that he wasn't with his kid at all. He admits he told Reeves to go get a cup of coffee. And while Wade was out of the cab, Smyth gets in and starts whacking the machine up against the wall. Till your Mr. Valiant falls down dead. Douggie here did the interview. We have a signed confession. The case is closed."

Peralta looked down at Douggie. A couple of hours in a room with him and most people would confess to murdering their own mother. Not to mention that Smyth certainly didn't have a lawyer for this interview. Didn't know that the police can say whatever they want to you when they interview you. Can lie. Can say they found your fingerprints somewhere they didn't. They can say that another witness has identified you as being on the scene. They can tell you that you're facing the death penalty and only if you open up to them and tell them what you actually did, do you have any chance of seeing your family again. Your kid. Your wife.

The old-fashioned way of interrogating suspects was basically to find the guy with the best motive and hit him over the head until he confessed. Somewhere along the way, someone had told the police that they weren't allowed to do the hitting-over-the-head part any more. But that didn't mean they had to play fair. Peralta looked from one detective to the other. They had just arrested a man who was almost certainly innocent. And they were proud of it.

"And where is Mr. Smyth now?"

"Oh, he's locked up in the six-seven. Don't worry, Detective. We'll put your name on the paperwork and everything. You can tell your kids you helped solve a real honest-to-god murder. Can't she, Douggie?"

Douggie was done with his bagel, so there was no real reason to open his mouth. Instead he just shrugged.

"So we were going to kick back a little. I mean, we gave the confession to the ADA. We'll close out the rest of the paperwork maybe tomorrow. But you can go back to OCCB. Find someone running a fake handbag ring or something."

"What about Manny Reeves?"

"What about him? Valiant wasn't sleeping with his ex-wife. He didn't kill the guy."

"Who pushed him into the air shaft? What was he doing at 80 Smithdale? Why did he leave the scene and go to that building that afternoon? What happened to getting a cup of coffee, if you think he did that?"

The tall one took a long, slow sip of his own cup of coffee. He looked genuinely puzzled for a moment. When he spoke, he didn't address Peralta at all. Instead he looked to his squat buddy on the couch.

"Douggie, did the guy in the hospital, Reeves, did he die?"

"No. Guy in the hospital asked for a lawyer. Lawyer hadn't shown up. So we went out and solved the case."

"But he isn't dead?"

"No."

"So whoever pushed him off the air shaft didn't murder him."

"No."

The tall one looked back to Peralta. He took another sip of his coffee.

"Well, I guess, Detective, given that I'm a homicide detective, and Mr. Reeves is not in fact dead, that I don't give a rat's ass who pushed him, do I? I don't investigate assaults."

Peralta could have asked other questions. She could have asked how they thought Gabriel Smyth had gotten home to Queens after slipping into the cab of the crane and killing Valiant. How it was that none of the other people on the site reported him as being there. Who he left watching his son while he traipsed around town on his murder spree. But that would be missing the point, Peralta figured. Because the point was that these men had grown soft while their jobs had become easy. With only three hundred and thirty murders a year, spread through the five boroughs, and a couple of squads per borough-wide division, this team of four yahoos was likely to investigate no more than fifteen or twenty cases a year. You would think they would take their time. That they would walk down every possible lead in every case that came their way. They could certainly afford to. But they had settled into their routine twenty years ago—pound away until you get someone in lockup, and then move on to the next one. And if the next one is just an afternoon eating a bagel on the couch, so much the better. Joining the homicide bureau wasn't a step up after all. Peralta tugged the index card with her name on it off the door.

"Okay, Detectives. Mulino could use me on the missing kid, I'm sure."

"Call us if the kid shows up dead."

"I'm sure someone will."

With that, she turned down the hallway. The lounge didn't look so special anymore. Nowhere to bounce around theories on the latest murder. Instead it was a break room at the factory, a place where thick men gathered with lunchboxes to pass the time until they had to go back out to the smelter. She would have thought it was funny if it wasn't so terribly sad.

As she shifted down the stairway, her cell phone started ringing. Maybe Mulino, following up on the missing kid. It would be good to get back to him. To help on a case where it would really matter. Where a life can still be saved. She pulled out the phone. It was a Manhattan area code. Unfamiliar.

"Detective Peralta."

"Peralta. This is Detective Simmons. Fraud Investigations Unit."

A lot of good that would do now. She stopped in the stairwell.

"Hello, Detective."

"I did some work on those companies you gave me. I found something that I thought you might want to know."

Peralta looked over her shoulder, back toward the homicide detectives' lounge. No point in telling them, whatever Simmons was going to say.

"Shoot."

"One of the companies. One of the entities that bought a property, it's based in Malaysia. It's just an investment fund. Buys things all over the world. The land it bought probably isn't much more than a blip on its portfolio. But you're right it was oversold. It paid fourteen million for a plot that now it can't sell. Last time it tried to market it was for eight."

This was pretty much what Leonard had said was going on. The land was all pumped up to unreasonable prices. Then the outsiders got stuck with the bill. "Okay. That should be true of pretty much all of them."

"It is. But this one has an unusual transaction. About three weeks ago, this company made a big payment. It translates into nearly two hundred thousand dollars. And the payment went to another real estate company here in Brooklyn. But no one bought any land. There is no other side of the transaction. They just shipped a lot of money to a rival of your Hill and Associates."

"What company is it?" But she already knew.

"It's an LLC. The members' names aren't public. But it's named after one of the buildings it owns."

"And which building is that?"

"80 Smithdale Street. It's called 80 Smithdale, LLC."

Peralta held the phone for a moment, catching her breath. "And it's not just named after that building, Simmons? You confirmed that it owns the building too?"

"Absolutely. Isn't that the building where your witness fell down the air shaft?"

"Thank you, Detective. He didn't fall down the air shaft. He was pushed."

CHAPTER TWENTY-NINE

Detective Peralta stewed. If the homicide squad didn't want her, they didn't want her. But for them to make such an obvious hash of the investigation made her feel sick. Some dad from Queens was sitting in a holding cell and the two sneering detectives were going to railroad him into twenty years in prison. Nothing in the Patrol Guide tells you what to do when you see a couple of incompetents bumbling into convicting an innocent man. If nothing else, she could get her bearings back at OCCB. She could tell Mulino what was going on. He might figure out a way to do something about it.

There were two uniforms at the cubicle she had shared with Bruder. Both of them on the phone, speaking softly, taking notes. As soon as one of them hung up, the phone would ring again and he'd pick up. That would be the hotline for the kidnapping. That would be every crazy in the city promising he had the boy in his basement, hoping to end up on the cover of the *Post*. Peralta still ached knowing that Homicide had reached into Gabriel Smyth and dragged out a lie, and yet here was a flurry of false confessions, each of them self-important, willful, and meaningless.

She nodded to the two unis and their stacks of notes and turned to Mulino's closed door. She knocked.

"Yeah, go ahead."

She swung the door open and there was Mulino, his leg propped up on the little stool. In front of him sat a stack of cards, the leads that were coming in from the hotline. Welcome to your promotion. You get to read through a thousand index cards and separate the true lunatics from the merely wrong. And in the seat across from him was the civilian. Leonard Mitchell. Peralta figured that if Leonard got this much time with the supervisory detective, he couldn't be all bad. Truth be told, she was kind of warming to him. He didn't really think like a cop and he didn't really hit the street, but he seemed smart enough and his head was in the right place. Working as a plant in the real estate office isn't easy. Always worrying about whether you're going to be found out. There must be some toughness under that cheap suit after all.

Mulino looked up at her. "Detective Peralta."

At least Mulino would always remember her name. "So the homicide guys have locked someone up for the Valiant murder."

"I got a call."

"I think it's the wrong guy."

"That's for the DA to figure out."

"Those guys. Those Homicide detectives? They don't listen at all. They just went out and found this guy. Their theory doesn't make any sense."

Mulino and Leonard looked at each other. Peralta almost noticed Leonard laugh a little. Mulino opened up with a broad, wan smile. She wasn't saying anything he didn't already know. The creases in the corners of Ralph Mulino's eyes told Peralta that he had been through hundreds of mornings like the one she had just suffered. Her education was really just getting started. Then he spoke.

"Detective Peralta, we can only control what we can control. Homicide likes to close cases. They get their numbers that way. They get the wrong guy, let's hope he gets a good lawyer. Let's hope the ADA tells them that their case is nonsense. But I go in and tell the chief of detectives you think they have the wrong guy? You think I have that much suck? That way we both end up in traffic enforcement."

Peralta looked over to Leonard. A civilian, he wouldn't be able to help either. He had been at a city agency though, even if it was DIMAC. He had suffered his own indignities. Suffering indignity, Peralta was just starting to figure out, was a big part of being a police officer. You get it from the person who doesn't want to get a summons for carrying around a beer and asks you why you aren't out catching murderers. And when you work your butt off and give a thousand of those summonses, and a couple of hundred arrests, and they make you a detective, then you get it from the murder guys who think you aren't fit for more than handing out summonses.

"I have something else, though."

"Shoot."

"I gave those companies to Frauds. The ones Leonard found out about. One of them has been giving a lot of money to 80 Smithdale Street."

After she had been at Frauds, she had run off a couple of dozen reports on the building. You get money from the city, there is a lot that you are supposed to file. Management reports. Registration regarding the units. Tax abatement forms. The Department of Buildings and the Department of Housing Preservation and Development had them all, and they are all very cooperative with detectives. Leonard reached out first and took her stack of paper.

While Leonard started on the documents, Mulino looked up at Peralta. "You know, Detective. Manny Reeves is in his hospital bed and he has a lawyer and he's not going to say anything. He's happy that Homicide is looking at someone else for a murder he committed. But he's still afraid of whoever pushed him off a building. Because I think whoever pushed him off the building was trying to tie up loose ends."

Peralta nodded. "I'd thought of that."

"And Leonard has just been telling me a very interesting story about a guy who used to embezzle from Eleanor Hill. Using Valiant as a beard. Fake invoices, fake deliveries, real money. Robert Armstrong. Maybe too common a name. But there are a lot of databases you could look in to track him down. I gotta keep working the kidnapping. Leonard is going to help me on that. But I can call it an OCCB investigation of the embezzlement if you want to try it. And if you get the guy, who knows what he might confess to?"

Detective Peralta didn't like the idea of being a lone wolf. But there was a man in jail who was wrongly accused. And she knew enough to know that once you're wrongly accused, you are more than halfway to being wrongly convicted. Mulino was offering her the chance to find a man who might have orchestrated a murder. She wouldn't have interference from the blowhards at Homicide, and she wouldn't have to babysit Timmy Bruder.

"Sure, Detective. Thanks for thinking of me."

Leonard pulled a paper out of the stack from Peralta. He held it out as though inspecting it, but also like he might be afraid it could hurt him. "The first step would be finding Mr. Armstrong. Except you already found him. According to the filing with HPD, 80 Smithdale hired him six months ago to be its managing agent."

Leonard smiled at Peralta. Mulino too. Both of them were proud of her, she sensed. She had done good work. She had always done good work, and she had always been proud of it herself. But there were some people in the PD who couldn't see that. She took the paper from Leonard. It had a name, an address. A house in Sheepshead Bay. Way out in Brooklyn. Far enough out that it is almost a different city. Peralta would go there alone.

"Thanks, guys. I'll let you know."

The men nodded to her. She folded the paper and turned on her heel, now on her own personal quest.

CHAPTER THIRTY

The elevators again. At least this time, Leonard was alone. At least he didn't have a nervous man worried about his missing son, tapping his foot next to him. But that man would be waiting for him upstairs, if the elevator ever came. Adam Davenport had been cooped up in Leonard's apartment all day. Leonard trusted that Adam could find a way to make himself a sandwich or something, but enough was enough and he ought to cut him loose for dinner. He had told Mulino he would bring him by OCCB. Keep an eye on him. Keep him safe. People in this kind of situation are likely to do just about anything.

Mulino had praised Peralta after she had left. A real legwork detective. She hadn't run over to OCCB as soon as she got the news of the payout, either. She had collected her paper, gotten the reports from HPD. And that was how they'd found Armstrong. Bruder sat on his hands for two days waiting for a call back from TARU. Peralta had initiative. And Mulino had taught her that. Finish the work. Get the details. Do it right.

"I could be getting used to this being a boss thing after all," Mulino had said.

"Don't. Once you've got more than three or four of them to watch over, you can't keep control of them. Eventually you can't even keep them all straight." Leonard spoke from experience. At DIMAC, working under Christine Davenport, he had managed sixty-five investigators. And the truth was that when the tougher cases came in, he still had to do most of the work alone.

The elevator finally came. The lobby was empty. The bright renovation hadn't brought in any market-rate renters. It was hard to lure newcomers to Ebbets Field when there was new construction just south and east and west and even north of it. Never mind that the new construction was made mainly with Sheetrock, would start to leak after the second heavy rain, and half the buildings were in litigation within a year. Ebbets Field had its problems, but exterior leaks were not among them. Small windows mean heavy brick construction. The building was there to stay.

Leonard stepped into the elevator and pressed his floor. It waited, as though deciding whether it was going to work today, and lurched upward suddenly, catching Leonard off guard. It was always like that.

Mulino had stayed behind. He was running down the miserable stack of hopeless leads. To Mulino, Leonard was just running an errand. Bring back Adam Davenport. Better to have him watched at OCCB then fiddle around in the apartment. But Leonard was still thinking about what he had found at Eleanor Hill's office. Not just about Armstrong stealing. And not just about him writing to Wade Valiant, but about the note from Veronica Dean. If someone thought that Christine had found even more damaging information, then they would still want to find it. Maybe they had been looking the whole year that Adam had been in New Jersey. Maybe he had been right to hide out. Look what had happened as soon as he put his name on a mortgage. The fact that Christine herself was already dead wouldn't really make a difference. Maybe someone had taken the kid to find out what Christine had left behind. Maybe someone thought the kid knew. Or the father. There was always something the victim didn't tell you.

Mulino hadn't bought it. Why would someone kidnap a child for information his mother had found a year ago? Why take the risk? And they had Davenport's investigation, after all. There was nothing more to it. So even if Armstrong had been feeding information to Dean—and Mulino didn't doubt it, the investor had been scouring the world for leaks and tips, after all—that didn't mean that he had anything to do with the kidnapping.

"You just bring Adam back, Len," Mulino had said. "You let me worry about the boy. We are going to keep doing everything we can. We don't need you making it any harder than it's supposed to be. You've done good work, after all."

Leonard had chafed, but nodded. Maybe Mulino was right. And Mulino, after all, was in charge now. That was part of the deal, taking the gig spying on Hill and Associates. He was back in the thick of it, back doing a real investigation, but he was reporting up the chain of command. And the PD was a chain-of-command organization, after all.

But Mulino hadn't said Leonard couldn't talk to Adam. Couldn't ask if he had seen someone matching the description Evangeline had given Peralta. A description of a man Leonard now knew must be Robert Armstrong: about sixty, with a bit of a stoop. No one could stop him from asking Adam how much he knew about what Christine had found out. Whether she had ever said anything more, had ever implied there was more yet to find. Once he got to the apartment he was going to have to bring the guy downstairs and downtown anyway. Plenty of time to talk. And maybe after being cooped up at Leonard's for a few hours, Adam would have something new to say.

The elevator dinged. The door heaved and opened restlessly. It was a short walk down the hallway to Leonard's unit. He noticed, for the first time in months, the sweet smell that used to fill the building almost every day. He had almost forgotten it. It reminded him, if he needed reminding, of the summer before.

He turned the corner. Something was out of place. It took him a moment to notice that his door was ajar. Just a half an inch, as though someone had left it to close without pushing it all the way shut and it had drifted into place. But no one would do that here. Because while Ebbets Field was not the crime scene it used to be, it wasn't yet the kind of place where you would walk away with your door a little bit open. Nowhere in New York was. He crept down the hallway and nudged the door.

"Hello? Adam, are you in there?"

Cautiously, he swung the door open. His apartment was unchanged. The sheets were folded and set on the coffee table. But Adam Davenport was gone.

Leonard's first thought was to call Mulino. He worried that Adam might hurt himself. Or take matters into his own hands and start running through the streets trying desperately to find his son. Leonard knew the little boy wasn't going to be found just walking down the street somewhere, but parents do what they think they can. They go a little bit mad. Mulino had to know; the detective would have to start looking for two missing persons now.

But then Leonard had a second thought. Because if he wasn't taking Adam Davenport back to OCCB, that meant he could follow his instincts. And his instincts said that Armstrong hadn't just killed Valiant. His instincts said that Armstrong was still trying to get something from Christine Davenport. Something she had maybe hidden. Something that would be in the house where Adam had moved all of her possessions, only a few blocks away. Mulino had told him to back off; he wouldn't be able to say he was there on OCCB business, or NYPD business at all, really. Because he wouldn't be. The house was being guarded by a police officer, but that wasn't something that would trouble Leonard. He didn't have a badge anymore, not like he did at DIMAC, but there were other ways inside a building.

It would mean striking out on his own after Mulino told him not to. It would mean following an investigation that he wasn't supposed to be involved in at all. But he had followed his hunches once before, last year, and found out a deeper and broader conspiracy than even he had expected. If Christine Davenport had found more, there would be some evidence of it somewhere in her house. He went back out into the hallway, pulled the door to his own apartment shut, and locked it. He turned back toward the elevator. He was going out.

CHAPTER THIRTY-ONE

When Leonard stole out of the Ebbets Field Apartments, it was early but already dark. The cars turning up Bedford from Empire had their lights on, alert to teenagers who still dashed across the middle of the street. It was a little chilly, but not bad yet. Thanksgiving was around the corner, but there wasn't any snow. There wasn't much wind. And with what Leonard was planning, he had to stay nimble.

When he reached Empire, he took in the massive ruined block. Dull, tired businesses. A used tire store on one side, storage units and a carpet wholesaler on the other. Somehow, incredibly, a series of storefronts with a couple of national chains: pizzas, Slurpees. Leonard wondered how they had hung on against the rush of artisan pies and cupcake stores. Other than that, the buildings were boarded up. Commercial storefronts had been sold and shuttered, bought by speculators hoping to flip them to developers. In the meanwhile, padlocks had been picked and wood had been pried off of windows and who knew what was actually going on behind the closed doors.

Leonard crossed Empire. Davenport's house was on Guilder Street, the next block down. His yard would front one of these buildings. There would be no way in on the Guilder Street side; the row houses were entirely attached. And if Leonard tried to go in the front door, the cop posted there would call Mulino, and that would be the end of that.

But getting into the backyard meant getting through, or over, these buildings. None of them would have a door that just opened into the yards beyond. The last building, at the end of the block, was an enormous grocery store with a massive parking lot. Leonard had been in there once; it had a cold storage room with sides of beef actually hanging from hooks. It stank. There was no way into the yards from there.

He could try scaling fences all the way toward the house. But he had never seen the yards. There could be alarms. The fences could be twelve feet tall. Adam Davenport's house was the seventh in from the edge. That meant seven fences, seven yards, seven separate acts of trespassing. The smart move was to get in through the commercial side. He would get in a building, hit the roof, and find a way to drop down.

Leonard scanned the traffic up and down Empire. The cars cruised by, oblivious. Around the corner, on Flatbush, the street would be thick with people, walking home from the subway or heading out for a drink. But since all the buildings had closed up on Empire, there was no reason for anyone to walk it. So there was no reason for anyone to stumble onto Leonard as he broke into a storefront. Even the methadone clinic had closed.

Leonard snuck up to an abandoned storefront; hanging on it was a small sign: "Music lessons for all ages." Once upon a time, kids had swung 'round to learn to play guitar and piano in here. Maybe they had even come down from Ebbets Field. Once upon a time, like six months ago, maybe. The front door was locked, but there was a window to the side that was ajar by about an inch. That meant the lock had been sprung. Another quick peek on to Empire to make sure he wasn't being watched. Leonard tugged at the window and slipped inside.

The room was a mess. Broken glass, mainly. The counter at the front, cash register askew, had been battered with a crowbar. There had once been cases on the walls, probably holding instruments for sale. All of it had been shattered. Someone had come through with a hammer and a crowbar and simply wrecked the place. Funny that they would have locked the door after they left. Most likely whoever did it hadn't found anything of value. Even in this environment, people get ninety days' notice before they have to clear out. It's not like someone would have closed the business and left the register full. Or maybe someone had just visited his rage on whatever was nearby, breakable, and abandoned. Leonard walked through the lobby toward the back of the building.

Through the lobby, there was a hallway leading to six or seven rehearsal rooms. Each was behind a soundproof door; each was about six feet square. Leonard had a momentary vision of the place filled with kids, working on their scales, a patient teacher popping in from one room to the next. It was a vision of another era. The back wall had no door, no window. If it had an opening, it would have gone straight into somebody's yard. The best bet was going to be the roof.

Leonard had missed the stairway by going in the window. The front door opened straight into it, with the music store actually on the left. That meant apartments above. People would come in the door and hike up the stairs to a couple of floors of two-bedroom units. So there had been a few people living on Empire before the whole thing was shut down after all. Whether it was legal or not, whether there were proper certificates of occupancy or whether the boiler was approved for residential use and hours, that was another story. Maybe if you want to give music lessons in the middle of Brooklyn, the best way to do it is to get a building and rent out a few apartments above your shop. Even if no one comes in to learn the French horn, the tenants above you are paying your nut. Maybe you take one of those apartments yourself. Makes for an awfully short commute.

Leonard reached the landing; there were two doors and another flight up. These would be apartments. There might be windows into the back, but as Leonard had counted, it probably wasn't the right yard. The best plan would be to get to the roof and cross from there. Somehow he would find a way to get down three stories. He turned up the next flight of stairs.

It was dark. There probably hadn't been power in the building for months. The ground floor had been fine, still aglow with streetlights. Even upstairs there had still been a hint of light. But now on the third floor, Leonard was feeling his way in near-total blackness. One hand gripped the railing, the other stuck ahead of him, to find whatever he was heading for before he walked into it. There would be one final turn, then either a stairway or a ladder or something to get to the roof.

He reached the top landing. Dark still. He would need a little light to get his bearings, to figure out how to get upstairs. He pulled out his phone and swiped on the flashlight app. It wasn't great, but it would do. He was on a narrow landing. There were once again two doors on either side. Apartments that had long since been abandoned. And a ladder on the back wall. No stairway. He walked toward it, his phone guiding him.

Something on the floor caught his foot. He slipped and flew forward, landing on his left arm, hoping to protect the phone with his right. There was decades-old carpeting on the landing. Thick, dull, and carrying a faded moldy stench, but good enough to break his fall. He was fine, but it had been loud. He stood up and continued toward the ladder.

"Who's there?" A man's voice, not afraid, not worried. But harsh and hostile. Someone who was being invaded and wanted to protect himself.

Leonard froze. There was someone behind one of the doors. A squatter. Someone who makes his home in a completely abandoned apartment might be doing it just to save on rent. But there would be no water, no power, no heat; he would really be roughing it. More likely—much more likely—was that whoever was behind that door had his reasons not to be found. Not by the police, not by the building inspectors, not by whoever used to be his landlord. And especially not by Leonard Mitchell, sneaking around to break into one of the houses on Guilder Street. Leonard slipped his phone back into his pocket. He grabbed the ladder. He started up, the cold rungs bearing deep into his hands.

One rung, then another, and then he heard the door to one of the apartments open. The voice again. "Who's there? What are you doing out there?" It was pitch black. Leonard couldn't see anything. Maybe that meant the man couldn't see him either. Slowly, cautiously, he started up the ladder again. He could hear the man pacing back and forth downstairs. Maybe waving his arms, hoping to run into whoever he had heard stumbling around. Leonard reached his hand up and felt a latch. The roof. He fingered the metal grate above him.

He saw a light below him. The man had turned on a flashlight and was shining it down the stairway. Leonard couldn't see the man at all, just the beam as it lit up the stairwell. "You gotta tell me your business, whoever it is down there. You've got no business in here, I can tell you that."

Leonard took a breath and tugged at the latch to the roof. It swung open. He popped open the grate and pulled himself toward the roof. As soon as he did, light streamed into the building. Leonard could hear the man below swinging around but didn't turn to look. He scrambled out, tugging his legs up onto the flat tar roof, and shut the grate behind him. He looked down at it. There was no way to secure it from the outside. If the man wanted to follow him out, he would be there in a moment.

Leonard stood. He was on one of a row of roofs, all connected, all about twenty to thirty feet over the backyards of Guilder Street. He looked down toward the giant grocery at the end of the block, into the dozen or so yards, each divided from the next by a vinyl fence. He counted seven in from the edge, to Adam Davenport's house. A broad deck, a brick patio below it, and where the other houses had yards, there was just a thicket of growth. Whatever was growing, it was four, maybe five feet tall. Even this late, even in November, the weeds were nearly as tall as a field of grown men. But it was only a few buildings down. Leonard turned. He ran across the roofs until he was face to face with Adam's house, the field of weeds below and the lights entirely dark.

Behind him, he heard a creak. The squatter was opening the grate, was following him onto the roof. Leonard scurried to the lip of the building. He slid to the edge, turned onto his belly, and started to slide down. Three stories wouldn't kill him if he could lower himself far enough before dropping. His whole body was dangling, fingertips on the lip of the building. And those weeds were pretty tall too. He held the ledge with his fingers. The armpits of his suit jacket strained, and he thought he heard some of the seams popping. His shoes bounced against the wall and he could hear a man's footsteps approaching above. He winced, pushed off from the ledge, and let go.

He flew into the weeds but came down on both feet, stalks crashing around him. He landed and crumpled into a ball. The weeds were thick and hairy, maybe half an inch wide. At least there were no thorns. Leonard stood up. His ankle felt awful. He spun it in a circle and decided it was sprained, not broken. He had made it down safely. He shook himself off and turned around to face the house. There was no longer any noise above him. Whoever it was wasn't about to follow Leonard into somebody's yard. Leonard walked out of the weeds and onto the back patio.

Now all he needed to do was figure out how to get inside.

CHAPTER THIRTY-TWO

Of course the door below the deck wouldn't open. He had been desperate to try it, after slithering through the overgrown yard and stepping down the three steps under the pine deck. Every house Leonard had seen from the yard was basically the same: a deck across the first floor, a few steps to the basement below. Leonard tugged at the door again. It would head straight to the mechanical room, the vent from the furnace piped just above the door. Under the deck there was a small window, but it was too small even for Leonard to squeeze through.

Leonard backed away from the basement door up the short steps onto the patio. He wasn't safe yet. If either neighbor came out on the porch, there would be a quick call to the police. They all knew that Adam's son was gone, that Adam wasn't home, and there was a patrol officer stationed on the front stoop. And Mulino had expressly forbidden him from coming here, so it wasn't as though Leonard could talk his way out by dropping the detective's name. He crouched, hoping he wouldn't be seen if someone came outside.

There was always the chance that the door on the deck was open. Or the windows. Slowly, hoping to keep quiet, Leonard climbed up the wooden steps and onto the deck. It was brand new but had never been painted. The last owner had probably built it to sell the house but hadn't bothered to treat it, so it was already starting to warp. Someone ought to have told Adam Davenport what he needed to do in order to take care of his property. But the man had other things on his mind. Careful not to let the warping wood creak, Leonard crept to the door and tried it. No dice. Inside he could make out a kitchen, even in the dark. Some kind of construction was underway inside the house. Some kind of construction gone wrong: the kitchen ceiling was propped up with a pair of steel columns.

There were two broad windows going into the dining room. Leonard stood back on the deck and looked up and down the block. Every house had the same two windows, the same door. But every other house had iron bars, painted black, protecting those windows. Maybe Adam hadn't gotten to it yet. Or maybe he was a new arrival in Brooklyn, thinking he could live free from fear, that he didn't need to shower his windows in security grates because New York was safe now. But if you are trying to jump fences and break into living rooms, and there is only one house on the block without any metal grates over the windows, well, that's the one you're going to target. Leonard was lucky—the easy mark was the house he was trying to break into anyway.

He stood back from the window, lowered his center of gravity, and hurled his foot at the window. Immediately his hip hurt. He had twisted something in his midsection. His foot bounced harmlessly off the window. He crumpled in a ball in pain on the deck. After a moment, there was nothing but quiet. He stood up and looked around. He wasn't strong enough to kick in windows.

He stepped back down to the patio. It was laid out with interlocking hexagonal paving stones. Small ones, the size of a brick. Leonard crept down the stairs and tugged at one. It held fast; they were sunk deep into the mud of the backyard, stifling the growth of the monster weeds. But under the wooden stairway, he saw that there was a small stack of leftovers. Gifts from the seller again. Leonard took one of the bricks and hauled himself back up onto the deck.

He took off his jacket and wrapped it around the brick. It held tight and he tied it up, his sleeve the handle of a slingshot. Leonard spun the rock and hurled it at the window. The brick flew through the window and deep into the dining room, noisier than Leonard would have liked. He reached through the shattered window and tugged until it gave way. Avoiding the splintered glass, he climbed inside.

The house was dark. And a mess. A pile of boxes in the living room had been overturned and rummaged through. Books, clothes, and toys for the boy spilled out of them. There was no order to it. Leonard walked through the parlor and onto the stairs. It was a hundred years old, this house. Every time Leonard took a step it sounded like someone trying to bust out of a coffin.

What was he looking for, anyway? It could be anywhere. The house was a disaster, as though someone else had already torn through it. Upstairs, the dressers were open and the clothes were on the floor and the desk was a riot of paper. It was too much of a risk, being here. He turned back toward the grand and noisy staircase, started down, and froze.

At the bottom of the stairway, feet shoulder-length apart in a ready stance, was a uniform officer. He had both arms in the air and was holding a canister of pepper spray at Leonard. That was what it had come to. They had drilled it into the NYPD: don't lead with your gun. So here was a guy thinking he was doing the right thing by confronting an unknown intruder in a crime scene with a canister of pepper spray. The ACLU would have been proud of the guy. It was Leonard's only chance.

"Hello, Officer."

"Stay where you are and put your hands up."

Leonard put his hands up, but he kept walking slowly down the stairs. He was half-obeying, after all. He kept talking, too, calmly, slowly. And telling the truth, to the extent that that mattered.

"My name is Leonard Mitchell. I work with Ralph Mulino from OCCB. We investigated Christine Davenport's murder. I'm looking to see if there is anything linking the people who did that to the boy's kidnapping."

"You on the job?"

"I'm a civilian investigator. I'm not NYPD."

"Just stay where you are."

One more step. Maybe two, and he'd be in the clear.

"Why don't you call OCCB on the radio? Why don't you ask for Detective Mulino?"

The cop hesitated. He lowered the pepper spray a few inches, thinking about whether he should call. How many criminals even knew what OCCB stands for, he must have been thinking. The officer's moment of hesitation was enough for Leonard. He put his left hand on the bannister and leapt into the parlor room below. It was eight feet maybe, and his ankle stung again, but it was easier than coming off the back wall into the garden of weeds.

The officer wasn't blocking his way anymore. He had been guarding the front door, and now Leonard was running back toward the kitchen. He leapt forward and trucked full speed. If the cop had his gun out, he wouldn't have been able to fire. Not legally anyway. Not that that might have stopped him. But without his gun, with only his pepper spray, what did it matter? The pepper spray only affects the soft tissue of the nose, mouth, and eyes.

"Hey, stop!"

And Leonard could feel the spray as it was released into his hair. He could feel it dripping down his neck, and he could tell even then that it was stinging a little. Just don't put your hand up there and wipe your eyes. He ran toward the open window, leaping over the radiator and slipping out.

"Stop! Come back here!" The cop, in his weak and soft way, was demanding compliance. Now Leonard was out in the dark, and nowadays no cop was dumb enough to try to stop someone running away by pulling out his gun and firing. All Leonard had to do was get out.

The fence to his left was maybe six feet tall. On a good day it wouldn't be a problem. He leapt for it and grabbed the top. The pepper spray had dripped down onto his back, through his jacket. It felt like he had a sunburn across his shoulders and down his spine. As he lowered himself in the next yard, this one neat and manicured, he saw a light go on inside the house. The neighbors would be calling the police now, for sure. Through the yard and over another fence, Leonard left a trail of pepper spray. Then again, and into the next one. Behind him the cop, the neighbors, were all already looking for him. The last three fences were only waist high, and he was able to hop them quickly. He flipped the last one and landed in the parking lot. He was in the clear. He passed the parked cars in a hurry and skipped toward the subway.

Mulino would not have his back on this one. The detective believed in protocol and the chain of command. There was only one person who might take him in, who might understand. It meant spilling more than a few secrets. But that was okay with Leonard now. He slipped into the subway. A train pulled in and he dashed inside. It would be only a few minutes now.

CHAPTER THIRTY-THREE

As Detective Peralta made her way through the lobby of 80 Smithdale again, it was just as quiet as the first time. The front door was still unsecured. But the place had been cleaned up. The detritus spilling out past the doors and mailboxes had been swept. If the lobby wasn't clean, exactly, it was empty. That was a surprise. It had been only two days. When you run a slum-for-profit, you don't waste money on sanitation. The trash left in the lobby gets cleaned up when the rats eat it, and the rats get cleaned up by eventually eating each other. Even the speckled floor had something of a shine to it. Like maybe it had even been mopped. The main reason a slumlord would mop a lobby is that someone had died and he was cleaning up the new rental for the first and last time ever.

But 80 Smithdale wasn't even a rental building; the residents were forced there and the city was picking up the tab. That left the other reason to clean up. The landlord was expecting a visit from a housing inspector and had to hide what he had been doing for the last six years. Or he was expecting a visit from the police. Detective Peralta put her hand down to her waist, making sure her gun was where she expected it to be. Not enough of a worry to unholster it. But she wasn't in uniform, and you never know. She reached inside her sweatshirt and tugged out her shield.

"Hello?"

Silence. At least that hadn't changed. No doors in this building were open to strangers. Even less so to cops. When someone asks for help enough times and ends up being shuttled into a rat-infested pit without electricity, with a quarter of the living room ceiling in a state of collapse, she doesn't think people are coming to help her anymore. Whoever lived in this building had been screwed over so many times by the Department of Homeless Services, the Department of Housing Preservation and Development, and the Department of Buildings that the Police Department appeared as just one more incompetent mob. Peralta didn't bear a grudge. But she wasn't about to cut power cables to get someone's attention again. That had only barely worked out okay last time.

She had some real information on Robert Armstrong now. Leonard Mitchell had given her his date of birth, his home address, and the fact that he managed the slum. But she didn't want to barge in on him in his house in Sheepshead Bay without a little more. She didn't have a warrant. If he didn't want to open the door there was nothing more that she could do. So before leaving OCCB she had stopped and done what she should have done to begin with. She ran his name through the Booking, Arrests, and Dispositions System. BADS. Anyone who was up to something serious now had likely been up to something less serious once upon a time.

Turns out he had been arrested but never charged with a credit card scheme about ten years ago. Not enough to tie him in to anything now. Innocent until proven guilty, and for reasons that the database couldn't tell her, the PD or the DA or someone had figured they couldn't make the case. But he had been booked, which meant he had been fingerprinted and photographed. Which meant that Detective Peralta could print his mugshot and bring it to 80 Smithdale. If her friend Evangeline could give her a positive ID, that would be enough for a warrant.

The picture was ten years old, of course, but it was the kind of face that probably didn't look much different now. Armstrong's eyes were set deep and very dark; his cheeks were sharp and his chin was soft.

In the photo, his hair was just about half gray, still neatly parted and sprayed in place. His narrow, crisp eyebrows hadn't grayed yet. He wore a suit. That meant that he had probably turned himself in. Planned his morning and showed up with a lawyer and gotten photographed with a thin little smile. Probably walked in and out of the precinct on the same day, released on recognizance and never spent ten minutes in custody.

Peralta turned the corner up the stairway to the second floor. It had been cleaned too. Peralta wasn't afraid, exactly, but it was unnerving to know that someone had been through the building. Sweeping and scrubbing and then getting the hell out. At the top of the stairwell, she looked into the air shaft where Manny Reeves had fallen. That pile of trash was still there. Nobody's perfect. There were still power cords in the hallway running under the doors. Sending someone by to clean the hallways was one thing. Getting the dead sockets fixed would have taken real work. Peralta stopped at Evangeline's door and knocked.

"Evangeline? It's Detective Peralta. You spoke to me the other day."

Silence behind the door. Peralta didn't blame anyone in the building for keeping her door closed to strangers. She would have done the same. But she really wanted to speak with this woman.

"Evangeline? We spoke the other day? I have some more questions for you. I have a picture for you to look at."

Peralta could hear a rustling now behind the closed door. Someone was in there. Peralta remembered being inside Evangeline's apartment: it was neat, and you could find your way to the door in a hurry. It wasn't like the guy upstairs. Evangeline would not have to climb over a pile of abandoned paper and forgotten clothing to answer. Inside, it had been just like any other apartment. But that didn't mean that Evangeline lived free from fear. And it didn't mean that she would open wide for a detective, even one who had been here before.

Footsteps. Evangeline was right behind the door. The door was thin and cheap and Peralta could hear her straight through it.

"Detective."

"Evangeline, can you let me in?"

"I'm sorry."

"What happened? The building's been cleaned up."

"The trash got cleaned up. The building is the same as ever. Maybe worse."

Peralta looked up and down the hallway. There was no one there. A clean, empty hall with a few thick orange extension cords running across it. There was no reason Peralta could think of for Evangeline to keep her out.

"Let me in. I have a photo to show you."

"I'm sorry, Detective. I don't know when they might come back. You don't know what they'll do if they see me talking to you. I told you everything I could."

"They can't do anything to you while I'm here. I can protect you."

"But at some point, Detective, you're going to leave. You can't be here all day and all night."

Whoever had come by had done more than clean the hallways and lobby. They had issued a warning. They had injected an extra dose of fear into a building that was already brimming with it. They had reminded everyone that someone had been found basically dead in this building four days ago, and it wasn't as though it was on the front page of the papers. It wasn't as though the city cared very much about some stranger falling down an air shaft somewhere out in Flatbush. And if they didn't care the first time, then why would they care the next?

Peralta breathed out. She reached into her pocket and took out the piece of paper. She had folded it twice, neatly. She didn't like to carry a bag or a backpack, anything that might slow her down. She didn't need the full gun belt with a flashlight, pepper spray, and a memo book. She had a pair of slacks with a pocket big enough for her notebook. With the notebook and her handgun, she was good to go anywhere. The sweatshirt hung low enough so that most people couldn't see the gun, or the notebook for that matter. She unfolded the printout of the mugshot. She knelt on the tile and slid it underneath the door. She whispered.

"Evangeline, do you recognize this man? When you saw someone last week walking upstairs. Was this him?"

Silence on the other side of the door. Peralta worried for a minute that Evangeline would take the picture. That she'd be afraid to be caught with it in her apartment, and that she'd shred or burn it. Peralta stood up. She leaned back into the door again.

"Evangeline?"

There was the slightest sound from behind the door. Evangeline wasn't speaking, but she was doing something. There were footsteps. There was the sound of tapping, scratching maybe. Peralta was not naturally patient: the wait from behind the door was interminable. She was ready to try to force the handle of the door when the paper slid back out again, and the voice along with it.

"Now go away. Leave me alone. I'll manage much better without you."

Peralta crouched over and picked up the paper. It had been unfolded, written on, and folded again. She stood and opened it. Across the bottom of the page, below the mugshot, Evangeline had written two words in neat, formal script: "That's Him."

"Thank you, Evangeline."

But there was no answer from the door. The woman had already returned to her tea, her business, and her fear. Peralta made her way back to the stairs and out of the building. She had enough now. It was late, but that was on her side as well. The man was likely to be home. As she stepped out into the dark autumn night, Detective Peralta took a deep breath. Leonard and Mulino were still trying to find the missing boy. The homicide detectives were busy railroading an innocent man. She was the only one pursuing Robert Armstrong. She was about to solve a murder all on her own. And she was ready.

CHAPTER THIRTY-FOUR

Eleanor Hill turned the stack of paper to its side. She clicked it level on her desk. At night, with no secretaries around, everyone is her own assistant. After six hours of writing and two hours of review, the packet was complete for the closing in the morning. That meant having it ready to go last thing at night. As the only one left in her office, Eleanor would have to copy and staple and collate the whole thing and leave it on her secretary's desk for the morning. But it was all worthwhile, because after next week, she would be all square with her father and she could go back to running her business.

It had taken her a few days to put the idea together, but now it was ready. She had lured in the outside investors. They had come up with the astronomical number that her accountant told her she had to pay out. Her father might not hold her strictly to the deadline, but he wouldn't give her too much slack. So it was worth the time in the office, going over the bid, running through the numbers for the fourth or the fifth time. It was a funny world, real estate, where the best way to collect a bunch of cash was to go into even greater debt. But Eleanor was long used to that.

She collected the paper and stepped out of her office into the severe glass hallway. As she turned right, toward the copy room, she heard a sound behind her and froze. A smooth click; the elevator had opened around the corner. It was almost ten. The last employee had left by five-thirty. Janitorial had come and gone before eight. By this time, there wasn't even a night guard downstairs at the desk. You'd have to swipe in to the building and the elevator both. She turned, her back against the hallway. Someone would be turning that corner in only a few seconds. Copying the bid papers would have to wait, but she wasn't about to drop them on the floor. And it wasn't as though she kept a gun in the office. She reached her free hand into her pocket for her phone. She had been raised not to call the police. Once they show up, they follow their own rules. But she wanted to be ready to call somebody.

As soon as she saw what was turning the corner, she knew she wasn't going to need to call anyone after all. At least not yet. A thin white guy in a torn suit stumbled out of the elevator and toward her. Leonard Mitchell was a wreck. His pants were a mess, his shoes were thick with mud, and his coat and hands were drenched in an ocher oil that Eleanor recognized as pepper spray. If he touched his eyes, he would start convulsing in pain.

"Eleanor. I need your help."

How many times did she hear that in a week? "You need to clean up."

"The police are after me."

That was the last thing she needed, to start harboring a white guy in a suit from the police. As soon as they found him, she'd somehow be the one under arrest and he'd be getting a medal for turning her in. "Before you say anything else, Leonard, go down the hall to the bathroom. Wash your hands. Get the pepper spray off of them. Take off your jacket. If you get that in your eyes there is going to be nothing I can do for you."

Leonard nodded and turned. So much for hiring someone who was going to keep the place quiet. So much for making up for last summer. She had never imagined, when she started her business, how many problems would be caused by her own staff. She had been prepared to negotiate hard with sellers, with contractors, and even with the construction unions. She hadn't realized that every person she put on payroll was a potential thief, that her office administrator might be a mole for her competition.

It had been eye-opening, last summer, when the law firm had finally told her how much damage Robert Armstrong had done to her company. And over the past few days, she had learned that even then she had been, if anything, too soft. She had forgiven Wade Valiant. She had given him another chance. But Armstrong, or whoever was working with him, obviously hadn't. And now this.

Leonard came out from the bathroom. He had soaked his hands and scrubbed off the pepper spray. His face was clean but his hair was matted wild past his ears. His suit would never recover. His shoes were a waste. She would need to have the carpet cleaned. The easiest thing would be to fire him and kick him to the street. Let the cops deal with him. But the lessons of her father were too ingrained for that. Still, she didn't put down the phone.

"So what happened?"

"I have to go back a little." And he did. He had been working, he told her, with a cop. The detective investigating Wade Valiant's death. The supervisor, not the screwballs who had showed up at her father's church. Her last deputy had been a thief, and this one was a spy. Looking into her transactions, her deals, to see if there was any reason she would want to murder a construction worker, one who was a shop steward to boot. Maybe her motive was to end up in the papers as an unsafe business, delay putting her building up, and pay a death benefit to a union fund that would eventually go to political candidates who wanted to shut her down. The right kind of cops could come up with a theory for anything.

"What makes you think I would want to murder my own employees?"

"Someone you knew might. Or someone you dealt with. Because his death began to look very quickly like it wasn't an accident. You know that."

This much was true. And she had held back this much too. After all, why wouldn't she? The police could issue a report blaming the inspector at the Department of Buildings. She wasn't about to call them up and tell them about Robert Armstrong. She wasn't about to guess whether someone she had fired for stealing from her company maybe wanted to do in his accomplice. That simply wasn't good for business. It was a lesson learned, but a quiet one.

"I know about Robert Armstrong."

Eleanor gripped her phone. He really had been snooping. He must have been reading year-old emails to find out what had happened with Armstrong. And that meant that he knew Armstrong's connection to Valiant. Which meant he might have put together her own suspicions. She held still. She spoke softly. You are always more powerful when you speak slowly and softly.

"Okay."

"He was stealing from you. And Valiant was helping."

"I'm aware of that. That's why we got rid of him."

"But that's not all of it. Right? Because you don't actually make money here by putting up buildings. You put up buildings for show. You make money by swapping one piece of land back and forth with your friends until it actually costs too much to develop. And then you sell it to someone who doesn't know any better. And they get stuck with it."

So he knew. Eleanor had made plenty of money on a couple of townhouse flips back when she started. And sometimes you could sell and re-sell the same lot, taking a cut each time, and it would still be a steal in the hands of the last developer. But the easiest way to make money is to sell something for more than it is worth. And when you learn the contours of real estate in Brooklyn, pretty soon you learn that there are a lot of people out there willing to pay more for land than it is worth. And why shouldn't you let them? If a Kuwaiti sovereign wealth fund wants to pay double the market price for a plot of land in Brooklyn, why turn them down? She wasn't in this business to go broke, after all.

It starts that way, but pretty soon it is easy enough. There are enough buyers out there with enough loose money. At first you feel as though they have wandered into you, but pretty soon you start seeking them out. It's an easy flip, with the buyers in another country and maybe with reasons of their own to sink their money in a faraway city. So maybe it was true enough. True anyway that there were enough big deals that left enough foreign holding companies with overpriced land. And you never know. Sometimes it's the guy on the other side who knows more than you do. As she had told him on the first day he showed up, you have to have good reflexes to catch a falling knife.

"Every deal we make is above board. Every transaction is vetted. We buy land from the lowest seller and we sell it to the highest buyer. That's the way business works."

"Sure. But do all of your buyers agree? I mean, you've never had someone call you up and tell you that they think they got screwed? You're dealing with foreign companies, they may not always think they are bound by the rules you're using."

Of course they didn't agree. If you buy and sell twenty buildings, and nobody thinks that you screwed them, then they all probably screwed you instead. Eleanor didn't have to justify herself to him. She was beginning to get angry. He was in her office, wanted by the police, and accusing her of—what exactly? Being a capitalist?

"What are you trying to imply?"

"Do you know where Robert Armstrong works now?"

"I haven't kept up with him."

"Why would you? Why would you care who he is talking to? Or who is wiring him hundreds of thousands of dollars? But if I told you

191

he was working as the property manager for 80 Smithdale Street, you wouldn't be surprised."

"No." It would make sense. A crook working for a slumlord. A slumlord who didn't know how to manage his own building. Promoting misery was such a hard way to make money, too. Verringer seemed to enjoy inflicting pain on the people who lived in his rathole. And he was probably barely scraping by to boot. It wasn't rocket science to figure out how to turn an honest profit on a building like that. In fact, she was holding the answer in her hand. She pulled the stack of paper closer.

"And would it surprise you to learn that a Malaysian holding company paid 80 Smithdale two hundred thousand dollars last month? Would you imagine why they would want to do that?"

Eleanor's arm went cold. Her offer papers suddenly felt as though they were made out of solid iron. Her hand drooped to her waist but she kept her fingers clutched around them. The Malaysian fund. Eleanor had flipped a plot of land that was supposed to end up in the footprint of the arena going up on Atlantic Avenue. She had promised the buyer that it would be in the footprint, or at the very worst right next to it. Maybe open a sports bar. A luxury hotel for athletes and rock stars. But she hadn't told them that the zoning wasn't quite right.

When you are in Malaysia, it's not so easy to lobby the city council to flip your zoning to residential. So instead of a space for a forty-story market rate condo building, the plot was a car wash. And was going to stay a car wash. The community activists had fought to keep the zoning outside of the footprint exactly in place. They were preserving the community's character. And if the community's character was a McDonald's on one side of the street and a car wash on the other, so be it. It was just as Eleanor had suspected would happen. Not that she had told the buyer about her suspicions.

"You're saying they paid off Robert Armstrong."

"And maybe Armstrong paid off Manny Reeves. And maybe he wanted to kill Wade Valiant because he worried that Wade would turn him in. Or maybe he just wanted to get your business in the paper. In a bad way. Maybe he just wanted people to walk around thinking less-than-glorious thoughts about Hill and Associates. And maybe I'm not the villain anymore, Eleanor. Maybe I'm here to help."

It would be a way to get two birds with one stone. Kill off Wade Valiant and smear Eleanor Hill. And Robert Armstrong would be happy to do both of them. She hadn't told the police the rest of what she knew. That Manny Reeves had come to her twice in the past six months asking for an advance on his pay. He had said that his kid was sick, but Hill and Associates offered good medical. They always say their kid is sick when they want money. Maybe he had been out to Aqueduct too often. Maybe his wife wanted a new kitchen. She hadn't given in, and he had stopped asking. But that only meant that he had needed money. For something. She was holding the packet up to her chest now, her sleeve dangling down her forearm. Leonard was staring, now, at her wrist.

"What is that?"

She cocked her head to see where he was looking. The gray band that she wore around her wrist. "This?"

She grabbed the wristband with her left hand and snapped it open. The snap connecting it was a USB port on one side that slid seamlessly into the other. "It's a flash drive. I just got so sick of carrying paper around all the time. I barely notice it most of the time. I can keep everything in it."

Leonard stared at the wristband. There was something working in his mind. He was suddenly distracted. "I've never seen one of those before. I never thought of that."

"Well. You can find them almost anywhere."

But his head was racing now, she could see. She put down the papers. The bid was going to have to wait. The secretary could copy the whole thing tomorrow. She should have gone home an hour ago, to tell the truth.

When she turned out from the office, Leonard was on his phone. Intent, quiet. Maybe she was close to convincing him that she was a victim too, after all. A victim of Robert Armstrong. A victim of whoever ran the overseas fund. A victim of the community board that was trying to stop her from building nearly free apartments. A victim of her father, who was perfectly happy to profit off of her success until it meant a moment of worry for him. She was carrying the burden. She was the one doing everything: buying, selling, building. And somehow everyone turned back toward her, thought ill of her, complained of her.

Eleanor stared at Leonard as he slid his phone back into his pocket. His face was raw and gray; he looked even worse than he had when he had come in, covered with pepper spray.

"That was Detective Mulino. They have found a ping from Adam Davenport's phone. He's inside the Seventy-First Precinct. We have to find out what he's doing in there."

The man with the missing son. She had heard it on the radio that morning. Of course a little white boy would take immediate precedence over everything else. Eleanor sighed. She had, at least, set the papers down. Leonard might be able to help her clear her business's name. But for the time being, that meant following him as he tracked down the soft man from the community board.

"All right, then. Let's go."

CHAPTER THIRTY-FIVE

Leonard's fingernails dug into the armrest of Eleanor Hill's Lexus as she pulled it out onto Flatbush and peeled down toward the park. He couldn't settle into the soft luxury of the car. He didn't drive himself; he hadn't since he moved to the city. The only time he had found himself in a car had been on a police ride-along or the occasional splurge in a taxi. Like most forced comforts, this car made him feel tense, awkward. He stared at the road ahead, late enough that the traffic had cleared. The massive arena was empty, purposefully plated with rusted metal to look more artisan. That was Brooklyn nowadays. Corporations building ugly toys to fool people into thinking they were handmade.

Eleanor would help. He was grateful for that. He had realized, as soon as he escaped Davenport's house, that he needed an ally. And he realized as soon as he had told her what had happened that she wasn't a murderer. She might have sold a building for more than it was worth, but she hadn't killed Wade Valiant. And she hadn't kidnapped Adam's son.

Eleanor understood that the cops aren't always right, that sometimes you need to get around them in order to find the truth, that the line between victim and perpetrator isn't always so clean. Eleanor Hill was raised to distrust the police, and she would understand. And since Robert Armstrong was messed up in all of this, she might feel just responsible enough to help. At the very least, she would know what he looked like.

He couldn't stop thinking about Eleanor's wristband. As soon as he had seen it, he had known why Adam Davenport's son was missing. A storage device, in lieu of lots of paper. Davenport had been investigating, up to the moment of her death. He had found some of what she had discovered—all of it, he had thought at the time—hidden in a flash drive on a magnet on her fridge. It had been buried in plain sight. But the emails on the Hill and Associates servers had convinced him there was more. *Davenport is onto us.* Veronica Dean surfacing again. And he thought of Christine, desperate to hide what she had found. He could see her now, snapping a green wristband around her son's arm, telling him to keep it safe. Knowing what it contained. And all at once he saw a motive for snatching the boy. Finding Adam Davenport suddenly meant the world to Leonard.

Eleanor swung the Lexus through the roundabout at the entrance to the park. The towering arch, meant to mimic Paris's Arc de Triomphe, but a little more golden, a little more ostentatious. So American. The library slid by on their left and they cruised downhill on Flatbush Avenue, park on both sides of them and no lights in their way. Eleanor, eyes on the road, steady without rushing, finally spoke.

"Why would he go to the precinct?"

"He thought the cops weren't doing enough. Parents never do. But they make things worse when they get involved. Missing children don't just pop up on the street."

"But if the police haven't found anything out yet . . ."

Leonard had thought of that. And surely Adam Davenport had too. You can kidnap a child for a reason: you want ransom, you want to make a deal. But the police hadn't received a call. There was no list of demands. And if someone steals a child without making a demand, then giving the child back isn't part of the plan. The kidnapper wants something from the child itself. Something hideous, something ordinary. Or as Leonard thought now, information. Only once you get what you need from a child, now you have a witness. Giving the child back makes it so much more likely that you will be caught. And children are exceptionally easy to kill.

"We don't know if the police found anything or not. They could have a lead that they didn't share with Adam. But even if the investigation is stalled, confronting them in the precinct is going to make it worse. If that is what Adam did, things could go very badly." Leonard had seen those complaints too, once upon a day. People stricken with grief, anger, or fear. A man who had tried to push his way past the firefighters on his stoop, screaming that his daughter was in the upstairs bedroom. The police had pulled that man back and beaten him with their nightsticks. He had his reasons, but he was obstructing governmental administration. And his daughter was already dead. Adam Davenport didn't know the rules. He wouldn't know what he could and could not do. He was likely to storm the precinct looking for his son and end up in the hospital, or worse.

They came out of the park and sped past Eleanor's own building, the condo on Empire where Wade Valiant had fallen. The orange netting fluttered in the moonlight, promising momentary romance on future balconies. Eleanor didn't look up from the road, slowing as the car turned left down Empire. Leonard could see the row of empty businesses. He saw the door he had slipped through on his way to Adam Davenport's house. Where he had broken in and been pepper-sprayed by a cop. And now he was headed straight for the precinct.

He gritted his teeth. Mulino would be there. Mulino wouldn't let him get arrested. At least, not until after they had found the boy. They drove past the row of abandoned commercial lots—the planned footprint for Eleanor Hill's next project. She didn't bat an eye. She knew the whole block by heart.

"Here."

The precinct was squat, cement, square. Built in the 1970s when the urban planners took their cues from Soviet Brutalism. Square columns along the front, and tall, narrow slits for windows, no wider than six inches but almost eight feet high. Good luck getting an off-the-rack pane to replace one of those when it gives out. Eleanor slowed the car and pulled into the small lot. Leonard reminded himself to take it slowly. One small step at a time. Don't be surprised by anything. He wasn't a cop himself; he didn't have a gun. If there was a manic scene inside the precinct, his only tool for solving it would be his voice.

When Eleanor opened the door for him, he could see right away that something was wrong. They were in the peak of the four-to-twelve tour, when the guys who like to make arrests are usually bringing in a petty drug dealer or an addict or someone who picked a fight in a bar the moment he stepped inside. Even slow precincts are noisy and active at night, and the Seven-One was not ordinarily a slow precinct.

But it was dead silent when Eleanor and Leonard walked in. There was no sergeant at the desk. There was no row of Police Administrative Assistants typing carbon-copy forms through electric typewriters. No one in the holding cell. The main floor of the precinct was entirely deserted. Four steel-gauge desks, dating surely from when the place was first built, sat empty, case files and food wrappers left haphazardly on them. Leonard looked at Eleanor. Cops are social animals—if there is a reason for one to run down the hallway, there is every chance that ten of his buddies will follow suit. But for an entire tour to abandon a precinct, something has to be seriously out of whack. Desk sergeants do not leave their posts for nothing.

"Down there."

Eleanor had walked ahead of him. Leonard, through force of habit, never passed the desk sergeant without permission. The Seven-One had the traditional barrier—a waist-high swinging door, like an amusement park would use for its Wild West Saloon. But no one was about to invite him inside a deserted precinct, so he followed Eleanor. Across the room there was an open door leading to a stairway. As he approached, he could hear voices below. He couldn't make out what was being said. One voice was calm but authoritative, the way cops speak to a criminal or an emotionally disturbed person. Don't jump off the ledge. Put down the knife. Just step out of the car with your hands up and it will all be all right. Eleanor was at the top of the stairs when Leonard joined her. She started down them and he put his hand on her shoulder.

"We should wait, Eleanor."

"Why?"

"We're not cops. We could make things worse."

She gave him a sad, serious look. "You know this guy. None of them know this guy. Don't you want to help him?"

Leonard paused. Trying to help Christine Davenport last year hadn't done any good. Trying to find out what she had learned had almost gotten him killed, had gotten him six months at Moriah Shock while someone else took credit for what he had found out. What good would it do to help Adam Davenport? Maybe there was a standoff. Maybe they would burst in and a jittery cop would shoot them both. Or maybe he was just giving in to fear. Maybe he ought to listen to this woman, who a few days ago he thought might have conspired to kill her own employee. Now she was willing to walk into a room full of armed men to help someone she barely knew. He had badly underestimated her.

"Okay."

Eleanor led the way, Leonard a few steps behind. He wondered, for a moment, where Ralph Mulino was. Mulino had called them to say that Davenport was at the precinct, after all. He should have been there already. Maybe he was downstairs with everyone too.

They hit the basement floor and started down a wide hall. The same contractors, it seemed, had built all the public schools and half the police precincts sometime around 1972. Someone with a surplus of splattered light brown linoleum tile, the better to hide the dirt and blood that would spill on trips between holding cells. The voices were coming from the last door on the right. When Eleanor reached it, she turned the corner and Leonard followed.

The tiny room was impossibly crowded. Leonard and Eleanor could see only the backs of maybe fifty heads. Most of the officers were kneeling and most of them were uniformed. The crowd seemed a thick, dark brew of identical bodies, all of them focused on the small doorway at the back of the room. About a half dozen of the cops had their guns drawn. None of them spoke; they were a small army of identical soldiers, holding their ground, waiting for a command. Standing to the right in a white shirt was the captain. He was maybe fifty, his military haircut bleeding gray and his broad, dark face laced with worry. He was staring at the door too, but kept glancing to his right as well. His gun sat holstered on his left hip.

The figure on the right got Leonard's attention first. Adam Davenport was sitting in a blue, molded plastic chair that was too small for him, probably also swiped from a school some thirty years ago. He was holding his right knee and squinting. Blood trickled out from between the creases of his knuckles, down his fingers and into small plops on the floor. He squeezed tighter, both with his hands on the wound and with his eyes, either to keep the pain at bay or to keep from seeing what was in front of him.

Because in front of him, silhouetted in the back door, open to the air, was a boy. Around seven, Leonard would guess. Hair cut short with a mini-pompadour in the front, soft, small features, and as Leonard saw right away, a green wristband over his left wrist. But Leonard didn't say anything about the green wristband. No one in the room was paying attention to it, and neither was the boy. They were looking at only one thing—the gun being held to the boy's temple.

The child was quivering, and the captain was preparing to speak again. The row of cops with their guns drawn was silent. He noticed Leonard and Eleanor come in, but flashed only a quick look to silence them. He couldn't be distracted now. Leonard touched Eleanor's shoulder. She understood too. Don't intervene. They both stared at the man with the gun pointed at the boy.

Trim, white, young, the man holding the Davenport boy had a cop's posture and bearing even though he was out of uniform. Leonard noticed, behind the boy's head, the hint of a chain around the man's neck. There would be a detective's badge at the end of that. Then it hit him. Leonard recognized this guy. He had seen him on the building site when he spoke to Mulino after Valiant had died. Bruder. One of Mulino's detectives. The captain spoke.

"Just let us get the dad out of here, Timmy. Let us get a bus for him, get him to a hospital."

The detective shook his head. "We just needed a few days to search the house. Everything would have been fine. But you had to let him in here. Now if I don't take the boy with me, you're going to lock me up."

The house. The detective had taken the boy so that Davenport's house would be secure. He had known that the father would be sequestered. That police would guard the place. And if the police were in Armstrong's pocket, looking for what Davenport left behind, Bruder could scour the place at their leisure.

The detective went on. "You get your ambulance for the dad once I'm on the road. He's going to be fine."

Adam squeezed his knee again but the blood kept gurgling through. The puddle on the floor grew. The boy looked at his wounded father. The detective took a step back. One of the cops on the ground, one of the armed ones, looked to the captain. The captain shook his head. Detective Bruder took another step back.

If Bruder had searched the house and taken the boy, it meant he didn't know what the wristband meant. Otherwise, they would have just taken it to begin with. Bruder had spent two days with the boy and hadn't taken the wristband. That meant the boy likely didn't know either. Leonard slid to his right, so he could have a clearer view of the pair.

"Detective, you don't need the boy."

At once, half the heads in the precinct turned toward Leonard. The captain's eyes opened and a vein on the left side of his neck started throbbing. Cops hate it when things do not go according to protocol. And a civilian stepping into this kind of negotiation was not protocol. Bruder stared back at him. Leonard could tell that the detective didn't remember him.

"You don't know what I need."

"You're looking for the rest of the information Christine Davenport left behind. It's all in that wristband. The wristband has a flash drive in it. Just take it and leave the boy. Just walk away. They'll let you go. Won't you, Captain?"

The captain looked slowly from Leonard to Bruder. "Sure. Sure, Timmy. Take the wristband and you can go. We'll call an ambulance for the father."

"Like hell I can."

Bruder stepped back another yard, dragging the boy with him now. The child swung his arm behind his back. He didn't want the wristband taken off. They were almost out of the precinct when Bruder looked back at Leonard.

"Remember what I said. You guys follow me and there is no boy. But thanks for telling me about the wristband. It's going to save me a lot of trouble."

And they were out, around the corner and into the darkness. Two cops stood up to chase them. They stood at the door, weapons drawn. Leonard couldn't see what they saw, but he could see their eyes. And their eyes told him that they were afraid that if they chased down Bruder, the boy would be gone. One of them spoke.

"Captain, should we close in?"

But Leonard could tell that even the officer was afraid to tempt Bruder. He had seen the detective holding a gun to the child just like the rest of them.

"No. We'll have to try to track him somehow. Someone call for a bus for the father."

The disappointed uniforms turned back. One daggered a look at Leonard. If they were alone, Leonard thought maybe the guy would have shot him. He eased back toward the stairway leading back to the precinct.

Timmy Bruder. A detective working for Ralph Mulino had taken Adam Davenport's son. Was likely trying to get information on what Christine had found. If that boy's wristband even had anything of value. And this detective, or whoever he had been working for, had spent a year looking for Adam and his son, and only just found them when they came back onto the grid in Brooklyn. Mulino would take the news hard. Finally able to run your own squad, and one of your detectives is a psychopath. That kind of thing comes back to haunt you sometimes. Leonard looked up the stairway where the captain had disappeared. The one who had given up. Had said, anyway, that the best they could do was track Bruder. Leonard figured at the least that he could help with that. He turned up toward the precinct lobby, Eleanor following alongside.

Just as he started up the stairway he saw a figure blocking the light into the main floor of the precinct. A big man favoring one leg, his hand on the arm rail and a broad smile on his face.

Detective Mulino spoke. "Hey, Leonard. Did I miss anything?"

CHAPTER THIRTY-SIX

Peralta pulled her unmarked car toward the curb of a street lined with small, neat houses. Her headlights lit the porch of one house in particular; this far into Brooklyn there was only a single pair of streetlights every hundred yards. Sheepshead Bay could basically be a Long Island suburb. The cheap kind, with postage-stamp lawns and vinyl fences and a thousand miles from the mansions of the Hamptons, but a suburb nevertheless. The neighborhood had a subway stop, but no one who lived there used it. There are some parts of the city so far away from the bloodstream of the MTA that everyone owns a car. Peralta wasn't sure what precinct she was in; she had driven with her phone in the passenger seat, directing her farther south and farther east with each turn. She was lucky no one in traffic enforcement had pulled her over. Looking down to get directions from a smartphone wasn't exactly texting while driving, but it was frowned upon. And she didn't want to spend the time talking her way out of a ticket with Robert Armstrong waiting for her.

At least she hoped he was waiting. Every building that runs any kind of affordable housing program has to register with the Department of Housing Preservation and Development. The building has to give an address for the company that owns it. The company has to list its membership, and the name and address of a managing agent. Tenants hoping to compel their landlords to turn on the heat or fix the collapsed ceilings have to file papers in housing court, and those papers have to be sent somewhere for the landlord to ignore. The entity that owned 80 Smithdale was named "80 Smithdale Housing, LLC." The only member was David Verringer. The address for the company was this house, tucked away in Sheepshead Bay. The trim neighborhood was laid out in crisp streets surrounding a body of water that Detective Peralta, squinting at a map, had never thought looked much like a sheep's head. Robert Armstrong was listed as the managing agent, and this was his address too. The whole thing smelled. It was better than just a post office box, but not by a whole lot.

Evangeline had vouched that Armstrong was the man in the picture. And Detective Peralta had heard the name Verringer before. But she didn't have a picture of him, and wasn't sure Evangeline or any of the other tenants would have been able to identify him if she did. There was no reason to think that the man who actually owned the building had ever set foot in it. That's what men like Armstrong were for. But this was the address she had, so this was the best place she could look. She stepped out of the car and onto the curb. Her right hand drifted down to her gun. Sometimes even post office boxes fight back.

She walked up the short path to the door. It reminded her of home. There was space between houses and lawns, and every so often a tree. A light was on above the porch, illuminating the door and a patch of lawn and leaving the rest in darkness. Peralta took the last step up to the landing and was reaching for the doorbell when the door opened.

"Yes?"

Through the open doorway there was a heavy screen door blotting out the light. Behind that, Detective Peralta could make out a silhouette, over six feet tall, white, and younger than she had expected. Good posture too; it wasn't Armstrong. And the open door meant he had been watching her as she made her way up the path. She looked down to where the man's hands should be. Inside the house was dark; Peralta couldn't see a thing. She was on an empty street far from her fellow officers with a man who might have orchestrated a murder. And he could be doing anything with his hands. She tugged her own gun out of its holster. This wasn't a post office box anymore. She could feel her hand start to warm the rough plastic case.

"Are you Robert Armstrong?"

"No."

"David Verringer?"

No answer to this one. Her right hand still on the gun, Peralta reached down to her chrome chain. She moved slowly. She didn't want to surprise this man any more than she wanted him to surprise her. She held up the blue sunburst shield.

"Mr. Verringer, I'm Detective Peralta from the Organized Crime Control Bureau. I want to ask you a couple of questions about your building."

"The what?"

That was the thing about OCCB. On the force, it might be something of an inside joke that the bureau had nothing to do with organized crime. But out on the street, someone might be wary of the name. He might think that this detective was coming with a stack of receipts to tie him to the Bonannos. Detective Peralta could always play that kind of misunderstanding to her advantage.

"The Organized Crime Control Bureau, Mr. Verringer. I am investigating a number of suspicious transactions regarding your building at 80 Smithdale Street. You are the owner of the building at 80 Smithdale Street?"

"I was."

"What do you mean, you were?"

"We sold that building. It was too much of a headache. It should be closing today. Maybe right about now."

Peralta considered. He could sell the building, but it didn't mean he was off the hook for anything he had done while he ran it. Crimes are still crimes. Abuse of tenants doesn't go away with a change of property. She stepped up onto the doorstop and peered inside.

"Whether you sold it or not, I have some questions for you. I have spoken to some of the tenants. We're conducting an ongoing investigation. If you only closed today, our investigation covers your ownership."

The figure stepped back into the shadow. She had surprised him. Right now she couldn't go into the house. There hadn't been time to get a warrant. But most people don't know how quickly they can accidentally grant a police officer the right to enter. Hot pursuit, plain view, search incident to an arrest—the warrant requirement was shot through with a thousand exceptions, and Detective Peralta had studied them all. This man, with his hands out of view, being told his company was the subject of an investigation, didn't know the bind he was in. Maybe if he calmly stated that he was calling his lawyer and carefully shut the door, she would have to stay put. But any sudden motion, any dash back into the house, and that would be an exigent circumstance. And exigent circumstances were the very biggest hole in the warrant requirement. He was hovering in half darkness now, and Peralta was ready to toss open the screen door and rush him.

"You'll have to speak to Mr. Armstrong. He does all the books. He manages all the properties."

"And where is Mr. Armstrong now?"

"I don't know."

"Mr. Verringer, he's registered with HPD at this address. You've listed him as the managing agent with this address. If you listed this address fraudulently, that in and of itself is a crime."

The man turned into the darkened house, just quickly enough that Peralta gave herself the right to pursue him. She whipped open the screen door with her left hand, the right still on her gun. He hadn't even bothered to close the front door behind him. Peralta burst inside to find a neat little house, maybe the kind of place where a retired English schoolmarm would be at home. An oversized gray couch with colorful knit throws across it.

A circular cherry breakfast table, two places set. A single bookcase, no television, no mess at all. As she ran through the pretty little room, she wondered what kind of real estate magnate lives in a museum.

The man had fled straight toward the back. Peralta ran through the house and onto the back porch. The rear yard was as small as the front. Here the neat vinyl fencing in front gave way to ragged chain link, an old rusted fence that was littered with tangles and holes. Straight through the yard, opening into the next property, was a hole in the fencing big enough for a man to slip through. Past that yard, and you could run up the driveway and onto the next block. It was the only way he could have gone.

But there was no reason to follow him. She wasn't looking for Verringer, only his henchman. If she called in a man in flight, the local precinct would track him down. He would be on foot, since his car was likely one of the ones in front.

She turned back toward the house, but not before noting that the backyard was a mess, filled with a tangle of weeds, brambles, and wildflowers. She thought again for a moment that a man who owned seven apartment buildings throughout Brooklyn probably didn't live here. They kept the house to have an address to register at HPD.

But then why had the man been there? If Verringer and Armstrong used a deserted house as a mailbox, why had he been sitting in the little living room, peering out the window at Detective Peralta as she came up the path? He hadn't been waiting for her. But that didn't mean he hadn't been waiting for someone. He had been planning to meet Armstrong, or the people who had cleaned up the building and scared the residents. She wouldn't be alone for long. Detective Peralta walked up the steps and onto the rear porch. Somewhere in here she could find some kind of document tying Verringer, or his employee, to the crane collapse. She would have time, but not a lot of time. She had slipped her gun back into the holster while surveying the backyard. Before turning into the house, she took it out again. It looked like she was going to need it.

CHAPTER THIRTY-SEVEN

"We can't put it over the radio. He took the RMP."

It took a moment for Leonard to realize what the captain was telling him. No New York Police Department officer would ever refer to the blue-and-white marked police car as a cruiser, or a car, or anything at all other than a Radio Mobile Patrol. An RMP. But Leonard didn't need a lesson in the jargon. What the captain was telling him was that in an RMP, Bruder could hear any call that went out. And he had promised that if that happened, the boy would end up dead.

Adam Davenport was being loaded into an ambulance in the precinct parking lot, Mulino debriefing him. The EMTs had bound up the knee and leaned him back on the stretcher. The wound was ugly, but it would heal. A bullet in the kneecap was not the source of Adam Davenport's suffering right now.

Leonard watched the uniforms as they scuttled back to their desks. He tried to figure how Bruder had kept the boy secret for so long. A precinct is usually secure. The boy had been the source of hourly bulletins and an Amber Alert; his description had been read aloud at every Roll Call in the city. Bruder had had the kid for a day and a half. At his home, maybe even in the precinct. And at some point he had come into the precinct with him without getting arrested or shot. He had taken him somewhere familiar, somewhere secure, somewhere he thought he would be safe. Maybe he had snuck him in a side door without any cop in the precinct noticing. It was hard to believe.

But the alternative was hard to believe as well. Because the alternative was that someone had seen them. Someone did know. And the alternative was that one of these officers, maybe more, maybe all of them, had kept quiet about a kidnapped boy. At least for a little while. Maybe for longer. All to keep from turning on a fellow cop. Sure, they had their guns out when Bruder took his stand. But when the detective shot Davenport in the knee, no one had returned fire. It was almost as though they couldn't help it; loyalty had been drummed into them above all else. Maybe Bruder had counted on that too. And maybe Bruder had brought the boy to the precinct precisely because it was the one place he could stash the kid safely.

"You're not going to just let him drive off with the boy, are you?" Eleanor Hill's outrage was muted by her obvious shock. Leonard could tell she thought the whole precinct was bonkers. They had let the cop walk away. They had let him take the boy. Leonard imagined what Eleanor Hill's father would say. If that had been a twenty-four-year-old black man holding a gun to the kid in the doorway instead of a white cop, this game would already be over, one way or another.

"We aren't letting him do anything." The captain was speaking through his teeth. Leonard could tell he was at a loss. Winding through the last few days. Wondering what had gone wrong. Eleanor didn't let up.

"Can't these cars be tracked? Aren't they on GPS?"

"We can't put a call out over the radio. We can't follow him with another RMP. He will spot us right away."

Eleanor spoke. "I can drive. You just call us and tell us where it is. He won't see my car. He won't notice it. It isn't marked."

The captain's hands were in accidental fists; he was in danger of simply crushing the pencil in his right hand. But wherever he was directing his rage—himself, his men, the culture of his entire department—he was going to have to swallow it.

"You aren't an officer. Neither one of you. I can't let you run off after this guy. What if he shoots you? What kind of responsibility do I have then?"

Eleanor was nearly bursting out of her skin. Reluctant an hour ago, now she was furious that she wasn't going to be allowed to help. Leonard looked across the room at a stout man in the doorway, staring out at the parking lot.

"Captain, we'll take Mulino with us. It can be his operation. I can vouch for Eleanor. She'll stay safe. We'll do what the detective tells us."

Leonard could tell the captain didn't like it. He looked back and forth between Eleanor and Leonard, two people whose very lives, very careers, were spent accusing the police. But he had no choice, and two minutes later they were back in the Lexus, headlights flaring, now rolling down Empire past Eleanor Hill's new development, just as Empire abuts the park and turns into Ocean Avenue. Eleanor was driving cautiously, hewing to the speed limit, signaling as she changed lanes. Mulino, in front, slid the chair back with the electric control just enough to start to cramp Leonard. Leonard slid over from behind the detective to behind Eleanor. No reason to make a thing of it. The captain was giving Leonard directions through his cell phone.

"He went down Ocean and took the parkway. He's headed south."

Deeper into Brooklyn. Brighton Beach, maybe Coney Island. Less likely Borough Park, but you never know. Maybe Marine Park or Sheepshead Bay. Or maybe he would stay on Ocean Parkway until it fed into the Belt Parkway and he would cruise all the way out onto Long Island. There were miles of beaches, empty spaces where a carrier couldn't ping a cell phone for its location. There had been a half-dozen young women found buried on those beaches not so long ago, their killer never found. If you wanted to drop a body where it would stay dropped, the south shore of Long Island was as good a place as any.

"Pick it up a little, Eleanor. He's on a parkway and we're on the surface streets."

The car rumbled past the Parade Grounds and into the circle south of the park. As she lifted it up onto the parkway, Eleanor accelerated, and the Lexus began passing one lesser vehicle after another. It was Mulino who spoke.

"Timmy Bruder. If this guy worked half as hard at being a cop as he did at being a criminal, he would have had a pretty nice career. I mean, what has become of the job? This guy would rather kidnap kids than catch bad guys."

"Armstrong must have had his claws into Bruder for a while," Leonard said. "Bruder was just a tool. Armstrong was looking for information from the boy. He was looking for information about Christine. Armstrong was working with Veronica Dean. He had been sending emails. Back when he worked for . . ."

Leonard was going out on a limb, but it was the only explanation that made sense to him. Bruder wasn't smart enough to go on a kidnapping spree on his own. And when Leonard had mentioned the wristband, Bruder had known what he was talking about. He had been looking for something that only the boy had, after all. All signs suggested that Bruder had done this at Robert Armstrong's command.

And Leonard was worried for Eleanor. He didn't need to remind her how much of this went back to her office. She had known that Robert Armstrong had been stealing from her. And if she had only turned him in then, maybe Wade Valiant would be alive and the boy would never have been taken. For the daughter of McArthur Hill, it would have all been too much.

Mulino just nodded. "I thought we cleaned house last year. I don't know what else to say, Leonard. There is always another cop out there who can be turned."

Eleanor spoke, her eyes still locked to the road. "What are we going to do when we catch this guy, then? If you have someone who is willing to kidnap a child, who is happy to murder. Have you thought through what we are going to do when we reach him?"

Mulino sat up in his chair. "I've thought about it, yeah. We just need you to drive. Thank you for your help. Thank you for working with us."

"The least I can do. After you set up a sting operation to read my email and planted a fake employee in my office. Why wouldn't I help out a couple of detectives who thought I would engineer a construction accident to kill my own employees?"

"I'm not a detective. I'm a civilian investigator." Leonard wasn't sure that Eleanor thought this distinction mattered much. "We didn't think you did it." It wasn't a total lie. But it was enough to provide a little cover. To himself and Mulino both. "We thought maybe someone did it to you, and that we could find out who. And you know, we were right."

Before Eleanor could answer, Leonard's phone buzzed again. It was the captain. He swiped it on.

"Yes, Captain."

"Leonard, Bruder just got off Ocean Parkway. He took the exit at Avenue U. He's headed east. It looks like he's going to Sheepshead Bay."

"Thank you, Captain." Leonard slipped the phone off and leaned forward toward Eleanor. "Get off at Avenue U. It's the next one. We're closing in on him."

Eleanor glided the car to the right, and all three of them sat quiet for a moment. Mulino gripped his armrest. Leonard leaned forward, trying to spot mounted sirens on any of the cars ahead of them through the parade of taillights. It wouldn't be long now.

CHAPTER THIRTY-EIGHT

Detective Peralta took the steps carefully back down to the living room of the tiny house. The upstairs had been a bust. A couple of trim bedrooms, not a speck in the small bathroom. Peralta was sure of one thing as she'd dug through the covers and the cabinets upstairs: no one actually lived in this house. The beds sported neatly tucked duvets and there were doilies on the bedside tables, but the closets were bare. The medicine cabinet had been empty, not so much as a tube of toothpaste.

Even though the house was a front, Peralta was sure there must be something there. Something pointing to Armstrong's theft, to the abuse of the tenants at 80 Smithdale. If there wasn't, then Verringer could have answered her questions and been done with it. He could have given her a tour, could have thrown Armstrong under the bus. If the house was nothing more than a place to get mail, it didn't explain the fact that he was there at all. He had to have stored evidence somewhere. But if the upstairs and the front room were any indication, Peralta was going to have a hard time finding it.

The detective stood in the living room, turning toward the kitchen. A pantry door between the two rooms hung slightly open. She hadn't called the precinct to report that Verringer had run off. Now it was almost too late. She might as well check the cabinets. Verringer wasn't coming back here. And five more minutes wouldn't make a difference. Either he was wandering around the neighborhood, or he had made his way to a car and was already gone. If they needed to, they could find him soon enough. There was always the DMV database, the IRS if it came to it. You can get the mail for your shell company wherever you want, but in this day and age, you can't really stay off the grid. Finding anything that was hidden in this house—or confirming that there was nothing hidden at all—was more important. Peralta started in on the kitchen, tearing open a cabinet.

It was empty. So was the next one. There was silverware in a couple of drawers. The stove didn't look as though it had been run in months. Maybe someone got takeout now and again, but like the bedrooms, the kitchen wasn't being used for anything but show. She turned back toward the living room and pulled the pantry door all the way open.

It wasn't a pantry. There was a narrow stairway down to the basement, most likely a mechanical room. Maybe Peralta would get lucky and find a couple of boxes of documents down there. Or maybe she would be unlucky. She drew her gun and put her hand on the railing. Something about the house had rubbed her the wrong way from the moment she had come up the walk. It had been too clean, too neat. If Verringer and Armstrong were truly doing something more than just letting places go to rot, there would be a record of it somewhere. And maybe someone would stay down there to guard it.

Peralta stepped as cautiously as she could, but her footfalls were still audible on the stairs. If there was someone down there, she wasn't going to be able to surprise him. And if she couldn't surprise him, she might as well come in hard. She drew in a breath and shouted.

"Police! Anyone down there I want to see your hands up!" She rushed down the stairs, no longer concerned with the noise, and placed her back against the wall, gun out, to survey the room as soon as she landed.

The place was a disaster. Folding card tables propped up against the rough basement wall, a single light bulb dangling from a ceiling outlet.

In the corner there was a furnace and a water heater. But this wasn't just the mechanical room. On the tables were mounds of binders and a half-dozen laptops. A couple of power strips were stuffed with plugs. They snaked behind the furnace, maybe hot-wired into the low-water shutoff valve. Peralta marveled that the whole hand-rigged operation hadn't yet caught fire.

She opened the nearest binder. Printouts of leases, letters, some emails, some in English and many in other languages. The computers were running too. Another trove of data. They would have to get another team in here to figure out what was going on. Maybe her friend from Frauds could help. It would be nice for him to get out of One PP, she figured. He would be able to put it all together. Leonard had told her that Hill and Associates had screwed over some overseas investor. The investor had paid money to 80 Smithdale. Armstrong was working for Smithdale and had a beef against Wade Valiant.

There were pieces to fill in, and from the look of this room there was a lot else going on. But it was pretty clear that Robert Armstrong was up to something. Maybe he had pushed Manny Reeves off the building; maybe he had paid Reeves to do Valiant in. She had more than probable cause to nab her man. She thought, for a moment, of the innocent man who was being held by the Homicide Squad. Gabriel Smyth had been beaten or badgered into confessing to killing Valiant. Finding Armstrong was important for two reasons: not only to catch the real killer, but to free an innocent man from jail.

There was a noise upstairs. Footsteps. Had Verringer come back after all? Peralta turned away from the machines and started up the stairs, quiet. Her back hugged the wall as she crept further. The door above her was still half open. Her fingers felt warm as she trained her gun on the door. If anyone did open it, she would have only a moment to decide whether it was someone trying to kill her. If she chose wrong, then she could shoot an innocent civilian, stand trial, spend the rest of her life in jail. If she chose wrong the other way, she'd be dead.

Whoever was upstairs took another step. Not right by the door. Peralta guessed maybe in the living room. There was a voice too. A deep one, speaking slowly. She couldn't hear anyone answer. Maybe he was on a phone? Two more steps and she would be able to turn the corner. She kept her gun on the door. One more step.

She heard another noise from outside. A car engine, brakes squealing. The noise gave her enough cover to take the last step and whip around the corner from the basement pantry. Standing in the living room was a white man who looked to be in his late sixties, his hair a mess, a slight stoop in his right shoulder. Robert Armstrong. As soon as Peralta busted up the stairway, Armstrong turned; the cell phone he had been holding dropped to the floor. Peralta kept her eyes on his hands. Both were empty. She couldn't shoot.

"Put your hands above your head. Above your head!"

The old man's eyes flashed fear, then shut halfway. He put his hands up, slowly. He was watching her gun instead of her eyes. That was good. His hands were above his head, but he was shuffling. He was maybe ten, fifteen feet away from her and he was slipping a little bit toward his right. A little bit toward the door. One half-step at a time. His eyes darted from her gun to the door. He was measuring how far away he was.

"Stop moving. Stand still." Peralta didn't have handcuffs. She didn't have her radio. She was in plainclothes. It was a privilege of the promotion that you don't have to walk around with all of the trinkets of police work all the time. Except now, when a pair of handcuffs might have been worth something. There was a pair in the car. Maybe she could march him out to the street.

Through the corner of her eye, she saw that there was a car outside. It had skipped up the pavement and was parked right in the middle of the lawn. Its headlights were on, blaring bright into the night and onto the house. An RMP. A marked car. The lights were running hot on its roof, but the sirens were off. One of the local units had responded after all. The precinct cop would have handcuffs, pepper spray, all sorts of goodies to make Robert Armstrong compliant without having to kill him.

Peralta circled away from Armstrong and toward the front door. The man had stopped shuffling. His hands were still over his head. His eyes, though, were still alert. Still darting back and forth between the door and the gun, sometimes looking out the window. Peralta looked out herself. There was someone getting out of the RMP. She couldn't see much through the glare of the headlights. For a moment, she thought she recognized the cop getting out. He was pulling out his gun too. It would be over in a moment.

Peralta had made it to the door. Keeping her gun hand on Armstrong, she reached down with her left hand and unlatched it. They were both squinting; the headlights of the car were the only light cutting through the midnight darkness. She opened it. The cop was close now, right on the stoop. She turned to Armstrong.

"Okay, Mr. Armstrong. I want you to walk very slowly. The officer outside is going to cuff you and we are going to take you to the precinct. And then we're going to find out where your friend, David Verringer, has gone off to."

Armstrong started shuffling again, slowly toward the door. Watching Peralta's gun. Peralta kept her eye on Armstrong but called out to the cop outside.

"Okay, I want you to cuff this guy so we can take him in. You think you can do that?"

The voice that answered her was all too familiar. "No. I think you can put your gun down and step away."

Peralta turned toward the voice, worried for a moment that she was taking her eye off Armstrong. Standing not five feet from her was her partner, Detective Timothy Bruder. There was no reason for him to be in a sector car. There was no reason for him to be in Sheepshead Bay. But most of all, there was no reason for him to be pointing a nine-millimeter handgun directly at her heart.

CHAPTER THIRTY-NINE

Eleanor tried to keep her focus as she pulled the car up Avenue U. It wasn't easy. Mulino was tapping his foot and kept checking his holster for his gun. Leonard, in the back, was calling out directions to her, directions that he was getting over the phone from the captain in the precinct. It was dark and there weren't as many streetlights this far into Brooklyn. Not so much traffic either. What exactly had she volunteered for? She was chasing an armed detective who had kidnapped a boy. She had another armed detective in her car. Suppressing the worry that she was about to be caught in a shootout, she focused on the road. She kept to the speed limit.

"Here. Take a right here." Leonard was jabbing between them, one hand still pressed to his ear. He wasn't wearing a seat belt. Eleanor usually was picky about that sort of thing but it wasn't the time to bring it up.

"Okay." She turned the car onto a quiet residential street. Detached houses. Square lawns. Matching white vinyl fencing. Once upon a time, someone must have gone up and down the block taking a vote, getting uniform support for the brand of fence. It was dark; the streetlights were cast too far apart to flood the whole street. She pulled the car slowly down the road.

Mulino had his right hand on his holster now, his left across his chest holding the handle of the door. He was crouching in his seat, getting ready to whip open the door and take cover behind it. When you're driving there is nowhere to crouch, but Eleanor slipped a little lower into her seat. She could sense that her hands were beginning to sweat. Nothing on the street looked unusual at all. Her headlights revealed only a few cars parked along the curb.

Leonard held down the phone and spoke. "This is the block. We are getting close. I don't know that we're going to get any more precise than that."

"Look." It was Mulino this time, pointing to an ordinary sedan parked on the left curb about midway down the block.

"What?"

"That's Detective Peralta's car. See the antennas on the back?"

In the darkness, Eleanor hadn't noticed the cluster of antennas on the rear of the car. She saw them now. She thought, for a moment, of how many details in her city she missed on a typical day. She had never paid much attention to the police. Not like her father, who had been obsessed with them, who had seen them as an occupying army to be extracted from his fiefdom. McArthur Hill would have been able to recognize an unmarked detective car, just as he had been able to spot an undercover cop trying to infiltrate a rally or a protest. The house across the street from Peralta's car was bathed in light, but Eleanor couldn't see the source of it. She slowed the car some more.

"Stop the car." Mulino was leaning on the door. They were almost at the house across from Peralta's car. Eleanor was only too happy to oblige. She pulled the car onto the right-hand curb. There were three unfamiliar cars ahead of them, the last directly in front of the house with the lights on.

Leonard hung up the phone. "The captain is sending a couple of units. It isn't going over the scanner. They'll be here in about twenty minutes."

"Okay." Mulino drew his gun and opened the door. "Guys, I'm leading the way. That light is going to be them. Open your doors. Slip out. We are moving one car at a time. Stay behind me and stay behind the cars. If there are people out there with guns drawn, just come back here and wait for the units from the precinct. If it's all clear up there, I suppose I could use your help."

Mulino led Eleanor and Leonard as they stalked up behind the first car, then another. In the dark, they ducked behind an SUV on the right-hand curb; a hedge blocked their view of the house. There was an empty space, big enough for two parked cars, and a gray Volvo parked at the gate in the front lawn. Mulino stole ahead and ducked behind the rear wheels. Leonard was crouching, nearly to his knees, hiding behind the hedge before taking the last fifteen feet to reach the car. Eleanor was right behind him. Her heart was pounding now. She could feel her pulse in her wrists, her knees, her neck. She had never felt what she was feeling now, as though her blood was racing through her body and draining out of it at the same time. She was overwhelmed with this new and sudden brand of fear.

Mulino slipped toward the front of the Volvo. Crouched behind the left front wheel, he peered over the hood toward the house. He raised his gun onto it as well. Eleanor had never seen a detective carrying a revolver. She had only ever seen officers carrying nine-millimeter handguns. The weapon Mulino was holding over the hood looked almost like a toy to her, almost silly.

Leonard gestured to Eleanor. Time to move. She ducked and ran forward, eyes shut as they stole toward the car, hoping to duck in before anyone saw them. She made it behind the Volvo quick and out of breath, only a few feet behind Mulino. She could hear Leonard behind her. He had made the open dash as well. He was ducking almost at the rear bumper of the car. Eleanor looked across the trunk toward the light cutting through the night.

There was a marked police car splayed across the lawn. What had looked like floodlights were its brights, saturating the lawn and house. The picket fence was torn to vinyl shreds. The rear tires had dug up the lawn. The driver's door was open. There was a man standing next to the car. She could see him only from behind, just an outline in the darkness. But she figured that it was the detective from the precinct. And she could see that he had a gun.

He was pointing it at a woman standing on the landing of the house, squinting from the light bathing her. Eleanor recognized her. Peralta. The one who had pretended not to recognize her in the hospital. The woman was in plainclothes, her badge hanging outside her shirt. She was bending at the knees, keeping her back straight, and she was setting her gun on the ground. Behind her, just inside the house, Eleanor could see Robert Armstrong.

One cop was disarming another. If she hadn't seen Bruder kidnap a boy from the precinct, she would not have known which one was the criminal. Peralta's hand shook as she set her gun on the doormat.

Eleanor sensed movement behind her. She turned and saw Leonard swing around the rear bumper and start up the lawn. He was in the open, heading toward the detective in the headlights, unarmed. Leonard came at the police cruiser from behind, no longer protected by the parked car.

Eleanor turned to the left and caught Mulino's eyes. Mulino was still crouching, steady, his eyes just above the hood, his gun at the ready. Maybe he was trying to get a bead on Bruder. It would mean shooting a man in the back. A man who was holding a gun on a detective, but shooting a man in the back nevertheless. She saw Mulino watch Leonard creep up toward the lawn. This wasn't what they had promised the captain. But it wasn't as though calling out for him to come back would be any safer. As Leonard made his way toward the RMP, Eleanor hoped he wouldn't make enough noise for Detective Bruder to hear.

CHAPTER FORTY

Leonard scuttled up the lawn toward the police car. Almost on all fours. The lawn had been torn to shreds and the mud was all over his pants, but his suit couldn't get any worse than it already was. He peeked over the edge of the car at Detective Bruder. He was still looking at Peralta, in the doorway. He hadn't turned back toward the street. He didn't know that any of them—Leonard, Mulino, Eleanor—had made it to the curb. Leonard took another step forward. The boy had to still be in the back seat of that car. Alive or otherwise.

Detective Peralta, slowly rising after setting down her gun, her hands in the air, shifted her gaze over the car. She had seen him. She gave a quick flash of recognition and looked back at Bruder. She didn't want to give the other cop any ideas. Didn't want him looking off in the direction she had been staring. Instead she spoke.

"You want anything else, Detective? Or are you just going to drive off with this criminal now?"

Bruder walked toward her and reached down for the gun. It was Leonard's chance, with a little bit of noise and the detective crouching. He slipped open the car door and into the back seat.

The boy was strapped into the seat. Belt locked. The door wouldn't open from the inside. They transport prisoners this way, after all.

Leonard put a finger to his lips to shush the boy and did his best to unlatch the seat belt without making any noise. Bruder was standing back up, stepping away from Peralta, his gun still trained on her. The headlights were shining straight in his face. Leonard was lucky for that; Bruder's sight was compromised by his own car. Leonard slipped out of the car with the boy, both skidding in the mud.

As they crept back toward the curb, the door swung shut, securing itself with a satisfying click. Leonard winced. It was too much noise. Bruder had heard it.

Bruder swung around from in front of the car, his gun steady. Leonard and the boy were not ten feet away. They were just low enough to the ground that he couldn't see them, but if they stood up they would have been exposed to his fire. The boy's eyes were wide with fear.

"Who is that?" Bruder looked into the back of the empty car. Bruder's face contorted in the headlights, confused and angry, then determined. He stepped toward the hood and started to round the car.

Leonard pushed the boy toward the curb, and shouted, "Run!" Henry leapt and trucked toward the curb. Eleanor scuttled to the rear of the Volvo, showing him the path between the bumpers of the parked cars. The boy bolted toward her.

Leonard saw Eleanor whisk the boy to safety. He turned back toward the car and expected to see Bruder pointing a gun at him. Instead, the cop was looking behind him and to his left, where Mulino stood holding his revolver.

"Detective Bruder, put down your weapon."

But Bruder had a semiautomatic handgun and Mulino had only a revolver. And Bruder was quick, young, and trigger-happy. Instead of answering, he fired at Mulino and took cover behind the front bumper of the RMP. Four bullets dug hot into the hood of the Volvo. Mulino hadn't been hit, but he couldn't stand in the clear and fire. He knelt behind the car, breathing deep and slowly.

Leonard was backing away from the police car toward the curb, but it left him stuck in the open, and still too far from the curb to join Mulino and Eleanor behind the Volvo. Bruder rose slowly from the front of the squad car. The headlights were tearing into him. If the detective had been able to see, he could have gotten a bead on Leonard and shot. Leonard bent on all fours, backing toward the sidewalk, his eyes glued to Bruder. If he stood up, the cop would see him over the car. But he was moving too slowly as he crawled back toward the sidewalk.

Bruder stepped out of the headlights and toward the right side of the car's front bumper. Around the car, his eyes met Leonard's. Leonard leapt to his feet to turn and run back toward Eleanor. But it was too late. He felt the pain before he even heard the shot, a swift hot spear barreling through his right shoulder, just below his collarbone. As if he had been yanked to the ground by an enormous hook. Because that was the other thing he noticed before he heard the shot. He was already on the ground. He couldn't move his right arm. He didn't have a gun. He pressed himself up with his left arm, expecting to see Bruder close in and shoot him again, and that was where he was standing when he heard the second shot.

He didn't feel a thing. It took Leonard a moment to realize that the second shot had not hit him. He looked up at Bruder, staggering toward him. The detective gasped and dropped his gun as both hands reached to his throat. His throat had been entirely ripped away. Bruder slipped onto his right knee and collapsed, his life seeping dark into the grass from the hole that used to be his neck.

Detective Peralta stepped down from the stairs, through the headlights, holding a small gun. A twenty-two. Barely bigger than a toy. But easy enough to keep strapped in an ankle holster without drawing too much attention. She was training it on Bruder, making sure that he wasn't about to jump up and start firing again. She didn't have to worry.

Leonard was rolling on the ground, clutching the shoulder. He could hear Mulino, kneeling by him, speaking softly. "Hang on, Len.

You did good. Hang on. It's just your shoulder. We'll get you in a bus and they'll stitch you up and you'll be fine."

Leonard let out a sound that wasn't quite a scream and wasn't quite a sigh. He clenched his teeth again, trying to bite on something that wasn't there, trying to force the pain out of his body. To pull his mind away from the wound and the blood and the seared flesh. He twisted on the ground, but could see behind him that Henry was safe, standing with Eleanor Hill.

Eleanor spoke to the boy. "Are you okay?" The child nodded. But he almost certainly wasn't okay. Not in the way any adult would understand the word.

As Leonard rolled back toward them in the mud, struggling to speak, he heard a car starting. The RMP, right in front of him, was revving up. He rolled out of the way so it wouldn't crush him on its way out of the lawn. The car spun in the grass and revved back toward the street, tearing out a new patch of fence, throwing up a new splatter of mud. Behind the wheel, Leonard saw the stringy white mane of Robert Armstrong.

He had slipped right by them and taken off in Bruder's car. He was already on the street, tearing away, before Peralta and Mulino stood up. It was Mulino who spoke.

"Aurelia, get these people to a hospital. I'll follow him. Let the dad know that his boy is okay."

By the time Mulino was in the car, Armstrong had already turned the corner at the end of the street. Leonard could feel that his whole shoulder, his whole suit now, was wet. With blood or mud or sweat it didn't matter. At least it meant he could feel something. Eleanor was still talking to Adam Davenport's son.

"We're going to get you back to your dad. Okay?"

The boy nodded, a thin tear streaking the left side of his cheek.

CHAPTER FORTY-ONE

Mulino had to wrench the seat in Peralta's sedan back. His right knee was killing him. But it wasn't as though he could wait for the precinct units. He flicked a switch and the blue-and-red lights came to life through the front grill. Down the street, turning back toward the parkway, Mulino could make out the lights of the RMP. Armstrong was running without lights and sirens, but Mulino wouldn't have any trouble keeping a bead on it. Plus there wasn't a hostage anymore. They didn't need to worry about keeping it off the scanner. Mulino flipped on the radio. He reached the captain at the seven-one.

"Captain, can you put the RMP we've been chasing over the scanner? We have the boy. Leonard has been shot. They are getting a bus but I'm following the car. We can let him know we're on to him."

"Okay."

Mulino hadn't mentioned that Bruder had been shot. Likely dead. Maybe the captain had known him. Mulino had been supervising detectives for only six months, and already one had been shot by the other. And the shooter was the good one. Maybe management wasn't really for him. Maybe he was a legwork detective after all. He would have to have a hard conversation with Chief Travis when this was over.

But he had already made up his mind about a few things that were going to make that conversation shorter.

The RMP had hopped onto the Belt Parkway. It was headed out to Long Island. Maybe Armstrong thought he would lose the NYPD if he left the jurisdiction. As though Mulino couldn't call Nassau County on the radio. As though half the Nassau County officers weren't retired NYPD anyway. Mulino swerved past the parting traffic and onto the freeway. Mulino would gain on him on the open road.

Bruder had been in league with them all along, and Mulino hadn't even seen it. He should have noticed when the detective abandoned his post at the hospital. No one is quite that lazy. It explained why the boy went with a stranger. Anyone shows a police shield to a child, and the child will follow. A seven-year-old hasn't been taught yet to be skeptical, to think that some cops are dirty, are holding out for their own sinister objectives. Bruder could have told the boy that there was news about his mother. That his father was in the hospital. A child who has lost a parent, filled with fear and anger that he doesn't understand, is an easy mark.

And Leonard had probably been right. If Bruder had been working with Armstrong, then they were looking for something that was left behind by the boy's mother. Adam had thought it was paranoid to hide under the radar with his kid for a year, but in fact they had been looking the whole time. When he bought the house he had made himself a target to Armstrong and whoever else wanted some clue that they could profit by. Mulino had put that part of last year's escapade out of his head. Not only had there been cops sabotaging the city, there had been someone profiting off of it. He had caught the cops, but Veronica had gotten away. That had been too much for Mulino. This part of the job was simpler. Just hunt down the shooter and lock him up. Maybe, Mulino thought, he really wasn't cut out to be a supervisor after all.

He had nearly caught the car. What little traffic was on the road this late was slowing, parting, giving way to the scene. An unmarked car running its lights, chasing a marked RMP running without them. It must have been confusing to the other drivers, no one sure which driver was the good guy and which was the bad guy, or if maybe the two of them were both chasing somebody else.

Mulino's headlights were close enough to shine an outline on Armstrong behind the wheel. The man was leaning over the dashboard as he drove. He didn't know how to turn on the lights and sirens. He didn't know how to run the radio. He was just an ordinary real estate scammer, after all. Mulino could see Armstrong fiddling, and suddenly find the switch. The RMP blossomed to life. Now cars ahead were parting for him as well. Mulino pushed the gas. If it came to racing down a straightaway, Armstrong would be able to lose him.

Armstrong had been the boots on the ground, Mulino figured. He had gotten one workman on the site to kill another. Likely he bribed him, but he could have had something else too. You always find a mark with a weakness. You tell him how easy it will be to make it look like an accident. And whatever dark moment there was in Manny Reeves's past, Armstrong would have promised him he could make it go away. And if Armstrong had been paid by the overseas fund, so much the better. He had, Mulino figured, probably taken the money to do something that he had been planning to do anyway. But as soon as it didn't look so much like an accident, Reeves himself had to be cleaned up.

As Mulino struggled to keep up with the now-surging sector car, he thought that he was right where he ought to be. He was the guy who chases down someone who pushes someone else over a ledge. That was straightforward, ordinary crime, the kind that Mulino understood.

They weren't out of the city yet. They were in East New York, heading north toward the airport and eventually Queens and Nassau County. The RMP hit the brakes, veering suddenly for an exit. Mulino was taken by surprise. He swung his foot to the brake and his knee felt like hell. He hit it too hard, too soon, and started to spin out. There were no other cars around, but he skidded past the exit ramp as the RMP careened down.

He had overshot the exit. He looked over his shoulder, flipped the car into reverse, and hit the gas with his aching leg. An oncoming car swerved out of his way. He still had the siren running hot; it was still police business. Still, he felt foolish swerving the car around to the off-ramp. He aligned the car and swept down toward where he had last seen the RMP.

The exit curled underneath the parkway and then back up toward the city. At the bottom of the ramp, the street was bordered by a three-foot retaining wall on each side. Over the wall to the left was a scrappy little beach and Buttermilk Channel beyond. To his right, a thick mess of tall grass covering murky growth. It was pitch dark here; the streetlights hadn't worked for years. You could hear the water, even if you couldn't see it. Mulino followed the ramp down, then a quarter mile to an intersection. The RMP was parked at the light. But it was empty.

Mulino stepped out of Peralta's car, the headlights flooding the car Armstrong had taken. He pulled out his gun. He walked up to the abandoned RMP. He checked the back seat, gun drawn, just in case Armstrong was planning an ambush. He cleared the front seat the same way. But there was no one in the car. It hadn't been five minutes since he had overshot the exit ramp. If Armstrong had left on foot, he couldn't have gotten far. Mulino swung his flashlight over the swamp to one side and the beach to the other. If someone had run to the right, the plants would have been trampled. There would have been signs of flight. On the beach, Armstrong would have been exposed.

Mulino wasn't in any shape to give chase into the weeds anyway. His leg hurt. He was out of breath. Even back at the house in Sheepshead Bay, he hadn't pulled the trigger. He had a bead on Bruder, just before Bruder had come around the car and shot Leonard. But he hadn't felt right pulling the trigger. A year ago, he had shot someone, and killing a man does something to you. At least, it had done something to Detective Ralph Mulino. Standing by the open car, wondering where Armstrong had fled but unready to give chase, Mulino wondered if he would ever have the stomach to pull the trigger again. And if he didn't have the stomach for that, another decision was already made.

He figured that Armstrong had reached out to someone. He had been picked up. It was easy enough to make a call while you're driving. Armstrong had been working with the building owner, after all. Something with a V. Peralta had shown him the name when she had come into the office, all excited. Every time you look up the chain, there is always someone else. Mulino had been duped again. Had run down the suspect only to have him slip out of his grasp. He had helped them catch Bruder. But once again, the dirty cop had just been the tip of the spear. Reeves had toppled Wade Valiant. Bruder had kidnapped the child. But these were the dupes, the stooges, the people who were doing someone else's dirty work and who were being set up to be caught anyway. The people who orchestrated it were gone. Mulino slammed his fist onto the hood of the car. His best work had, once again, only gotten him part of the way home. That conversation with Chief Travis couldn't come soon enough.

Mulino leaned back against the RMP and sighed. There wasn't another car visible on the road. The intersection threaded back under the parkway and into the city. Armstrong would be in a civilian vehicle: no scanner, no description, no trace. They would put it over the radio. A man in his sixties, white, matted white hair, and a slight stoop. Half of Borough Park would get thrown up against the wall in the next two days, but Mulino knew that they wouldn't catch Robert Armstrong. Staring toward the unforgiving ocean, Mulino wished for a cigarette for the first time in a decade. Instead, he closed the doors of the sector car, got back into the unmarked detective's vehicle, and turned on the radio. The other precinct officers would be there soon enough.

CHAPTER FORTY-TWO

"You can go in now. He's awake."

The receptionist had actually startled Eleanor Hill. Sitting in the squat, uncomfortable chair, she had been reviewing binders of leasing statistics. Her vacancy rates were higher than they should be. So much for the boom. That would be a problem for tomorrow. With its dull tiles and cheap Sheetrock, the waiting room could have been the Post Office or the DMV instead of a supposedly quality hospital. A lot of money gets spent in hospitals, mainly on high-end equipment and doctors' salaries. Surgical waiting rooms couldn't make visitors comfortable if they were plush, so why bother.

The receptionist directed her upstairs, to the seventh floor. The hospital was quieter than she'd imagined. On your way to recovery, there is no hurry. All the panic has already happened somewhere else.

Leonard Mitchell was propped by the window in an outdated hospital bed. In a hospital gown, his shoulder bulging comically with layer upon layer of bandage, he looked thinner and older than he had in a suit in her office. She noticed for the first time that his hair was thin and receding, with a hint of gray at the temples. He had been such a tempest of energy before that she had never really stopped to get a good look at him.

And he wasn't alone. Sitting by the window was the other detective. Peralta. The one who had shot her partner. The one who had saved Leonard's life. She was in her trim slacks and had her badge out over her shirt. Police don't have to wait in the same lobby as everyone else. Peralta's own hair was tied tight and her eyes didn't leave Leonard's face, even as he looked up to Eleanor.

"I brought flowers." They were from the bodega on the corner. There was a florist in the hospital, but the flowers looked just as tired in there and they cost four times as much as the ones out on the corner. Eleanor hadn't gotten where she was in life by wasting money. She handed Leonard the crinkled plastic package, wrapped and stapled. There was no vase in the room. Leonard cradled them to his body with his good arm.

"Thanks, Eleanor."

"I'm sorry about all this, Leonard."

Leonard sighed. "I'm sorry too, Eleanor. I shouldn't have lied to you about why I was there. We should have knocked on your front door and asked what we needed to know."

"But I might not have told you."

Leonard smiled. "Well, we all have our regrets."

Peralta was staring Eleanor down, blaming her. Eleanor looked at the floor. She had berated this woman in front of her father's church. She hadn't told the detectives about Robert Armstrong right after the accident. It had never occurred to her that he was capable of killing someone. She probably deserved to get a little of it back. She met the detective's gaze.

"I'm sorry."

Peralta almost smiled. "Like Leonard said, we all make mistakes."

"Okay."

"I've got one question, though." Peralta's eyes held fast on Eleanor, just as they had on Leonard. This was someone who was never distracted.

Who would never flinch from what she had to see and what she had to do. Eleanor recognized why Peralta was a good cop.

"What is it?"

"When I first went in, when I spoke to Verringer. He said he didn't own that building any more. 80 Smithdale. He said he had sold it. You know anything about that?"

Eleanor hadn't been planning to tell them yet. But after all this, it wouldn't do for her to still look as though she was holding out. Armstrong and Verringer were gone. They would prosecute Manny Reeves, as soon as he was well enough, but that would be little consolation. So they were not done asking her questions, and Eleanor figured it was time to come clean.

"I bought it." The closing papers were still being filed. But the transaction was done. It meant that Verringer had his money. That he could get himself almost anywhere in the world.

"I thought you might have. You getting into the slumlord business?"

"My father owns almost a quarter of my company. He wanted out. I had to raise money to buy him out, and I know it might not make sense to you, but the best way to raise money is to get investors to pitch in to buy something new."

"So have you paid off your father yet?"

"No." This part she had raised with him. He hadn't agreed yet, but she knew he would. It would allow him to appear powerful and to do the right thing all at once, and she knew her father wouldn't be able to resist that. "I'm going to give him the building. In payment of his shares. He can use it to house congregants if they hit hard times. And Hill and Associates will do all the rehab. We'll bring it up to code, we'll fix the wiring, we'll put everything in order. And once people are housed there, we will keep it that way. But the building will be his."

"That's very big of you. And I'm sure you're getting some kind of tax break to thank you."

"You want to run an audit on us, you just give the word. Leonard knows just about everything we've ever done anyway."

Leonard shifted in bed at the sound of his name. "I know you did your best, Eleanor. I know you didn't want any of this to happen. You should go back to your business."

"Thanks."

He turned toward the window, to the detective. He moved slowly, his shoulder in obvious pain with every shift of his weight.

"Aurelia." Eleanor hadn't known the detective's first name. None of these police people seemed to address each other by their first name. Leonard, his strength sapped and his body busted, seemed almost childlike addressing the cop so casually. "Did they find the wristband the boy had been wearing? It was green, and it snapped together. There was a flash drive on it."

Eleanor reached across to feel her own plastic flash drive bracelet. She knew the answer to this already. Peralta spoke.

"No. They searched the car that Bruder had taken. The searched the house. Armstrong must have taken it with him when he vanished. But it means you were right. You knew why the boy was taken."

"Have they spoken to him?"

"The boy? They have him back with his father. We have a foot post on the street to protect him. The kid is vulnerable. Turns out that Bruder had gotten him to go with him by saying he had news about his mother. That boy would leap in front of a car if he thought it would help bring Christine Davenport back."

Leonard grimaced. Eleanor knew this name too. The boy's mother. The woman who had been killed last year. Leonard had worked with her. Leonard went on.

"And the father?"

"He's recovering. His knee wasn't as bad as your shoulder, even. A lot of blood but the patella is intact. He's downstairs, actually."

"Did we debrief him yet?"

Peralta sighed. "He doesn't want to talk. He hasn't had a great week with regards to the NYPD. We parked him in your apartment and he ran to the precinct to get help. They had some way of helping him, shooting him and running off with his boy. How would you feel, frankly? Would you want to sit in an interview room with a cop anytime soon?"

Eleanor turned to Leonard. "What are you going to do now?"

"I don't know. Detective Mulino said that if this worked out I could come join him at OCCB. As some kind of civilian support. I don't know if he would consider this working out or not. I don't think I'm going back to the Parks Department."

"If you're interested in working in real estate, you can come talk to me. For real, not just as a spy for the police department. I think we could use you."

"Thanks. I'll think about that. I figure I have to think about a lot of things."

Peralta put a hand on Leonard's good shoulder. "You have to talk to Mulino. I don't know what he told you before you started. But I think there are some things going on you have to talk to him about."

Leonard nodded. "Okay."

"And I have to go talk to the Homicide Division. They've been keeping some innocent guy in lockup for three days now. If we don't get it taken care of, we're going to end up with a lawsuit."

"Yeah."

Peralta took her hand off of Leonard's shoulder and turned from the window. Eleanor watched her. Did she notice a closeness, a tenderness in that touch? In the way they addressed each other by their first names? This woman had just saved Leonard's life, after all. It wouldn't be altogether surprising for that to be personal. But that wasn't all Eleanor thought was going on. Maybe it wasn't any of her business anyway.

Leonard watched Peralta go, then turned back to Eleanor. "I should get some rest."

"Of course."

"Thank you for the flowers."

"You're welcome. I am glad you're going to be all right."

Leonard pulled himself up in the bed again. Another grimace. He was going to be all right, but he was not all right just yet. "So am I."

Eleanor shifted her feet. "So I guess I should go. Let you rest." She hadn't quite said what she meant to say. That she was angry at him for spying on her but glad that he had found out what Armstrong had done. That her father had raised her to be skeptical of the police, and she knew he was right, but that she had learned in the past few weeks that there are some good cops out there in addition to some very bad ones.

She knew he wasn't going to come work for her. She most likely was never going to see him again. She would pay her penance to her father, keep 80 Smithdale in tip-top shape, and go on making money by putting up new buildings and charging through the roof for them. People would admire her for the 80 Smithdale work, and maybe that way they wouldn't give her too much flack for everything else. She was, in the end, one of the good guys. That's what she thought. That's what she wanted to tell Leonard, what she wanted him to tell her. But his eyes were shut. He was already drifting off to sleep. His hand slipped from the bouquet of bodega flowers. She reached over and tucked it under his blanket so it would not fall off his bed. She patted it in place, turned, and left him to his sleep.

CHAPTER FORTY-THREE

Leonard looked across Flatbush Avenue and the park beyond. His shoulder was killing him. They had given Leonard some meds. Lortab. Oversized white pills flecked with green, as though they were mint candy. They took away the pain, but they put his head somewhere he never wanted it to be. At least it meant he could go home, even if most of the day at home he just sat on the couch and stared. Without the medicine, he could get up and about. But without the medicine, his shoulder attacked him all day long. Today, it was worth it.

Detective Mulino had asked to meet him in the park, so he had made do with a couple of aspirin. On the Lortab he would likely wander out into traffic. Six days after a bullet to the shoulder, four days after being discharged from the hospital, a couple of aspirin were not going to cut it. But he had told the detective he would show up, so he gritted his teeth and squirmed through the pain as he crossed Flatbush.

He looked up at the construction site. It was only a little over a week ago that he had come out here to get a statement on the crane collapse and found Mulino on the scene. The site was up and running again. A new crane, new members of the crew, business back to usual in the never-ending rush upward. Maybe they would finish the thing by spring after all. Twenty percent of the units were supposed to be designated as affordable. Maybe he would call Eleanor Hill, see if a unit could be reserved for him. Civil servants make almost enough to live in affordable housing, after all.

But he wasn't sure he even was a civil servant anymore. Even if he could talk his commissioner at the Parks Department into having him back, he couldn't convince himself that he really wanted to go. He had been back in action with Mulino, and he knew he had missed it. Two decades investigating corruption at DIMAC couldn't be washed out of his system so quickly. He had agreed to see Mulino to find out whether the deal was still on, to learn if he could still join the detective's team at OCCB for good.

Mulino wanted to meet at Lakeside. In the summer, they ran sprinklers and kids ran through ankle-deep water squirting each other with plastic spray bottles provided by parents who frowned on actual squirt guns. In winter it was a skating rink. Now, in the tail end of November, it was mainly empty. The water had been turned off months ago, but they hadn't laid down the ice yet for the winter. As Leonard crossed into the park and along the narrow path toward the rink, he practiced what he would say to Mulino.

He had a whole speech ready, on what he had contributed to the investigation. He only hoped that Mulino didn't make too much of the part where Adam Davenport had snuck out while he was supposed to be in Leonard's apartment. Or the part where Leonard had nearly gotten himself killed until Peralta had saved his life.

Detective Mulino was standing with a cup of coffee, staring over the broad field of concrete and toward the lake beyond. Something looked off about the cop, but Leonard couldn't quite place it. He was standing a little straighter, maybe, not favoring his right leg quite so much. Or maybe that he was dressed up a little, more like a lawyer on a Friday afternoon than a detective. Or maybe it was the smile. Because Mulino was wearing a broad, guileless smile, showing off a casual happiness that Leonard had never seen in him. For the first time that Leonard had seen him in two years, Detective Mulino appeared genuinely untroubled.

"Detective."

"Leonard."

"You look well."

"You look like hell. You look like a guy that got shot and shouldn't even be out of bed yet."

Mulino was right. The shoulder hadn't stopped hurting since the last Lortab had worn off hours ago. "You could have always come by the apartment to see me, Detective. If you're so worried about whether I should be out of bed."

Mulino moved to pat Leonard on the back but held off. Worried, maybe, that he would hurt him more if he slapped him in the wrong place. "You'll be all right, Len. I spoke to the doctors. You're going to be just fine. I know a couple of guys who have been shot. Nice clean exit wounds like you have, they end up good as new in a couple of months, blessing their luck the whole way."

"I certainly was lucky." Leonard cocked his head, trying to take Mulino in. He wasn't sure whether it was time to raise the question. Maybe he should come out and just say it: *Remember how you said you would take me on your squad? Are you going to follow through with that?* But maybe that would be too forward. The detective had called him out here. So he had something to say. Or at least Leonard hoped he did. Mulino took a long sip of his coffee.

"I have some news for you, Leonard."

"Okay." Mulino still had that smile on. But just because he was happy didn't mean that he had good news for Leonard.

"You heard about how they changed the pension rules." Leonard didn't follow the inner workings of the police department. But he had heard about some changes in city rules. Instead of paying out a pension based on your last year, they'd pay it out now based on an average of any three years of your choosing. The point was to keep people from piling on fake overtime in their final year.

"I heard a little."

"Well, you know I've had my twenty for a while. And I had a couple of fat years back when everyone had them." It dawned on Leonard what Mulino was about to tell him. Like most cops, he had probably put in a ton of overtime after 9/11. The department had lost a lot of officers to retirement right after, guys who could get the pension calculated on a big year. Now, with the new rules, Mulino would be able to throw that year in the mix. Mulino was done with the NYPD.

"So when are you going to put in?"

"I did it this morning. That's why I wanted to tell you right away."

Leonard wasn't going to join a team after all. There wasn't going to be a team. Mulino couldn't force anyone else to bring on a civilian who once investigated cops and had a six-month stint in prison on his resume. Leonard tried not to show his disappointment.

"Congratulations."

"Thanks."

"So is that it for you?" Retired cops don't have many options. You can't go work at a different city agency—your pension gets withheld until you're retired from city service entirely. You can work in the private sector, but that mainly means sitting at the desk of an office building, signing people in until something goes wrong. Mulino couldn't take that. A lot of retired NYPD spend the last twenty years of their lives puttering around a workshop in a basement in Long Island.

"I've actually got something lined up."

"And what's that?"

"I'm going to be a special advisor in another department. Mainly training. Some investigations."

Another department, Leonard knew, meant another city, likely another state. "Where are you going?"

"Scottsdale. Arizona." And Leonard could see, suddenly, why Mulino looked so different. He had shrugged off thirty years of danger. Thirty years of never knowing what was behind the door. Thirty years of always having someone above you tell you precisely what you did wrong during that moment when you were afraid for your life. And he was going to go somewhere where it was never cold, where everyone has a swimming pool, and where anything that amounts to real crime is committed well outside the city limits and handled by ATF or the DEA anyway. Leonard knew what these retirement gigs were like: it basically amounted to coming into a precinct a couple of times a week to tell war stories to the new cadets. Mulino was cashing in and would be taking it easy from here on out. Because after all, why shouldn't he?

"Okay. Well, Detective, it was an honor working with you."

"Thanks, Leonard." Mulino held out his hand. "No hard feelings."

Leonard reached out his good arm, the painless arm, and shook the cop's hand. "No hard feelings, Detective."

"And I know I told you that you could come work for the squad. After all this. And I know you deserve it. I put in a word for you. Obviously, I don't make the decision anymore. But I said they should still do it. And the new SDS said you should come by."

Leonard nodded. What Ralph Mulino's word meant to some newly promoted detective was anyone's guess. But it was better than nothing. He saw that Mulino was holding out a business card.

"You should give a call."

Leonard reached out and took the card from Mulino. He looked down at it, then back at the detective. Mulino was still wearing his new, easy smile. He would probably wear it for the rest of his life. Leonard looked back down at the card, marveling at the familiar name on it. He still had one stop to make.

CHAPTER FORTY-FOUR

Aurelia Peralta looked over the desk. It was old. She opened one of the steel drawers, grimacing at the screech. There wouldn't be any gliding runners here. There was a hardware store up the street; she would go get a can of WD-40 and it would be working by tomorrow. She was never one to call up and ask for maintenance to come fix it. They would take too long and probably do it wrong anyway. A creaky, old steel desk was a small price to pay for the promotion.

She had almost fainted when the bureau chief had told her. Promotion to SDS, only eighteen months after making detective at all. Bruder was dead and Mulino was retiring. She would be able to staff up her own squad. And she would be in Mulino's old office, which meant that she would have a door she could close off to the rest of the squad. Not quite thirty and she had her own office. It might seem routine to her classmates at Nutley High, now working as lawyers or accountants, but to have your own office in the NYPD meant that they trusted you. The powers that be recognized that, left to your own devices, you were not going to just close the door and play games on your phone all afternoon. In this organization, that was a higher bar than you'd think.

Chief Travis had called her in the day after the shooting. There was going to be an investigation, sure. The Firearms Discharge Control

Board was involved; DIMAC would run through the paces; she had taken and passed the Breathalyzer on the scene. Her gun was in safekeeping for a few days while she sat in a cubicle and wrote up a couple of twenty-page reports summarizing the investigation. But shootings don't get much cleaner than this one. Bruder had abducted a child in front of forty sworn officers. He had shot a civilian just before being killed. There wasn't going to be a protest for him. No one was going to wonder why Peralta wasn't going before the Grand Jury. She supposed, looking over her desk, that she shouldn't have been surprised. The tabloid stories were making her out as a hero. They managed to leave out the part where she'd been surprised and disarmed by Bruder to begin with. She was doing her best to forget that part at all.

Even more than the promotion, she had been glad to see that Gabriel Smyth was let out. And the Homicide detectives had been dressed down. There was going to be an internal investigation there, too. Did the officers coerce a confession? Did they have a conflict of interest? The sort of thing that usually happens only twenty years after the guy is convicted when some eager young lawyer gets his hands on subpoena power for the first time. She wished she had been able to see the faces of those proud, fat, white guys when they got the news. Generally, she wasn't the kind to gloat, but there is always a little room for an exception.

Chief Travis had walked her through the assignment. Based in Brooklyn, she would have citywide jurisdiction. The same deal Mulino had. She would get two detectives. There was a stack of twenty resumes in a manila folder sitting on her desk. That was what her afternoon was going to be. Looking through those and picking one. Because she had already picked the first one.

"Aurelia."

She turned around from the desk. Standing in the doorway—her doorway—was Leonard Mitchell. His shoulder was still bandaged, but it was no longer so heavily bundled as to look absurd.

"Leonard. Good to see that you're out."

"Mulino told me that he put in his papers."

"Can you believe that? Scottsdale." Peralta waited a moment to see if Leonard asked if she had ever been. If maybe he, like the Homicide guys or the cadets in her Academy class, thought that every woman with a Spanish name was actually Mexican, and had probably snuck through Nogales as a kid. But Leonard wasn't that type. That was a good sign.

"And he told me that you wanted to talk to me."

"Yeah. I'm taking over the squad."

"I know. Congratulations."

It was time for the pitch. Not that he could refuse. She knew he wouldn't refuse. But she wasn't comfortable with wielding power yet. She didn't know that she didn't have to sell anything, she only had to command.

She hesitated as she asked, suddenly feeling almost as though she were in high school again. *Spit it out*, she told herself. "Leonard, you did good work on this case. You helped out Mulino a lot. You helped out me. And I want to know, if you want in on this, well, we would love to have you."

"And I'm supposed to thank you for saving my life, Detective."

"I wish I'd gotten him before he hit you once."

Leonard nodded. Peralta thought for a moment that he was thinking it over. She didn't want to get to the point of talking about money. Civilians in the department have their own pay scale. When he spoke, he said maybe the one thing that could have surprised her.

"I can't carry a gun. I don't know how much help I can be."

"You don't investigate with a gun, Leonard. You investigate with your eyes and your ears and your brain. We'd like to have you on board."

"Then I guess I can't say no."

Peralta reached out to shake his hand. It was dry and thin, but firm. Inside the wiry frame was a man who had been beaten down, pepper-sprayed, imprisoned, and shot. And he was signing up for more. Peralta knew she could use him for what was coming. She knew that Armstrong had gotten away, that he had stolen something from the boy. Chief Travis talked to her about that too. But that was for later. Now she just had to get Leonard on board. He grimaced a little. The shoulder would have to hurt still. But he was toughing it out. She appreciated that.

Peralta stepped back. "I've got to look through these. I'm getting one more team member. You go rest that shoulder, talk to HR. I expect to see you tomorrow at eight."

"Of course, Detective." And as Leonard smiled, Peralta saw why she wanted to work with him. His smile showed that, like her, he would never be happier doing anything else in the world. He didn't need to have a gun, because she would always have hers. He would be her eyes and her ears and he would always owe her one. He would always owe her his life.

This was going to be fun.

ACKNOWLEDGMENTS

To Jacque Ben-Zekry at Thomas & Mercer, who championed *The Big Fear* and shepherded this sequel, thank you for your continued commitment to my work and for all the support you have offered to me in the past eighteen months. To the rest of the Thomas & Mercer team—Sarah Shaw, Grace Doyle, Dennelle Catlett, and many others—you have created an incredible project that feels more like a family than a publisher, and I am honored to be a part of it.

To Kim Witherspoon and Monika Woods at InkWell Management, who took me on two years ago and have never stopped fighting for me, I am in awe of your dedication and devotion to writers, and feel so grateful to be in your hands.

To my editor Charlotte Herscher, who fought (sometimes with me) to make the first book and this one better, I owe a great debt for your clear and honest feedback, always in service of the work. I am grateful for Jeff Quick's insights and Ray Vallese's careful eye; they both added clarity and force to the book. Having an ally like Sarah Burningham of Little Bird Publicity is an enormous honor, and I cannot be more grateful to her for her efforts in publicizing my books.

I received terrific early feedback from family and friends who read early drafts of this book. My father, Claude Case, gave invaluable insight on both the book and its subject matter. Robin Hessman, Wade Carper, and Lorin Wortheimer all gave terrific notes on early drafts, and this book is better for all of their efforts. There is much in *A Falling Knife* that comes from my work and my life in a changing Brooklyn, and many of those who I came across, spoke to, and worked with on these issues did not know their thoughts might end up in a book, so it would be improper to name them. But they are in my thoughts and I have thanked them in person when I could.

Most of all I want to thank my wife, Claudia Case, who not only read and gave feedback on the book but offered incredible support throughout the process of creating it, and my two curious and inspirational children, David and Helen, without whom none of this would be possible.

ABOUT THE AUTHOR

Photo © 2015 Trevor Williams

Andrew Case is the author of the novel *The Big Fear* and the stage plays *The Electric Century*, *The Rant*, and many others. He has been a member of the New American Writers Group at Primary Stages, a participating playwright at the Eugene O'Neill Theatre Center, and a member of the PEN America Center. For nearly a decade he served as an investigator, spokesman, and policy director at the Civilian Complaint Review Board, which investigates allegations of misconduct by New York City Police Department officers. Andrew has written on police reform for *Newsweek*, the *Columbia Human Rights Law Review*, and other publications. *A Falling Knife*, the sequel to *The Big Fear*, is the second novel in the Hollow City series. He lives in Flatbush, Brooklyn, with his wife, Claudia, and their two children.